Brian McGilloway is the author of eleven crime novels including the Ben Devlin mysteries and the Lucy Black series, the first of which, *Little Girl Lost*, became a *New York Times* and UK No.1 bestseller. In addition to being shortlisted for a CWA Dagger and Irish Book Award, he is a past recipient of the Ulster University McCrea Literary Award and won the BBC Tony Doyle Award for his screenplay, *Little Emperors*. His standalone novel, *The Last Crossing*, is shortlisted for The Theakston's Old Peculier Crime Novel of the Year 2021. Brian currently teaches in Strabane, where he lives with his wife and four children.

Praise for Brian McGilloway

'**Poetic, humane and gripping** . . . reminded me of Bernard MacLaverty's early work. Yes, it's that good'

Ian Rankin

'**Moving and powerful**, this is an important book, which everyone should read'

Ann Cleeves

'[A] superb book . . . **thoughtful and insightful**, wrenching and utterly compelling. It says something truly profound and universal about love, loyalty and revenge . . . If you want to understand Northern Ireland, or any society that has experienced conflict, put it on your list. And **the writing is exquisite**'

Jane Casey

'An **extraordinary** novel from one of Ireland's crime fiction masters'

Adrian McKinty

'A gentle, reflective book about a violent situation seems like an oxymoron but that's what Brian McGilloway has achieved with *The Last Crossing*. **An eye-opening read**'

Sinead Crowley

'This IS important. This book is the peak of what crime fiction can do. **Brian McGilloway writes like an angel**'

Steve Cavanagh

'As **heart-stopping and thrilling** as it is exquisitely written and prescient. A work of fiction which looks unapologetically at the legacy of our troubled past'

Claire Allan

'**Utterly stunning** and beautifully written'

Liz Nugent

'A cool, controlled, **immensely powerful** novel. McGilloway brings a forensic and compassionate eye to bear on the post-Troubles settlement in this thoughtful, morally complex book'

Irish Times

'**Outstanding**. From its harrowing opening scene to its equally violent conclusion, this is an **utterly compelling** story of how Northern Ireland's violent history has affected generations'

Irish Independent

By Brian McGilloway

The Inspector Devlin series
Borderlands
Gallows Lane
Bleed a River Deep
The Rising
The Nameless Dead
Blood Ties

The D.S. Lucy Black Books
Little Girl Lost
Hurt
Preserve the Dead
Bad Blood

Standalone title
The Last Crossing

BLOOD TIES

BRIAN McGILLOWAY

CONSTABLE

CONSTABLE

First published in Great Britain in 2021 by Constable

This edition published in 2021 by Constable

1 3 5 7 9 10 8 6 4 2

A CIP catalogue record for this book
is available from the British Library.

ISBN: 978-1-47213-326-7

Typeset by Hewer Text UK Ltd, Edinburgh
Printed and bound in Great Britain by Clays Ltd, Elcograf S.p.A.

Papers used by Constable are from well-managed
forests and other responsible sources.

MIX
Paper from
responsible sources
FSC® C104740

Constable
An imprint of
Little, Brown Book Group
Carmelite House
50 Victoria Embankment
London EC4Y 0DZ

An Hachette UK Company
www.hachette.co.uk

www.littlebrown.co.uk

In loving memory of my father, Laurence.

'When I decide I shall assemble you'

'Identity' by Elizabeth Jennings

Prologue

26 June 2020

I have seen too much of death, have known it too closely.

I have stood in rooms where it lingers still, have smelt its peculiar odour clinging to me, a stench that carries on for days, contaminating food, perfume, life. I have seen its face among the Rorschach of blood spatter, glimpsed it in the fleeting movement at the corner of my eye as I stand at the centre of the minor industry that develops at each crime scene. I have felt its coldness in those flats we've broken into when neighbours haven't been seen for days, seen the effects of its gorging on those we've pulled from rivers, turned away from its devastation at car-accident sites.

And more recently, I had seen it intimately, watching as it took the breath from my father, took the warmth from his hands, robbed him of his voice, his laugh, his being. Despite years of propinquity with its effects through my work, I was still unprepared for such a personal incursion in my life and the lives of those I love. That its kiss was gentle in my father's final moments did little to assuage the grief it left in its wake.

Yes, I have seen too much of death and wish to know it no further. And yet, I find myself constantly drawn back to it, find myself looking at it daily, in any one of its multitude of manifestations.

Day One

9 March 2020

Chapter One

In the early spring of 2020, the manifestation of death I faced was one of violence and passion, seemingly fuelled by hatred. We'd been called to a house on the road out of Lifford by a postman who'd noticed the curtains undrawn in a house. The first officer on the scene found a broken pane in the back door and, on entering, discovered the occupant, murdered.

The dead man lay on his side, hanging half off the bed. His upper body, exposed over the tangle of bedclothes that acted as a loincloth of sorts, carried a number of puncture wounds, a thin trail of blood arching up the wall and across the ceiling above him, drawn in the wake of whatever had been used to stab him to death during one of the more violent swings, as surely as the moon pulls the tide. The blood was unnaturally bright, lit by the fluorescence of the floodlights that the Scene of Crime Officers had set up at each corner of the room to reduce the shadow fall from those moving around this *memento mori*. The air was sharp and ferric with the taste of blood.

I stepped from one metal footpad to the next, angling my head to better see the dead man. Fifteen years ago, I might instantly have known him for a stranger. Back then, Lifford was still small enough that everyone knew everyone else, the population static, save for the occasional passing or birth. But that had all changed.

Lifford straddles the border between the north and south of Ireland. Once a frontier point and customs post during the darkest days of the country's recent history, the end of violence and the demilitarisation of the border made the crossing point almost invisible, a slight change in the tarmac quality on the roads, and the change in signage from kilometres to miles the only indication of the place where one jurisdiction merged into the other.

The housing bubble in those years of the early 2000s had brought with it an explosion in developments, while the relative weakness of the Euro, compared to the pound at the time had brought in an influx of buyers from the north. The recession, and austerity measures in the south, drove those same buyers back across the border again ten years later and left the area peppered with houses either lying empty or, more often, being rented out on short-term leases. Added to that, the Brexit vote had caused nothing but concern about the likely direction the area would take as one of the few places where the UK abutted the EU with a land border – a fact given scant consideration throughout the debate by those braying for a return to the days of splendid isolationism.

The combination of all these factors led to further move-ment as people shifted sides in preparation for the possible fallout of the vote. As a result, the population of the town was ever changing, and strangers no longer stood out.

'Does anyone recognise him?' I asked. 'There's something about him that's familiar.' The room, though alive with movement, was surprisingly quiet, each person going about their own work, passing one another with balletic agility at times, in the cramped space. A few shook their heads; the others, non-locals, said nothing.

I stepped closer, examined him more carefully. I knew his face, somehow, his profile eliciting in me a form of déjà vu that always left me feeling unsettled, as if grasping at the scraps of a dream, ephemeral as mist.

He wore black boxer shorts, his legs thin and wiry. His arms, one of which seemed entangled in the bedsheet, were decorated with a number of tattoos, several of which, I could tell, were home-made. One, of a spider's web, traversed the skin between his forefinger and thumb. His trunk, in addition to the wounds which I'd already seen, was marked with small, perfectly round scars, perhaps half a dozen, no bigger than a 10c coin. His body, though almost lupine, was toned and hard, even in death.

On the floor rested the nest of his trousers and a T-shirt pulled inside out. They had clearly been discarded that way before he'd got into bed. His boots lay not far beyond, a black sock balled up inside the leg of each, a gesture of neatness and control that seemed antithetical to the manner in which he had discarded the rest of his clothing, as if it was something done through muscle memory or habit.

I glanced around the room, noting the décor: magnolia paint with cheaply framed art prints on the wall; a scented candle, unused, sitting on the bedside cabinet atop a lace doily. A small non-brand TV set sat on an occasional table in the corner, the remote control hanging in a plastic holster stuck to its side.

There was something about the dead man which did not seem to match the room, nor indeed the house itself. The hallway leading to this room had been similarly sparingly decorated, the magnolia walls bearing the occasional print of vases of flowers. The windowsills housed potpourri bowls sitting in front of damp traps. There was nothing personal, nothing that seemed to reflect *him* in the house.

While there was a small closet in the bedroom, I guessed it was empty by the rattle and clatter of unused coat hangers as I gripped the door handle. Sure enough, it was bare inside. In the far corner of the room, an overnight bag spilled clothes onto the floor. Carefully, I took a quick scan through the contents: a change of underwear, socks and a spare T-shirt. Whoever he was, he was most likely a visitor and one who'd not been planning on staying long – a night or two at most. Unzipping the front pocket, I found a set of headphones, a packet of antacid tablets and a box of condoms.

The small bathroom next door seemingly confirmed the transient nature of his visit – a toothbrush, single disposable razor and a small bar of soap lay on the sink.

Perhaps he was unlucky, a visitor to the area who'd been caught up in a burglary gone wrong, I thought. But I dismissed the thought; the level of wounding on his body, the intensity of the stabbing he'd suffered, suggested this killing had been personal and targeted. Someone had passionately wanted to hurt this man. They'd succeeded.

I checked the final rooms of the bungalow. In the living area, the TV and Sky box were present and correct; there were no signs of disturbance, of someone having searched the house, of anything taken.

I stepped back out into the narrow hallway. A SOCO was kneeling on the floor, setting up a small marker card with a number on it.

'Watch your step, sir,' she said. 'A few blood drops out along here.'

I edged along the corridor, noting the spacing of the drops, every metre or so along the laminated wood of the floor.

'Is it the victim's?' The dead man was lying as though killed in his bed. Nothing suggested he'd made it out to the hallway.

'Hard to say. It's isolated from the rest of the scene,' she said. 'Maybe the killer's on their way in or out.'

The killer or killers had, undoubtedly, come in through the back door. One small pane in the door out to the yard had been broken and the door then unlocked, the key having seemingly been left in the locked door. The garden beyond was surrounded by tall hedging which provided it with such a degree of privacy from the neighbouring properties, all bungalows as well, that they could have broken in safe in the knowledge that they would not be spotted. I stood at the door, scanning the property boundaries in vain for any glimpse of the surrounding housing. I would need to assign uniforms to do house to house but I could already tell that the houses were so secluded in their own grounds that there was a high probability we'd get little actionable information.

'Sir!' someone called from the bedroom. I moved back up and was met at the doorway by a SOCO holding a phone. 'It'd fallen down the back of the bedside cabinet,' she explained. 'It must have been on the charger but the cable had pulled free of the plug.'

I took the phone, which I recognised as an older model of my own, and clicked on the home button. It was locked, unsurprisingly, the battery indicator at 2 per cent. Moving quickly, I brought it across to where the victim lay and, using his thumb, unlocked the device. I clicked on the phone app, hoping that a home number might be immediately visible, but he had no contacts listed on his phone.

I looked at recent calls. One had been dialled repeatedly, though none had been assigned Caller IDs, so they meant nothing to me. Moving into the messages as the battery indicator dropped, I found an array of messages. Many were from an 0115 number. Clicking on them, I found they were messages from Airbnb. Coming back out, I scrolled up to the most recent message, which had come from a southern mobile. I only managed to read, 'Hi George. Sorry – my dad—' when the phone went dead. I had, at least, a first name for the dead man now. 'George.'

'The pathologist is on his way, sir,' the SOCO offered.

'Perfect,' I said, handing her the phone. 'I want all communications copied off this. I'll leave you to get on with it. I have enough to get started.'

To be honest, I was relieved to be out of there, away from the hushed business, the smell, the damp chill: Death's calling card.

Chapter Two

It didn't take long to get the names of the house owners for they were still on the electoral register: Andrew and Sinead McDonald. A quick check in the phone directory for the north revealed that they were now living just over the border, in our neighbouring town of Strabane.

As a courtesy, I contacted my counterpart in the north, Jim Hendry, to explain that I intended to call with the McDonald's. Hendry agreed to meet me at the border and head across with me, just to smooth over any jurisdictional issues. Truth be told, we frequently crossed the border to speak to people without need of chaperones from the other side and, for a while, most people accepted it without comment. Once again, Brexit, and the accompanying reinforcement of the psychological border that most people had forgotten about, brought with it an increase in those who would challenge your right to come across to speak to them. Whatever else about it, the whole issue had already begun to impact on the minor practicalities of policing a frontier.

'You bored?' I asked, climbing into Hendry's car at the petrol station on the border. 'Or just looking to get out of the station for an hour?'

'I've not seen you in a bit,' Hendry said. 'Thought I'd catch up before they build the wall and we never meet again.'

'That's America you're thinking of,' I joked.

'Is it now?' Hendry arched an eyebrow as he started the engine. He'd aged since last I saw him, his hair more grey now than sandy, his moustache thinning and similarly more sabled. 'So you've a murder?'

'Indeed. Stabbed while he was sleeping, by the looks of it.'

'Just like Macbeth.'

'Except he was the one doing the stabbing,' I said. Debbie, my wife, was an English teacher and had forced me to sit through an admittedly good performance of the play the previous year by Chris Eccleston. I'd gone primarily because he was Doctor Who; I'd watched it with my kids when they were younger. I explained this to Hendry.

'Was he any good?'

'He was,' I said. He had been too and, despite my better efforts, I'd got caught up in the story, even if almost everyone did die at the end. This, Debs had explained, was necessary; everyone touched by the initial corrupt act had to die for justice to be done and order restored. That part had appealed to me. I didn't tell Hendry that though. 'I enjoyed it, at any rate,' I said instead.

'Fat lot of use that'll be in finding out who killed your dead man. Unless it was Shakespeare. What have you got so far?'

'I think the victim is called George,' I said. 'He looks like he wasn't planning on staying long so . . .'.

'Either he was followed here or he was in the wrong place at the wrong time.'

I nodded. 'I want to get his details off the McDonalds,' I said. 'He'd a lot of contacts from Airbnb, so I'm guessing

12

they rented out the house to him. And, seeing as it was their house, I want to see if there's any chance they were the intended targets.'

They lived in a house off Bradley Way, just past the bus station. It was a new development of white town houses, squeezed together like slices of wedding cake on a narrow plate. Inside their home, the décor was almost identical to that in the house in Lifford; more magnolia and scented candles proliferated. The key difference was that, in this house, the pictures had a more personal quality than the generic prints in the Lifford house.

The McDonalds were a young couple, with two children, a boy and a girl, whose photogenic qualities had been exploited at every opportunity in their development, based on the range of family portraits that graced the walls.

'Is there a problem with the house over there?' Mr McDonald asked as we all sat in their living room. He glanced nervously at his wife.

'You rent it out on Airbnb, is that right?' I asked.

The man glanced at his wife again, then nodded. 'We moved out a year or two ago and the place was getting run down, lying empty. The market had collapsed and we couldn't afford to sell it – we'd have been in negative equity. So we only rent it out to keep someone in it every so often; stop the floors from swelling with the damp, you know? We're making almost nothing from it. In fact, most of it goes back into redecorating, upkeep of the garden and that.'

Hendry looked at me and lightly raised an eyebrow. It was an unnecessarily detailed response to a simple question.

'I'm not here about tax, if that's what you think,' I offered. The barely perceptible slump of both husband and wife indicated that this indeed had been their fear.

'Well, what's wrong, then?' Mrs McDonald now asked. Despite both of them being almost twenty years younger than either Hendry or myself, neither had indicated that we should call them anything other than Mr or Mrs McDonald. 'Has the current tenant done something wrong?'

'He's died,' I said.

'My God,' Mrs McDonald said, turning to her husband. 'I told you there was something odd about him,' she added, as if eccentricity was an indicator of impending mortality.

Her husband was more interested in the details, though. 'Was it a heart attack or something? It wasn't suicide, was it?'

'It's too early to say,' I replied. 'We do suspect another party to have been involved.'

'Was he murdered?'

'As I said, it's too early to speculate.'

I could tell the man wasn't satisfied with the response.

'We'd best check the house,' he said, motioning to stand. 'Is it bad?'

'The house will be out of bounds for a while,' I said. 'It's a crime scene. What can you tell me about the tenant there?'

McDonald shrugged. 'Not much. He booked last week for one night then contacted us the night before last and

14

booked another night. I was planning on calling across this evening to check the place over once he'd gone.'

'What was his name?' I asked.

'Geoff Dallas.'

'Geoff? Not George?'

'That's the name on his Airbnb profile.'

'Do you have any contact details for him?'

'We contacted him through Airbnb,' Mrs McDonald explained.

'You had suspicions about him, though,' Hendry said. 'Why?'

'He didn't answer any messages,' she said, though without conviction.

'Is that all?'

She shrugged. 'He didn't have a social-media profile anywhere. No Facebook, Twitter, nothing.'

'We always check,' her husband offered by way of explanation. 'We're not stalkers or anything.'

'You get a sense of someone very quickly,' his wife continued, taking control of the conversation. 'If someone's posting pictures of themselves out drinking all the time or partying or whatever, we're less inclined to agree to the booking. We don't want the house trashed. There's nothing wrong in it – everyone does it who rents out places.'

'It's our college fund for the kids, you see,' Mr McDonald explained, nodding towards where a portrait of the aforementioned children dominated the room from over the fireplace.

'My eldest has just gone to uni,' I said, somewhat unnecessarily. 'You'll need every cent you can get.'

15

'Was Mr Dallas here for business or pleasure?' Hendry asked.

'Pleasure, I think,' Mrs McDonald answered. 'I'm not sure.'

I'd deliberately left the only other question I had until last so as not to spook the couple too much. 'Can you think of anyone who might wish to cause either of *you* harm?'

'Us? Harm?' the man asked, his arm automatically snaking around his wife's back where she sat next to him.

'Has anyone ever threatened you? Threatened to harm either of you?'

'Lord, no,' he replied. 'We're not that sort of people. Why?'

'Just something I have to ask,' I said.

I stopped myself from asking which sort of people ended up being victims of threats, and instead thanked them for their help. In truth, all we'd learned was that the victim's name was Geoff, not George, and I began to suspect that perhaps I'd misread the text in the fleeting view I'd had of it before the phone had died.

'So Penny's at university now?' Hendry commented when we'd stepped out into the freshening afternoon.

'In Dublin,' I said.

'How's that going?'

'Fine, I think. She started last autumn. English Literature, like her mother.'

'I meant for you.'

'Fine,' I repeated. I considered the number of nights I'd not been able to get to sleep, wondering if she was in her digs okay, wondering if she was homesick, wondering. And the mornings when I'd woken at 5 a.m. and watched the dawn's light creep across the walls from where it seeped around our bedroom curtain, and realised the immensity of the silence in the house, a silence that seemed to be growing slowly around me. I'd spent so long thinking of myself primarily as a 'father', I wasn't sure I knew what to be once the kids moved on. Was 'fine' an adequate summation of all that? Possibly.

'And how's things since? You know, with . . . your dad and that?'

I shrugged. 'You know . . .' I offered, as if this was in itself a response.

My father had been sick on and off for some time, but his eventual diagnosis of chronic heart failure simultaneously confirmed a long-held fear and blindsided me in equal measure. We'd lost my mother a few years back; my father was the person who tied my family, my brother Tom and I, together, our childhood home the hub through which we met and kept abreast of each other's news.

'He's moving in with us for a while,' I said. 'This coronavirus thing. The lockdowns in Europe panicked me a bit in case it happens here and we can't get down to see him. He needs a bit of help getting himself sorted in the mornings and that.'

'You should take compassionate leave,' Hendry suggested. 'If it gets too much.'

'It'll be fine,' I said. That word again.

Hendry nodded. 'It's not easy.'

'It's not,' I agreed. 'How's all with you?'

'Fine,' he said, an echo of my earlier response. 'Fine.'

'What's up?'

He shook his head and looked past me, as if avoiding my gaze would allow him to avoid the conversation. 'I'm thinking of getting out early.'

'Of the police?'

He nodded. 'I've a few years on you. I feel like I've done my bit. We've a new head honcho in D district. Might be time to get out before everything changes.'

'What would you do?'

'Always work for a retired cop,' he said. 'Take up painting, maybe. Bit of rugby coaching.'

'I never took you for a rugby player,' I laughed. His physique, whippet thin, did not square with my impression of the sport.

'Space for all shapes and sizes on the rugby pitch,' he said, trotting out what sounded like a rote response.

'You don't think you'd be bored?'

'I'm not fully decided. Just thinking about it,' he said, snuffling his hand against his nose and clearing his throat. 'Let me know if you need anything more on this, all right?'

As I drove back across the border, I could not help but feel a rising sense that everything was changing at a pace with which I could not keep up.

18

Chapter Three

The station in Letterkenny was buzzing with activity when I went in, the usual business of An Garda supplemented by Brexit planning, which had seen a marked increase in meetings and briefings that I'd done my best to avoid attending. I'd spent most of my career working out of the small station in Lifford, a frontier post of sorts, sitting only a few hundred yards from the bridge through which the border ran. The same austerity measures that had sent families like the McDonalds back over to the north had seen the closure of such satellite stations and all teams being centralised in the larger stations like Letterkenny.

I missed Lifford station, its quirks and peculiarities, the rattling of its water pipes when someone flushed the toilet, the uneven heat distribution that left those in the main office wearing coats on days those in the upper offices were in short sleeves. The building was still there, the Garda sign still outside the door, but in reality, it was rarely used.

I made my way up to the incident room. Sergeant Joe McCready, with whom I'd worked for a few years now, had just arrived back from an earlier call-out regarding a burglary just outside Letterkenny. He was hunched over at his computer, inputting the list of all that was stolen, primarily to generate an incident number that the victims could use to claim insurance, for there was little chance of most burglaries being solved these days, resources being stretched as they were.

'Anything interesting?' I asked him as I passed.

'A digger,' he said. 'A few other pieces of machinery too, but the digger is the big one. I'm sending an email out to all the local banks to keep an eye on ATMs.'

There'd been a spate of late-night robberies in the north where diggers had been used to literally rip ATM machines from the walls of convenience stores that had housed them for their customers.

'I heard you got a call-out to a death. How was it?'

'Violent,' I said. 'I'll fill you in in a bit.'

I googled Airbnb's main office and put together a request for information on Geoff Dallas, based on the evidence I'd been provided by the McDonalds, which I entered into Airbnb's Law Enforcement Portal and faxed through to them as well, to speed things up. While I waited for a reply, I got McCready caught up to speed on what I'd learned. It was, admittedly, a brief conversation.

I did a cursory search on social media for Dallas, though was unsurprised to find nothing in light of the McDonalds' warning; I guessed Mrs McDonald would have been forensic in her own searches and she'd come up empty handed.

Just then, a reply came through from Airbnb. Geoff Dallas had paid with a debit card registered to Gerard Dawson who lived in Limavady.

Jim Hendry had called ahead to the station in Limavady to smooth things over for me. As I made my way up to the set of houses at the edge of the estate where I'd parked, I realised that what had looked to be semi-detached homes were, in fact, sets of apartments. Beside each door was an intercom with three flats marked. When I found the correct house number, I'd need then to know Dawson's apartment letter too. In the end, the intercom outside Dawson's carried two buttons with names filled in – neither of them his – and one with no name attached. I hedged my bets and tried that one first, but there was no response.

As I rang a second time, a young man came shuffling up the pathway, eyeing me with some suspicion.

'Excuse me,' he said, moving past me and fitting a key into the door.

'You're not Gerard Dawson by any chance, are you?' I asked.

He looked askance at me, then shook his head. 'Gerard's in flat B.'

It was the bell not marked with a name. 'Is he about?'

The youth shrugged, his head lowered. 'Marty up on the third floor will know.' He opened the door and stepped in, holding it open for me.

I reached the second floor and knocked on the door of flat B, but to no avail, so made my way up to the top flat to speak to 'Marty'. The man who answered was older than I was expecting, possibly in his late fifties. He was barrel-chested and tall enough that, as he stepped through the doorway, he had to dip a little to avoid hitting his head on the jamb. 'Yes?' he asked, without introduction.

'I'm looking for Gerard Dawson,' I said. 'The fella on the bottom floor said you might be able to help.'

'I'm assuming you've knocked at his door. Who's asking?'

'I'm a Garda inspector, Ben Devlin.'

'You're off your patch,' he said, straightening as he hitched his jeans up a little by the belt loops on either side. 'What's he done?'

'I need to speak to him in connection with a death in Donegal.'

'Deliberate?'

'Too early to say, sir,' I said.

'I'm ex-probation service,' Marty said, as if this information would allow me to share more with him. It didn't.

'The person whose death we're investigating was a younger man. Late twenties, early thirties maybe. Wiry, black hair cut in a longer style. Tattoos on his arms, including a home-made spiderweb on his hand. We don't have an ID for him yet, but Dawson's name has come up in our enquiries.'

Marty nodded. 'That sounds a bit like Gerard himself, to be honest.'

'Have you any way of contacting him? Any way of checking if he's—'

'Not your victim?'

I nodded.

'Give me a sec.'

He ducked as he turned and slouched into the rear of his flat, appearing a moment or two later with a bunch of keys and his phone. He opened the phone first and scrolled through something before presenting it to me. It was a picture taken at a party. Several men stood together, bottles of beer in hand, staring at the camera. Towering above them was Marty, his arms draped across the shoulders of men to either side of him. None of the others embraced or touched in any way, all standing slightly apart from each other.

'We'd a bonfire out on the green last Eleventh night. Someone took a picture of me and some of the lads from the flats around here; I look after this and three other blocks.'

I scanned the faces of the men standing either side of Marty. One of them bore enough of a resemblance to the dead man I'd looked at earlier to suggest to me that he was the same person. He stood to the outer edge of the group, a bottle of beer in one hand, the other stuffed in his pocket. He wore black jeans and a T-shirt. He seemed ill at ease, even among such a rag-tag assembly. Again, something insubstantial, at the edges of my memory, stirred in recognition of the man's face. I'd seen him before, I knew. But he'd been younger, less weathered, then. I still couldn't pinpoint whence I'd known him and the name Gerard Dawson meant nothing to me.

'That looks like him,' I said, pointing him out.

'That's Gerard all right,' Marty said, grimly.

'Can we check his flat?'

'Have you a warrant?'

'I've a suspicion that the victim of the crime lives downstairs, if that's of any use to you?'

Marty shrugged and stomped down the stairs ahead of me, though not before pulling his door shut and shaking the handle to check it was closed. He saw me catching him in the movement and smirked. 'Old habits,' he said. 'Can't be too careful.'

Chapter Four

Marty explained, as we made our way downstairs, that the housing block was all sheltered accommodation for younger people who had struggled to find permanent housing. He'd been hired in after retirement as a caretaker of sorts, his previous employment seemingly well placing him for such a role. I thought of Hendry and his own plans for retirement. I tried, in vain, to see him as a doorman for the dispossessed.

He went into Dawson's flat first to check whether the young man was there before agreeing to allow me in simply to see if I could find contact details for next of kin.

While the house in Lifford had clearly seemed anomalous to the man we found there, this flat was no better a reflection of his personality. It was sparsely furnished, the hallway opening out into a living area and kitchenette. There were no paintings on the wall, nothing but a poster for *Inglourious Basterds* that peeled at one corner, hanging over a small electric fire. Off from the main living area was a cramped toilet and shower room and, next to that, a bedroom. The whole place was painted in gunmetal grey, the floor covered with charcoal carpet squares. The walls in the bedroom were similarly bare, save for a series of photographs that had been tacked to the wall next to the bed. I had no doubt now that

Gerard Dawson was indeed the man we'd found in Lifford. He featured in several of the photographs alongside two other youths. There were no pictures of family that I could see, nor girlfriends or partners. No children.

There was, however, a sketch I recognised to be the dead man, drawn in a cartoon style I knew to be anime: large, rounded eyes, a thin line for a mouth, the hair and ears exaggeratedly pointed. My own kids had watched reruns of *Pokémon* for a while.

'Do you know any of the people in those photos?' I asked Marty. He glanced at the pictures and shook his head.

'Was he not allowed to decorate?' I asked, glancing around the space.

'Yeah,' Marty said. 'Within reason. I just don't think he was the home-décor type.'

'Clearly not,' I said. 'How long had he been here for?'

'Just shy of a year. Start of last summer he came here.'

'Is he a local?'

Marty shrugged again. 'He's from the north, for sure, from his accent,' he said. 'I don't know if he's Limavady originally, though. I don't think so. I never saw any family or that. Then again, most of the kids living here are the same. If they'd family that cared, they'd not be living here, most of them.'

The bedroom was as sparely furnished as the rest of the flat: a bed with a cabinet next to it and a built-in wardrobe against the far wall. While Marty opened the wardrobe, I checked the drawer of the bedside cabinet, but it was locked. There was undoubtedly something heavy inside, for I could hear it rattling.

'Have you a key?' I asked.

Marty was initially reluctant.

'Dawson's not being investigated,' I said. 'He's the victim here. I need to find something that leads me to his family.'

Marty nodded. 'I've no key, but these things are useless; there's one in each of the flats. If you tip it up, you can pull the mechanism down and unlock it that way.'

'That's a neat life hack,' I said as I lowered the cabinet onto its back and pulled down the metallic bar which ran up one side of its inners.

Marty shrugged. 'Trick of the trade.'

I felt the fitting click into place and, righting the unit, opened the larger bottom drawer. Inside was a laptop and an assortment of tablet boxes and medicine bottles, which rolled around the base. I lifted out the laptop and laid it to one side, then lifted some of the tablets. The first box contained Risperdal and carried a pharmacy label with Dawson's name on it.

Marty had been leaning over my shoulder. 'That's an antipsychotic,' he said. He clearly caught my look for he added, 'Not my first rodeo.'

I lifted another bottle. This one contained Pregabalin and had been dispensed by a pharmacy in Omagh a year earlier. The name on the label, however, was a woman's – Mavis Holmes. I knew it as an anti-anxiety medication; for a while its nickname had been Bud because it gave the same buzz as having had a few beers for a fraction of the cost. A second bottle rattled with tablets as I lifted it. Even through the brown plastic I could tell what they were; large, blue and diamond-shaped.

'Viagra?' I said. 'I'd have thought Dawson was a bit young to need it. Maybe he's selling them.'

'You can buy them over the counter,' Marty offered. 'Apparently. Wouldn't have thought there would be much trade for them illegally.'

I closed the lower drawer and opened the top one, the movement again marked with a heavy clunk of something inside hitting the rear of the unit. The front of the drawer held a few loose condoms and socks and underwear. I pulled it out and emptied it onto the floor, lest he'd needles secreted in there among the clothes. The last thing I needed was to get stabbed with a user's needle.

A squat handgun clattered to the floor.

'Looks like Dawson was expecting trouble after all,' I said.

Chapter Five

I made my way back to Letterkenny, Dawson's gun, tablets and laptop all safely stored in evidence bags. Before leaving, I'd taken pictures of the various photographs pinned to the wall to help identify some of Dawson's friends.

I contacted Hendry and asked him to check for me whether Dawson had had a licence to own a gun. He had also agreed to run Dawson's prints through the Northern system to officially confirm his identity and to check if he had a record quickly, bypassing the wait involved in going through Europol. He'd already come back to me about the former; I was not wholly surprised to learn that Dawson hadn't applied for a licence. The gun was Eastern European, I guessed, though the date and serial number had both been filed off, suggesting it was bought illegally. Jim told me that our SOCO team had just sent him through Dawson's prints, as I'd requested. He'd come back to me if he found anything.

When I went back into the station, Joe McCready was still sitting at his desk, the phone wedged between his cheek and shoulder. I assumed he'd been calling round the various local convenience stores, warning them about the digger theft.

I'd just set down the items I'd brought from Dawson's when Chief Superintendent Patterson's door opened and he beckoned me across. I followed him back into his office.

'Shut the door. Sit down,' he instructed gruffly as he dropped into his own chair behind his desk. Patterson had been a contemporary of mine and indeed, at one stage, we'd both gone for the same promotion. For some time afterwards, our relationship had been strained, but since moving up to Letterkenny, he was so stretched himself, I suspected he had little time for personal gripes and, seeing the issues he'd had to deal with in his post, I'd long ago contented myself to going no further in the force. As a result, we'd reached an informal *entente cordiale* of sorts.

'What's the story with the killing?'

I filled him in on the details, including the finds in the flat in Limavady.

'Someone followed him here?'

I shrugged. 'Possibly. Though his plan to stay an extra night seems to have been a spur-of-the-moment thing.'

'What are your thoughts?'

I shrugged. 'None at the moment. If I had to say, I'd peg him for an ex-con. The home-made tattoos, the accommodation block where he was living, the prescription drugs belonging to other people, the handgun. All of it. Perhaps he was selling, though if he was, it's hard to know where his money went because his flat was bare. He had scars on him, but not injection trails that I noticed. The PM will tell us for sure.'

'So what made him our problem? Why was he in Lifford?'

'Again, I'm not sure. I've handed his phone in for examination. I'm going to call up and see what they found and take them in the laptop I took from his flat. Between the two we might learn something. I know his face though. I've seen him before, but I can't think where.'

I handed Patterson my phone, displaying an image of Dawson, cropped from one of the pictures on his bedroom wall. He examined him briefly and, shrugging, handed back the phone.

'They all start looking the same after a while,' he said.

'How are you?' I ventured. Normally he'd dismiss me with a wave of his hand, but not today, which I took to be his own peculiar form of an invitation to talk.

'Okay. I've twelve years done here this year.'

I nodded, unsure what response he expected. 'You're not thinking of leaving, are you?' I asked, reminded again of my earlier conversation with Hendry.

'No,' he said, though without conviction. 'You get a bit sick of it, though. Don't you? All this shit.'

It was my turn to shrug. 'You just keep going. Better that than the alternative.'

'Do you think things are better here? Than they were?'

I suspected he was reflecting on his legacy. Things had certainly changed in his time, though most of those changes had been imposed on us rather than being of his making. Twelve years ago, we'd been competing for this job. Would I have done anything different from him? Would I have been able to?

I tried to think of something reassuring to offer him, but nothing obvious came to mind. 'I'll take a run up to Gerry with this stuff,' I said, standing.

'Keep me updated. If this was some Northern drugs feud that crossed the border, we can get them to do the spade work on their side,' he said, already retreating again into his work.

I found Gerry Carter on the second floor. He worked out of a newly installed IT room. An assortment of devices and skeletons of computers were scattered across the work-space he occupied, each encased in evidence bags and labelled.

'Ben,' he said, when I knocked on his door and stepped in. 'I was looking for you. I got your phone charged and pulled what I could find off it.'

'I was in Limavady,' I explained. 'I've more of Dawson's things for you.' I presented him with the laptop.

'Hopefully I'll have more joy with this,' he said. 'The phone you sent me was pretty new. I did pull his messages though. Looks like he was meant to be meeting up with someone. What age did you say he was?'

'Late twenties or more, maybe,' I said. 'Why?'

'He's contacting girls who seem a bit younger than that. Look.'

He handed me a few sheets of paper on which he'd printed out the messages from Dawson's phone. In turn, I handed him the laptop, which he set to removing from the evidence bag.

The first page held the most recent message – the one I'd started to read in the house in Lifford.

Hi George. Sorry – my dad said I'm not allowed down to see you today. He's a wanker. ☺ *I really want to see you. I'm so sorry. Helenxxx*

George had replied:

That's really annoying. I came all this way. Is there no way you can make it down? I'm dying to see you.

It was followed an hour or so later by a second message:

I might be able to get down tomorrow instead. Can you stay for a day? Hx

Finally, George had replied:

Okay. But I can't afford more than one night. This was meant to be special for us. xx

'Any ideas who this Helen is?'

'Flick back a few pages and you'll see. She sent him a picture about a week ago,' Gerry said as he unscrewed the base of the laptop I'd handed him. I was surprised to see him working on it straight away; normally there was a triage of sorts with Gerry before he'd get to analysing whatever he'd been given.

I flicked through the pages until I came to a colour image. It featured a girl, topless, her bra pulled down to her waist. She was smiling into the camera, though there was a filter applied to the picture, which gave her a dog's nose and tongue and two cartoon ears each side of her head. My initial suspicion was that the girl pictured was in her teens, though I couldn't be sure due to the filter and the graininess of the image. Irrespective, I found something profoundly saddening about the innocence of the dog ears being applied over such an image.

'She looks underage,' I said, covering the picture and reading through the earlier messages.

'That's what I thought,' Gerry said. 'That's why I'm keen to see what's on here. The only things on that phone were those messages – nothing else – so it's probably a burner phone. I suspect we'll find a bigger cache of messages here.'

As I read through the texts, I could trace the development of their relationship over the past few weeks. Clearly, from the first message, they'd already been in contact on an alternative platform, but the phone was being used expressly to arrange a meeting.

Helen was meant to have met 'George' two days earlier, on the first day of his stay in Lifford. They had arranged to meet at the border, near the site of the old customs post, opposite where the bus from Letterkenny stopped on its way through to our neighbouring town of Strabane. Both had expressed enthusiasm for meeting the other and the image that had been sent was, on the evidence of the messages around it, unsolicited. There was still no doubt though that Helen was younger than George, even based on the tone of the texts and the manner of abbreviations she used.

'Can you trace her phone?' I asked Gerry, who already had the laptop dismantled and was attaching the hard drive to cables running from his own workstation.

'I already have,' he said. 'It's one of three on an account belonging to Peter Shaw. His address is in town here.'

'I wonder if he knew his daughter was meeting with Dawson?'

Gerry's screen flickered to life as he accessed Dawson's hard drive. Just at that, my phone rang. It was Jim Hendry.

'Ben, I've got news.'

'You've a hit on Dawson?'

'More than that. He is, or was, Brooklyn Harris.'

The instant he said the name, the dead man came alive to me. I remembered now where last I'd seen him and in what context. None of it made me feel better.

Chapter Six

Brooklyn Harris first met Hannah Row when he was sixteen, she fifteen, in 2001. He'd seen her before a few times at school; she was the type of girl boys noticed, he said. Smiling at everyone, always happy, bubbly, the centre of groups of friends.

By contrast, Brooklyn was quieter, reserved. He'd a handful of friends. At best they'd drifted around him in a loose orbit, occasional satellites drawn by the gravity of his misdemeanours. When he was causing problems in school, his popularity rose a little, with the consequence that he tended to play up when he was feeling most isolated, keen to have the momentary adulation of those who took a vicarious thrill in his head-to-heads with his teachers. Only two, Riley Mullan and Charlie McDaid, stuck with him.

Hannah had spoken to him a few times, but once, in the canteen, had really stood out. She'd asked to get by him to get cutlery: he'd stepped back and let her past, been paid with the sterling of her smile. He watched her as she moved in front of him, her tray in her hands, waiting to pay for her lunch, kept watching even after one of her friends, who'd turned to say something to her, noticed his gaze and told Hannah of his attention. She'd turned and regarded him with a faint smile, then flicking her hair, turned back to her friends who laughed in feigned embarrassment at the frankness of his stare.

But she'd smiled at him, he remembered. She'd liked knowing that he was watching her, he decided.

After that, he'd kept an eye out for her in school, never missed the chance to watch her. On the corridors, at times he would walk behind her after class, when the crowds thronged towards the exits to freedom. If she knew of this, he was not aware, though afterwards her friends would say that she'd found him a bit of a creep, even if he was cute.

They'd met again, properly, at a nightclub in Letterkenny on 29 June 2001 during a 'Start of Summer' disco. The school discos had been running for a while, fairly successfully. The bar did not serve alcohol because of the age of the attendees, though there was an increasing problem with kids arriving already drunk or high.

On that night, Brooklyn had met up with two friends – Riley Mullan and Charlie McDaid – in Omagh, where they all lived, and while waiting for the bus, shared speed, which one of the boys had bought – Brooklyn either couldn't remember or wouldn't say which. They dissolved it in a bottle of water that they shared between them on the bus. Brooklyn had lifted six cans of Carling Black Label from his father's stash in the house and he gave the others a can each while he drained the remaining ones.

By the time the bus was approaching the outskirts of Letterkenny, forty-five minutes later, he could feel the buzz building. He'd seen Hannah on the bus, sitting with a group of her friends near the front. She'd had her hair curled for the evening, wore a vest top that showed off the gold of her shoulders, the strip of her bra visible beneath stirring something in him. His friends continued chatting, singing, but Brooklyn grew quieter, more intense as the journey wore on. Hannah, as if aware of his focus on her, seemed to preen herself a little, flashed him that smile, kept glancing back at him. She liked him, he knew it.

He took his time in the club. He'd been able to act sober at the door, but once inside, the heat, and the lights, and the music, and the thousand bodies shifting together in the thudding ambience drove him onward. He and his mates danced for the first hour or so, bouncing around the floor, barely aware of other people beyond the occasional shunt when he got too close to other dancers. Not that it mattered. He was sixteen, he was free from home for the night, staying with his mates in a sleepover. And there was Hannah, shifting in time to the music, her eyes closed, her teeth digging into her bottom lip as she concentrated on the rhythm, swaying to the beat.

As the music had slowed for the love-song set, she'd moved towards the bar with her friends. Some of them had already started chatting to some boys and she was alone. Brooklyn had taken his chance, believing she was waiting for him, had deliberately separated herself a little so that he should have the chance to speak to her. And so he did, offering to buy her a drink, insisting when she said no. The bar only sold soft drinks and water, so he'd bought two Cokes and crumbled a bit of the residue of the speed into both glasses.

The music was so loud, he'd had to lean right in towards her to speak to her and she to him. He could remember the thrill that accompanied the feeling of her breath against his neck, the heat that she radiated. They danced to one song, 'Ms Jackson', and he knew that everyone in the place was watching them. He'd put his hand on her back as they danced. He'd hugged her at the end, tried to kiss her. She must have been embarrassed, he thought, for she kept her mouth closed, her kiss prim and controlled. It just made him want more, want to get her away from her friends where she wouldn't be so self-conscious.

She'd thanked him for the drink, explained that she needed to see where her friends were. For the rest of the evening, Brooklyn, his confidence building commensurate with his frustration at the chasteness of her kiss, shadowed her. She pretended not to see him, he knew, but every so often he caught her eye, caught her looking for him, and he knew he was right. She wanted him near, waiting for the chance to get away from her friends, pretending an interest in his instead.

That chance came in Strabane. They'd all piled back onto the bus, the seating arrangement a little different now as those who had paired up through the evening took double seats together. Some sat alone, dozing against the bus windows, whatever they had taken or drunk already worn off. The bus was making a drop off in the centre of town and some others took the chance to ask for a toilet stop, which developed into a burger stop, despite one having already been made in Letterkenny. For the kids, it was a way to make the night last that little bit longer, to dissect the details of the evening's events or to spend that extra twenty minutes in the embrace of a longed-for classmate.

Throughout the journey back, Brooklyn had watched Hannah, noted how she'd grown more agitated as the evening had worn on. He guessed it was the speed – maybe she wasn't used to it. After she got off the bus, she'd vanished. He couldn't remember where or how, but all at once, she was there, waiting for him, inviting him. He'd followed her down the side street to the canal basin where the trees lining the street diffused the light from the streetlamps. There, among the shadows dancing along the pavement in the breeze, shadows that spoke to him, urging him on in voices he did not recognise and could not quite remember, they'd had sex.

This was how he described the events of the evening in the statement he later gave to the Royal Ulster Constabulary, the police force in operation before becoming the Police Service of Northern Ireland later that same year.

It was half an hour before anyone noticed Hannah was missing and another twenty minutes before she was found. The bus driver had already left by this stage, getting everyone else home to Omagh, Brooklyn included. Hannah's friends had stayed behind, one calling her parents to explain that they couldn't find her.

When her friends finally did locate her, Hannah was lying among a flower bed in the basin, half hidden from view. She had been knocked unconscious with a blow to the back of her head, which had stained the wall near her almost black in the streetlamp's glow. She had been sexually assaulted.

Hannah Row did not recover from the injury she'd suffered at Harris' hand. She remained in a non-responsive state for around six days before dying, her final gift to the world being an organ donation of her heart.

I'd worked the case at the time in a supportive role; we'd been tasked to scour through footage from the security cameras in the nightclub looking for images of Harris with Hannah Row, it being in the Irish Republic. The investigation had been led by the RUC in the north. It had been one of the first times I'd met Jim Hendry, who'd been part of the team working the case.

The footage we'd sourced had supported Hannah's friends' statements that Brooklyn Harris had been harassing their friend through the evening, had insisted on giving her a drink she had not wanted and had touched her repeatedly while she danced with her friends. He'd been off his face, they'd said. His behaviour in the footage, moving as if his limbs were not under his control, like a dummy with the strings all cut, supported the claim that he'd taken something before entering the club.

The police tied him to the scene because of traces of Hannah's blood found on his trainer. He admitted being there, admitted pushing her, admitted that they'd had sex, but claimed it was consensual and that he couldn't quite remember any of it and had hallucinated his way through the whole episode anyway. The damage to Hannah Row's skull had left her in a vegetative state, the doctors who examined her said; there was no possible way that she could have given consent.

Eventually, Harris was charged with the attack, found guilty, and was sent inside. That had been the last I'd heard of him. The last time I'd seen him had been in the footage we'd provided to the RUC, with the result that I'd not recognised the now adult Harris when I saw him.

But knowing that someone had now stabbed him to death, less than a mile from the spot across the border where he'd left Hannah Row to die, filled me with an unease I could not easily dispel.

Chapter Seven

I explained all of this to Patterson as we sat once more in his office. Patterson hadn't been stationed in Lifford at the time and, while aware of the killing, had played no part in the investigation.

'That puts things in a different light,' he said. 'Would anyone here have recognised him, do you think? Taken revenge?'

I shrugged. 'He wasn't from Strabane. The fact that he chose it as the locus for the attack was purely opportunistic. Maybe someone knew him but the chances of a random person spotting him and recognising him are slim. *I* didn't recognise him and I worked an element of the case.'

'Where the hell did Gerard Dawson or whatever the name was come from?'

'He was given a new identity after he was released,' I explained. 'He'd received death threats even during his trial. His legal team argued that he needed a whole new life if he was going to survive out of prison.'

'How long has he been out?'

'Five years. He fulfilled all his release conditions, apparently. His behaviour since then would suggest otherwise.'

I passed over a set of printouts taken from Harris' computer. There were over a hundred images in total, many of which appeared to be selfies, featuring a range of young girls. All looked to be in their mid-teens. Gerry was still working through the internet searches Harris had made, but it was already apparent that he'd been contacting young girls through chat rooms on various sites and striking up friendships. The images in front of us were the result of these friendships.

Patterson glanced through the images, grimacing as he did so. 'The fucker got what he deserved then, no matter which way you look. Where do you start though? The family of the victim then? The father of one of these lassies? The list of people who'd have wanted him dead must be a mile long.'

'Possibly,' I said, a little uneasily. 'We need to inform his next of kin. And Hannah Row's as well.'

'So where are you starting?'

'There was a text on his phone from a girl in Letterkenny. She was meant to be meeting Harris but cancelled at the last moment, saying her father wouldn't let her come down to Lifford.'

'Good for him,' Patterson grunted.

'She said she'd meet him the following day. I think that's why Harris took the house for another day, in the expectation that she'd manage to find her way down to see him.'

'You think the father found out and came looking for him instead?'

I shrugged. 'We've no evidence that he knew where Harris was staying. He didn't share his address with the girl; they were to meet at the bus stop in Lifford.'

'Maybe she did go down to him the next night and the father followed her.'

'Possibly. We'll know when SOCO give us a rundown on what they found in the house. He also was clearly either buying or selling prescription medication. Maybe something there caught up with him. Or, as you say, Hannah Row's family finally found him.'

Patterson nodded. 'Whoever it was, there won't be many mourning his passing. Get it wrapped up quickly and don't waste too much time or resources on it.'

'His family will want answers.'

'They might,' Patterson said. 'Or they might be glad to have the whole thing closed and done with.'

'He's still a murder victim,' I said.

He cocked an eyebrow at me. 'Inform the next of kin, see what the SOCO find and do your best. But I'd not be losing sleep over this one.'

Before anyone else, I contacted Jim Hendry; Hendry had worked the case after all. I filled him in on what we'd found, including my conversation with Patterson. I needed to track down Harris' parents, if they were still alive. As he'd lived in the north, Hendry would find that information much more quickly than I would.

'Patterson's right, you know,' he said. 'Harris devastated the Row family. They fell apart after the wee girl's death. Rather than just pleading to it, he claimed diminished responsibility, tried to have the fact he was off his head used as mitigation. The defence cooked up a whole pile of shit about undiagnosed mental health problems. The best thing to do with the fucker is take him out to the Atlantic some-where and tip him overboard. He'd contaminate the ground he'd be laid in.'

'I need to track down his family nonetheless.'

'Are you sure they'll want to hear about it? If he'd a whole new identity – a new life – maybe he left them behind long ago. You could be reopening wounds here for a lot of people that are better left closed.'

'I don't choose the victims, Jim.'

'Victim?' he laughed mirthlessly. 'Hannah Row's head had been so badly damaged he'd collapsed in most of her skull. Then when she was dying in a pool of her own blood, he raped her. Then he left her lying there and fucked off back onto the bus and sat there like nothing had happened, went home and went to his bed. By the time we'd been put onto him, he'd his clothes in the washing machine. The thing that let us get him was the fact he stood in her blood. So do yourself and everyone else a favour and zip the body bag back up on the fucker after the PM and have him burned or something. If you're looking for justice in this case, justice has already been done, as far as I'm concerned.'

Chapter Eight

Before heading home, I called down to the office to see if Joe McCready was still about, but he'd gone home for the day. I knew the SOCO team would still be working at the house and the pathologist was planning on conducting the PM in the morning. I considered speaking to Peter Shaw, the father of the Letterkenny girl with whom Harris had been in contact, but thought it best to wait until SOCO established who else had been in the house. It would be harder for him to lie if I had evidence tying him to the scene.

I couldn't find music to suit my mood on the way home and flicked to the local station to see if there was any mention of the killing. We'd released a boilerplate statement to hold the press until we knew more; certainly at this stage, until both families had been informed, I didn't want word of Harris' identity leaking. I'd worked with Hendry long enough to know he'd say nothing.

Sure enough, the piece got a brief mention as a second story, following on from a prolonged focus on the coronavirus outbreak in Italy, which seemed to be devastating Lombardy. The story immediately following the murder was about the latest row in the north between the two parties in charge over pensions for Troubles victims and whether it should be available to all injured during the violence here, including those injured in perpetrating some of the attacks and, as a sidebar story, the latest complaints about the prosecution of ex-British Army soldiers for Troubles-related crimes.

Only in Ireland could we create a hierarchy of victimhood, I thought.

Shane was already at work by the time I made it back to the house, so Debbie and I ate alone in the kitchen. A stack of exercise books awaiting marking sat on the counter – my wife's evening activity. We talked about our respective days and, inevitably, the conversation came around to Harris.

'I know Helen Shaw,' she said, when I told of the phone messages. 'She's a quiet wee thing.'

'I'll have to speak to her father tomorrow,' I said. 'He's an obvious suspect.'

'He's a good man,' Debbie said. 'He comes into our school and coaches some of the after-school teams. Take it easy on him.'

'He's a suspect.'

'For what? Protecting his daughter?'

'Killing someone.'

'Someone who killed a girl. Someone who was clearly grooming his daughter.'

'Harris was stabbed repeatedly,' I said. 'It was vicious.'

'You reap what you sow.'

I looked at her, surprised.

'What?' she asked, a forkful of spaghetti raised to her lips.

'Harris is the victim. He's the one who's died.'

'Not all victims are equal,' Debbie said, simply, then continued eating.

I sat out in the garden for a moment after washing up, watching the sun dip in the west, a habit I'd developed when I smoked and wouldn't do so inside and which I now continued despite having given smoking up. The sky was burnished by the dying light, the sun, even in its passing, creating something beautiful with its final moments in my sight. I walked up to where our cherry blossom stood proud at the top of our garden. Beneath it, I could still see the slight rise of the earth where I'd buried our basset hound, Frank, a few years back after he'd passed. I patted the tree limb nearest me instinctively as if in substitute for the memory of the thickness of his now absent flank. The fields behind had been zoned for development and the grassland cleared the previous year, but no work had started on it.

'Penny's on the phone,' Debbie called, standing at the back door. She passed me her mobile as I came back down to the house.

'Hey, love,' I said, aiming for cheery.

'Hi, Dad, how's things?'

'Good. Yeah. You?'

'Yeah. Good.'

The silence buzzed on the line and I imagined her in her room, impatient to get on with her evening, her daily call to her parents completed for another day.

'Dublin treating you okay?'

'Yeah, good,' she repeated. 'How's Grandad?'

'He's good. I'm bringing him up here tomorrow to stay for a bit.'

'Tell him I said hi,' she said.

'I will. What are you doing this evening?'

'Some of the other girls in halls are ordering in pizza, just.'

'Enjoy it,' I said. 'Stay safe.'

'Will do. Speak to you tomorrow sure.'

'Watch yourself,' I said. 'Love you, darling.'

But I knew the line was already dead, my own fears and sudden awareness of mortality no concern of hers. Nor should it be, I reasoned.

Still, that evening, I could not help but check Find My iPhone on my phone, relieved to see the pulsating blue dot that represented my daughter centred over her halls on the satellite map of the app.

Shane drifted in after ten, smelling of petrol and bleach, his twin responsibilities being serving customers at the petrol pumps until the end of the evening when he had to wash down the floors. It wasn't quite what he'd expected from the world of work but was at least earning him a few euro to take him out at the weekend. He'd matured into a mixture of me and his mother. He'd inherited my obsessive nature. Thankfully, he had his mother's fineness of both feature and form, her simple binary thinking and her ability to cut straight to the chase in our discussions.

'Are you stalking Penny?' he asked, glancing over my shoulder at my phone as he reached into the fridge for chicken to fix himself a sandwich.

'I'm just checking she's okay,' I explained, shutting the app.

'That doesn't tell you she's okay,' he said. 'That tells you she's at home. I'll be turning that feature off the minute I get to uni.'

'I'll be more worried for your housemates than for you, whatever time you head off. They'll think you'd never seen a hoover or dishwasher being used before.'

He feigned a grin. 'She'll go mad if she finds out.'

'Then don't tell her,' I said. 'Besides,' I added, reflecting on the day's events, 'it's hard to be a parent and not to worry.'

'You know she's in her halls, now,' he said. 'What's to worry about?'

'You're right,' I said, telling myself I would not check again that evening.

I lied.

Day Two

10 March 2020

Chapter Nine

Joe Long was finishing his work on the body when I came into the pathology suite the following morning. I tended not to wish to see the post-mortem, trusting that the experts in that regard will tell me whatever I need to know, but, somewhat unusually, Long's assistant had called and asked that I attend. I wasn't going to refuse.

Harris lay naked on the metal table, his body still wet from where he had been washed down after the examination. A 'Y' incision traversed his trunk, stitched back together now, bloodlessly. I tried to avoid looking at him while I waited for Long to finish the paperwork on the main desk.

'Squeamish, Inspector?' he asked, without turning.

'I'm not long after my breakfast, Doctor Long,' I explained. 'I suspect neither of us wish to see it again.'

'I'll keep it quick then. Cause of death was, unsurprisingly, the trauma caused by multiple stab wounds, most notably the one that pierced the heart and four that punctured the lungs; three to the left lung, one to the right. Downward pressure and the angle of penetration would suggest you're looking for a right-handed assailant. Probably a taller man, judging by the arc of blood spatter relative to the wounds that I saw yesterday and the force with which the knife managed to break through the sternum. Our victim had no defensive wounds on his body – he was sleeping when the first strike was made – probably the one that crushed his sternum and ruptured the heart. There was no blood or skin under his nails, so he didn't strike or scratch his killer. So that's that.'

I nodded, unsure why he had asked me to call down to see him, considering all of this could have been emailed through to me.

'Which begs the question, why are you here?' he asked, seemingly reading my thoughts. 'I heard some of the chat this morning about who our victim is. Some concern that we're wasting resources doing anything other than burying him as quickly and cheaply as possible.'

'I've heard those same conversations. I don't subscribe to that view,' I said, feeling the need to defend myself even as he moved away from me and over to the body.

'I didn't think for a second that you would,' he said. 'That's why I wanted to show you this.'

He pointed across the body to the series of small pock-marked scars I had noticed when first I had seen Harris lying in the rented house in Lifford. 'They're old scars. Burn marks.'

'Cigarettes?' I guessed.

'Indeed,' Long said, nodding. 'I found ones behind his ears and on his neck too,' he added. 'Certainly not in positions that would suggest they were easily self-administered.'

He pointed out the mark behind the right ear. I squatted at the head of the table, breathing through my mouth, as I examined it.

'There's also a malunion on his leg and two smaller ones on his right arm. I had him X-rayed this morning. Look at the arm first.'

He opened up his iPad and showed me the negative image of Harris' arm. Stretching out the image, he highlighted one thicker area of bone, running diagonally up the length of the arm for several centimetres. Then he changed the image and showed me a second, similar image, closer to the wrist, I guessed, judging from the bones visible below it.

'Both of these are spiral fractures that weren't treated and so have slightly misaligned in the healing process. And here,' he added, flicking through to the next image, this time of the leg. 'The tibia. Do you see the lump here that leaves the lower part of the bone off alignment with the upper?'

I nodded; it was clear to see, though ran across the bone rather than diagonally through it as the arm fractures had.

'The spiral fractures on the ulna and radius suggest injuries caused by a twisting motion; that's what creates that tear running up the diagonal of the bone as the torsion of the twist works against each other, creating a shearing effect.'

'Someone twisted his arm hard enough to break the bone?'

'Twice. Two different bones, two different places. And they didn't take him to get it repaired.'

'I take it these are childhood fractures?'

'I'm getting a Dexa scan done to check density, but I'd bet money on it having been when he was a kid. Likewise for the leg injury.'

'It's not a twist though?'

'No. That's a straight transverse. Might have been caused falling off his bike, or out of a tree.'

'But?'

'But it would have hurt like hell and it wasn't fixed. It healed into a malunion. He'd probably have had a limp from it.'

'He was neglected?'

Long nodded. 'And, based on the spirals and the cigarette scars, possibly abused. But at the very least, no one cared about this child. Not his parents, not his school or his teachers. No one noticed these things or, if they did, no one intervened.'

Looking now at this grown man, lying naked on the table in front of us, I was struck by Long's use of the word 'child'. Somewhere, before my seeing him murdered, before Hannah Row's murder, he had been a child, suffering. No one had cared then and, I had the feeling, very few would care now.

'I'll send whatever else I have through to you when I get it all wrapped up,' Long said. 'I just thought you should know what you are dealing with here, Ben.'

'Thanks, Joe,' I said.

'I remember a former colleague claiming at a conference I attended that there's no such thing as an innocent victim,' he said. 'That everyone who is killed has made some choice, some decision, even if a subconscious one, that leads to their deaths.'

'Really?'

He nodded. 'He'd worked it all out. Even accidents are the result of a series of decisions by the victim, he contended:

which side of the road to walk on; which tool to use in the garden; which flight to take.'

'You don't believe that, do you?'

He shook his head. 'It annoyed me, the whole idea seemed antithetical to what I do. The nice thing about my job is I don't have to decide the worthiness of a victim. I just need to establish of what they were a victim. In the case of Mr Harris here, I suspect he was a victim twice over, first as a child and now more recently as a result of a stabbing which proved fatal, whatever other evil things he may have done in between times.'

As I headed out of the suite, the word *child* stayed with me.

Chapter Ten

I called back to the incident room and found Joe McCready who'd just arrived.

'I'd to drop David off at school,' he explained. 'There's talk they're going to shut them down if this virus keeps spreading.'

David, McCready's son, was seven now. If the primary schools closed, my own son's secondary school would probably do the same thing. I could only imagine how Shane would respond to being locked in the house for a few weeks.

'It's not looking good,' I agreed. 'I'm bringing my dad up this evening to stay with us for a while, just in case. It could go any number of ways.'

McCready nodded. 'How was the PM?'

I filled him in, both on Long's conclusion on cause of death and on his comments afterwards regarding Harris' childhood.

'Plenty of kids have a tough time of it,' McCready said. 'That doesn't mean they all go out and beat and rape someone. If he'd done something to my kid, I'd have taken a knife to him and not thought twice about it.'

I nodded, trying to keep Harris as a child separate from the person he had become, as if the two were discrete identities, one innate, one created by the force of others acting on whatever fault lines already ran through the youth's psyche.

'I'm heading out to speak to the parents of Helen Shaw, the young girl he had arranged to meet,' I said. 'Are you coming?'

Peter Shaw sat on the edge of the settee as we spoke. When first I arrived at the house, I explained that I needed to speak to him. Shaw was trim, a little shorter than me, with greying brown hair cut neatly. He wore rimless glasses that slipped down his nose as he spoke, for he repeatedly fixed them back up.

'We're investigating a crime in Lifford at the moment,' I explained. 'In the course of inquiries, your daughter's name has come up.'

'My daughter? Helen?'

I nodded, coughed a little as I worked out how best to phrase it. 'I believe your daughter was in contact with someone online whom she called George.'

Shaw sat back, his shoulders straightening, his hands moving to grip his knees. 'Him.'

'You know him?'

'I know of him. Helen told me she'd made friends with a boy online and he wanted to meet her.'

'What happened?'

'I refused to let her, obviously,' Shaw said, holding my gaze with a defiance incommensurate to our conversation.

'Did you speak to the boy in question?'

His face flushed a little, even as he shook his head.

'You'd no contact with him?'

'None. Your wife teaches up at the school, doesn't she?'

I nodded. 'You coach up there, is that right?'

'Sometimes,' he said, then continued, not to be deflected from his line of reasoning. 'What would you or your wife do if some stranger contacted your daughter?'

'You'd no contact with him, then?' I repeated, choosing not to respond to the question.

'None.'

'How did he respond after your daughter said she wasn't going to meet him?'

Shaw shrugged. 'What's this got to do with Helen? Has he done something to another child?'

I shook my head. 'He's been murdered,' I said.

If Shaw was feigning surprise, he was doing so very skil-fully. But behind the shock, I could detect something else, an uneasiness.

'How much contact did your daughter have with him?'

'How did he ...? You don't think I'd something to do with it? Or Helen?'

'How much contact did your daughter have with him?'

'Not much. They were texting one another. Met in a game group chat or something.'

'Just text messages?'

Again, I could see the flush rising along his throat.

'As far as I remember,' he said.

'No photographs, then? No images?'

He shook his head, his gaze sliding from mine. I wondered whether having two male officers sitting opposite him had been the wisest choice and, as on other such occasions, missed once more my old partner, Caroline Williams, who'd had a knack for assuaging the egoism of more than one interviewee.

'I'm a father myself, Mr Shaw, as you rightly pointed out,' I said. 'I understand how you might have felt knowing that your daughter had been in contact with someone. I'm going to ask you again – just text messages?'

His shoulders dropped a little, his hands moving together, clasped in his lap. 'She sent him pictures. Harmless at first. But he asked for more. She sent him one she shouldn't have.'

'Did Helen tell you this?'

He shook his head. 'My wife saw it. She checks Helen's phone every so often for things just like this. She couldn't believe it when she saw it.'

'Is your wife here?'

'No. She's a nurse,' he offered, as if by way of explanation.

'So what did you do?'

'We confronted Helen about it the next morning and told her she wasn't going to meet him. She contacted him and told him she wasn't allowed to see him.'

'Did she contact him again afterwards?'

Shaw shook his head. 'Why?'

Someone had contacted Harris after that message saying Helen couldn't come to see him and I wondered whether Helen had done so without her parents knowing, or whether Shaw or his wife had sent the message to keep Harris in the area for longer.

'I'd like to speak to Helen, if that's okay, sir?' I asked. 'You can sit in, but I'd like you to allow her to answer the questions. It'll just be a chat at the moment, nothing more. We'll also need to take her phone with us, just to let our forensics team see if they can track any more messages from our victim.'

'From Helen?'

'No. From the man she was contacting. He's the victim whose killing I'm investigating.'

'We've different ideas of what constitutes a victim,' Shaw said, defiantly.

'So everyone keeps telling me, sir,' I said.

Shaw stood and, moving across to the living-room door that he'd closed when I came in, opened it and called for Helen. The speed with which she appeared suggested she'd been nearby, listening to our conversation. I glanced at McCready who raised his shoulder lightly in acknowledgement of the tension in Shaw's responses.

Helen was a sheepish young girl, awkward in herself. She came into the room, the sleeves of her black shapeless top pulled down and balled in her fists, her feet slightly turned in on themselves as she shuffled over and sat beside her father.

'Hello, Helen. My name is Inspector Ben Devlin and this is Sergeant Joe McCready,' I explained. 'We want to talk to you about a young man you've been in contact with recently called George.'

She blushed, her shoulders curving, her arms gathering protectively in front of her chest. She looked to her father who nodded.

'Can you tell me how you first met him?'

'Anime,' she said hoarsely, then cleared her throat and repeated it a little louder.

'The comics?' I thought of the image on Harris' wall, the cartoon portrait.

'Me and my friends read anime. We draw some ourselves. I met him through a group chat. We both like Shonen.'

I shook my head lightly, indicating I was at a loss.

'It's a type of drawing. George can draw in the Shonen style. He asked me to send him a picture of me and he'd do me like in a comic, so I did.'

'That must have been nice. Having someone draw you. Taking an interest in you?'

Helen nodded, though I could see the twisting of her sleeves increasing.

'So what happened then?'

'After a while he said he wanted to meet me in real life. To do a proper drawing. He said he was coming to Lifford to meet up and would I meet him. I said I would.'

'Was that the only reason he gave for wanting to meet?' I asked, as delicately as I could. 'To draw you?'

She nodded, though could not meet my gaze.

'I know he'd booked somewhere to stay,' I said. 'Had he asked you to stay over with him?'

She demurred, though so quietly, I could barely hear her.

'I know you sent him a topless picture, Helen. You're not in any trouble for that, believe me. Did he ask you to send it?'

She shook her head, as if keen to defend him. 'He wanted to draw me. He mentioned it once but I said no. But the more I thought about it, the more I thought it was harmless. Plenty of the other girls in school are doing it. And the boys too.'

Her father motioned as if he would speak, but could tell from my expression as I glanced at him that he was to remain quiet.

'But not to me,' Helen added quickly, with just a hint of regret.

'So it was nice someone taking an interest just in you?' I asked, aware that the question was leading, but suspecting that the appeal of George had rested in just that.

She nodded. 'I knew he was more grown up than the boys in school. So I sent it to him – it was nothing special,' she added, feigning nonchalance. 'He said he would draw me something special for when we met.'

'Did you meet him?'

Again, a shake of the head. 'Dad wouldn't let me,' she said, a little petulantly, and I suspected that the argument that must have followed such an edict had not yet been fully resolved.

'You didn't see him anyway? I know when I tell my kids not to do something, they don't always listen.'

'I couldn't. Dad wouldn't let me.'

'You didn't try to see him the next day, did you?' I asked. 'I know that George stayed for an extra day in the hope he might see you.'

Again, the material of her top tautened as she twisted it. 'No. I didn't know he stayed longer.'

I knew that to be untrue from the text messages we'd pulled from Harris' phone, but said nothing about it for now.

'Were you here the next evening? All evening? Can you remember?'

'She went to her friend Ann's,' Peter Shaw said. 'Didn't you, love? We dropped her up.'

I tried not to show my annoyance at his answering, kept my attention focused on Helen. 'Is that what happened, Helen?'

The girl nodded.

'And did you stay in Ann's all evening?'

Shaw straightened beside her. 'We told Ann's mum to keep an extra close eye on her,' he said, winking lightly.

'Is George in trouble?' Helen asked, releasing her sleeves now. 'He didn't do anything wrong. I sent him the picture. He didn't pressurise me or anything.'

'Of course he did,' Shaw said. 'You just think—'

'You think I'm a child,' Helen snapped suddenly. 'I'm not. I'm fifteen! I'm allowed a boyfriend.'

'That's true,' I said, interrupting before Shaw had a chance to respond, for I knew if he did that I'd have no chance of getting any more answers. 'Just as a matter of interest, what age did George say he was?'

Helen squirmed a little where she sat, then seemed to reconcile herself to something and straightened a little herself. 'He's twenty-one.'

'Twenty-one?' her father said, turning on her. 'You said he was seventeen!'

Helen smiled lightly as her father tried to contain his rage, clearly struggling over with whom he should be most angry.

'He was thirty-five, Helen,' I said, watching her reaction to see if she'd known this. The smile froze on her lips, her sleeves balling up again instantly.

'Is he in trouble?' she asked again. 'What's happened to him?'

I began to suspect my use of the past tense had registered, for tears brightened her eyes and she seemed to shrink a little before me. Strangely, in imparting the news, I felt worse than I had for a long time, not because of Harris, but because of the damage the revelation of this truth about him had done to this child.

As we left the Shaw house, with Peter Shaw caught between scolding and consoling his daughter, I realised that the interview had simply complicated things.

'Someone contacted Harris through Helen's phone and promised to meet him the following day,' I explained to McCready. 'Maybe Helen was lying and had sent the message to Harris without her parent's knowledge, perhaps meaning she had managed to get to see him.'

'I can check with the parents of the friend, Ann,' McCready said, glancing at his notes. 'See if they stayed in the house that evening. Do you think the Shaws told them what had happened?'

I shrugged. 'On the one hand, you'd want them to keep an eye. On the other hand, he strikes me as the type who'd probably not want to be telling anyone else what his daughter had got involved in.'

'Would you even send your kid to someone else's house after finding that?' McCready asked. 'My instinct would be to keep them as close to me as possible, so I knew they were safe.'

I nodded. 'Shane criticised me last night because I was checking where Penny was.'

'Having a kid changes you, though,' McCready said. 'You're a different person as soon as someone calls you "Dad". What were you doing?'

'Checking her whereabouts on Find My iPhone.'

He laughed. 'That is a bit excessive, mind you,' he said. 'She's what? Twenty-two now?'

'That's irrelevant!' I joked. 'But it does bring me back to Shaw and his wife offloading Helen the day after they found out about her friendship with Harris.'

'Maybe they wanted to get the child offside to create an opportunity to confront Harris directly,' McCready suggested.

Whatever the reasons, I knew that someone was not being totally honest.

Chapter Eleven

We met in the incident room at 11 a.m. to gather together all that we had found to date, Patterson directing the team working the murder, though without the usual bluster and sense of business that attended his involvement in such incidents. He had already made up his mind about the worthiness of Brooklyn Harris as a victim as had, by extension, a number of the others gathered there.

I spoke first, outlining what I had learned from Dr Long in the post-mortem.

'He wasn't hit hard enough!' Patterson quipped *sotto voce* when I mentioned the historical injuries Long had identified on the body.

Next, Joe McCready ran over what we'd been told by Peter Shaw and his daughter, Helen. Then Gerry Carter spoke, running us through the timeline of Harris' interactions, first with Helen Shaw and then with a number of other children, stretching back months.

'This one is interesting,' Carter said. 'Last year, in late May, Harris struck up an online friendship with this girl.' A slide appeared up on the screen. The child in it was mid-teens, again. She had shoulder-length strawberry-blonde hair, brown eyes, tanned skin. 'Her name is Sara Burke. They met through an online forum for Ecchi anime.'

'Which is?' Patterson asked.

'A style of comic book. Ecchi tends to be sexual but not explicit. There's a stronger genre, hentai, which is much more graphic.'

'These are comics we're talking about?'

Carter nodded, then raised his shoulder lightly in a half shrug. 'It's an art form. It runs the range from suitable for young kids right through to extreme pornography. Anyway, after a bit of back and forth between them, Harris sent her this picture.'

A second image appeared on the screen now, next to the picture of the girl. It was a sketch, drawn in anime style, of the girl. Her face was more pixie-like, her eyes exaggerated in their size, her figure more sexualised, but it was, unmistakably, the same person.

'Was Harris an artist?' Patterson looked to me when he asked.

'I don't know. Helen Shaw mentioned him doing something similar with her. There was a sketch of Harris done in anime style on his flat wall; it could well have been a self-portrait.'

While I spoke, I could see McCready take out his phone and begin typing something.

'Certainly, this was enough to really grab Sara's interest,' Carter continued, pointing to the picture. 'They arranged to meet on 29 June. And they began sharing more explicit images.'

A series of pictures appeared on the screen in quick succession of various body parts in stages of undress.

'Then, after 29 June, their contact stops. Neither make any attempt to engage with the other.'

'Did something happen to Sara Burke?'

Carter nodded. 'She vanished. From a social-media perspective anyway.'

'Do we have any details about her?'

Carter shook his head. 'She has almost no social-media footprint. Her first account appeared at the start of the year. She shared images of herself and her dog, but that's about it.'

'Protective parents?'

Carter nodded. 'Possibly. Or a fake account.'

'Someone trying to target Harris?'

Again, Carter raised his shoulder in a mild shrug. 'I can't tell. But she made first contact with Harris in the forum, so . . .'

'See what you can find on this Burke girl. Maybe Harris did meet her and it went wrong.'

Carter nodded. 'I've Helen Shaw's phone and PC to examine as well,' Carter added. 'That may well throw up something of use.'

The next to speak was Lauren Clarke, one of the Scene of Crime team, who talked us through the scene. Harris' killer had come in through the back door, managing to break the small pane of glass and unlock it with the key that had been left hanging in the lock. Harris had been sleeping when the first blow was struck, as Joe Long had said. There then had continued a series of blows around the trunk, neck, arms and head.

'The assailant would have been fairly covered in blood,' Lauren said. 'We suspect they were wearing some form of protective gear though. We have hair and a huge amount of fibre samples being tested, but considering the house was a rental property, and the potential footfall moving through it, we can't be sure that they belong to our killer.'

'Maybe there was a whole squad of them,' Patterson joked to a ripple of laughter. 'They were lining up to stab him.'

The comment annoyed me. His interruption of me had been a muttered aside and Carter and McCready had not been interrupted by him at all, yet the first woman in the room to speak began and he cracked a joke in the middle of her work.

If Lauren realised this, and I was fairly sure she had, she continued as if he hadn't spoken. 'We did, however, find something of interest.'

She brought an image up on screen of the floor in the hallway.

'You can see these droplets here,' she said, pointing to a series of small drops of blood. 'We found these in the hallway and we know that Harris didn't make it out of the bed so we guessed they belonged to the killer.'

'Did Harris manage to hit his killer or wound them in some way?' I asked.

Lauren shook her head. 'There were no defensive wounds on Harris' arms, no skin under his nails.'

I nodded. Joe Long had told me as much himself. 'So what do you think happened to him?'

'I think our assailant may have taken a nosebleed from the exertion. The droplets and the distance they fell based on the particle spatters suggest it. We've run the blood through our databases, and I've sent a sample to the PSNI to do likewise with theirs. As soon as I have anything, I'll let you know. Obviously, it would be quicker and easier if we had something to compare the sample against.'

Patterson nodded his head. 'That's your job,' he said to me.

I nodded in reply as Joe McCready leaned across and held up his phone. On the screen was an image of a teenage girl, smiling towards the camera, the image grainy and aged. I recognised it to be Hannah Row.

'What do you notice about her? And Helen Shaw? And this girl Burke?'

I looked again at the image still visible on the screen and then back to the one on the phone. Like Helen Shaw, all the girls were soft featured, their hair strawberry blonde, their eyes wide set and round, their cheeks marked with dimples when they smiled.

'They're all similar looking.'

'They're all like Hannah Row,' McCready said.

'He arranged to meet Burke on the anniversary of the day he attacked Hannah, too,' I said. '29 June.'

'He'd not moved on from her, even twenty years later.'

I nodded, aware once more that I had yet to face Hannah Row's family, to tell them about the death of their daughter's killer. And while I suspected it might bring them a modicum of comfort or sense of justice, I knew it would do nothing to fill the gap her absence had left.

And before even that, I knew I had the harder job of breaking the news of Harris' death to his own family before it leaked out to the press.

Chapter Twelve

Joe Long's request for Brooklyn Harris' dental records from prison meant we'd been able to confirm his identity quickly to expedite the post-mortem and had not needed to locate his family to positively identify him. It had taken Jim Hendry until the mid-morning to get me the address, so it was just before lunchtime when I set off for Omagh, where they still lived.

I'd dreaded seeing Harris' family, if I'm honest. Part of it was the normal reluctance I feel when speaking to the recently bereaved, that sense of the meaninglessness of my words, the limits of language which means that every statement falls short in conveying condolences, the questions asked which either should not or can not be answered and, behind it all, the awareness that answering those questions does nothing to mitigate against the seismic shift that is occurring in someone's life, the breach which you are rending in their being that will never truly heal again.

Grief, like a broken bone, will always leave its mark, except that while bone grows back, albeit with a tell-tale thickening, grief creates a gulf that does not heal, that never closes. Instead, you accommodate it at your centre, carry it, gently, as if it was something fragile, precious. I did not want to look at its face again.

And, of course, the thought of broken bones simply reminded me that someone in Harris' childhood had caused the boy physical harm and none had acted to stop it or to bring him to medical aid.

The address I'd been given was in a residential estate of detached houses just on the outskirts of Omagh. The houses were all set back a little in their own grounds and at the centre of the estate lay a communal green area as well, strewn now with bicycles whose presumed owners played Chase up and down the pavements. They stared at me as I passed, driving along suspiciously slowly as I tried to work out which house was number 43. Finally I found it: a bungalow outside of which was parked a people carrier. As I got out of the car, the local kids gathered on the green opposite the house and openly watched me, waiting to see who I was and to which house I was bound.

One of those same children ran past me as I made my way up the drive, calling that she'd tell her mother I was here. Consequently, I stood at the doorstep and waited. The child, a girl whose age I put at six or seven, came back out and stared at me.

'Who are you?' she asked, her arms folded in a gesture I guessed she'd seen in adults and felt was right for this situation.

'I'm Ben,' I said, not wishing to worry the kid by announcing I was a police officer.

'Do you know my mum?'

I shook my head. 'Not yet,' I said, 'but I'd like to speak to her, please.'

'She's coming now. She's working with Granny. Do you know my granny, then?'

'I'm afraid not,' I said.

'Then who are you? Are you a doctor?'

'Do I look like a doctor?'

She shrugged. 'I don't really know what a doctor looks like.'

'No,' I said. 'I work in the south.'

The door opened behind the child and a woman stood there, clearly the child's mother by the level of maternal resemblance between the two. The woman was, I guessed, in her early forties. She seemed harried, a little breathless as she wiped her hands on a towel, her brow glistening with perspiration.

'Yes?' she asked, without introduction.

The child looked between us, waiting to hear the reason for my visit. 'Miss Harris?'

'Ford,' she corrected me, straightening a little, tensing, as she did so. 'I was Harris. Why? Who are you?'

'I'm Garda Inspector Ben Devlin. I'm an officer in Donegal.'

She raised her chin a little, as if this information confirmed something she'd been expecting. 'What's he done now?'

'Can we speak somewhere else?' I asked. 'Perhaps sit down somewhere,' I added, nodding lightly at the child still standing on the step next to us.

'We need to talk about your dad, love,' the woman said. 'Go on and play with the others.'

The child dropped her arms to her side in disappointment and stomped up the driveway before seeming to forget her incursion into the world of adults and sprinting off after her friends.

'What's he done?'

The question concerned me – her brother had been living in Limavady not Donegal, which made me suspect she thought I was here about someone else.

'I'm here about your brother, Brooklyn.'

'Brooklyn?' she repeated. 'I thought it was my ex you'd lifted again. What's Brooklyn done?'

'Can we sit down?' I asked again.

We sat in the kitchen. Three pictures of children, one of whom I recognised as my doorstep inquisitor, hung on the main wall, a darker square next to them, which highlighted how sun-bleached the rest of the wallpaper was, and which had, until recently, housed a fourth picture. I guessed it was one of the ex to whom she had referred.

Brenda, for that was, she told me, her name, sat opposite me at the table. She'd picked up a small orange from the bowl between us and was peeling at it absentmindedly.

'Murdered?'

I nodded. 'I'm sorry, Ms Ford.'

'Brenda,' she repeated. 'Who did it?'

'We don't know yet,' I said. 'We're following a few lines of inquiry. When was the last time you spoke with him?'

'Years back,' she said. 'My mum visited him for a bit after he was put away, then she took sick and that was that.'

'Is she still alive? Your mum?'

Brenda nodded. 'She's got her own room out the back. I was in helping her into bed when Marie called me.'

'Do you want me to break the news to her, or would you rather do it?'

She shrugged. 'Probably best if you do,' she said, standing up and motioning that I should follow her.

Mrs Harris was ensconced in what appeared to be a hospital bed set up in the rear room of the house. I suspected the space had originally been used as a playroom for, incongruously, an array of medicines and equipment sat atop a unit which held baskets of toys in each shelf. A low-level suspiration of oxygen hissed from the tank next to the bed, which was attached in turn to the nasal respirator the woman wore.

Even having not seen Mrs Harris in her younger years, I could see that she was little more than the shell of a person. She seemed to be turned in on herself, her spine curvature such that her head lolled forward, her shoulders rounded in such a way that she appeared concave.

'Mummy,' Brenda said, her tone hushed. 'There's a policeman here. About Brooklyn.'

The older woman gestured that I should approach with a light raising of her hand. Each movement was economical, as if designed to conserve energy.

'Mrs Harris,' I said, moving forward and standing by her bedside. 'My name is Ben Devlin. I'm a Garda officer in Donegal. I'm afraid I have some bad news. Brooklyn's remains were found yesterday in Lifford. He's . . . he's passed away, I'm afraid. I'm very sorry.'

The woman did not speak, her eyes swivelling from me to Brenda, as if to check the veracity of what I had said. Her daughter evidently confirmed my claims, for she flicked back to me again. Her hand flattened against the duvet as if smoothing it. She nodded, lightly, then seemed to slump as she released the breath she'd been holding.

'What happened to him?' she rasped. I heard a click in her throat as she spoke, her voice dry as rust. I found myself swallowing, involuntarily.

'He was killed, ma'am,' I said. 'We believe he was stabbed to death.'

She nodded a second time, as if this had confirmed her expectations. 'Thank you for ... for telling me,' she managed, her breath seeming to fail her mid-sentence.

'I'm sorry for your loss, Mrs Harris.'

'He died years ago,' she said, leaning back against the pillow and closing her eyes. She raised her fingers an inch off the duvet as a gesture of dismissal.

Brenda led me back into the kitchen and motioned that I should sit while she filled the kettle. 'She has COPD,' she said, seemingly feeling I needed some explanation for her mother's condition. 'She took sick a few years after Brooklyn went inside and never really came round again. She's not the same person she was then and she certainly can't look after herself. She ended up living with me.'

'That can't have been easy.'

'That's why my ex is my ex. That and his being an asshole,' she joked. 'Do you know yet who killed him? Brooklyn?'

I shook my head. 'Would you have any idea of anyone who might wish him harm?'

She scoffed mildly. 'The queue would run round the block. The Row family, I'm sure. Some of the people he was inside with. Brooklyn didn't make life easy for himself.'

'Any more recent altercations that you know of?'

'As I said, I've not seen him in a few years.'

'When did you last *speak* to him?'

'After he got out, he was living up in Dungannon for a while. He contacted me one day looking for money.'

'Would you remember the address?'

'I'll get it for you,' she said. 'He'd been located there once he was released. They'd given him a new name.'

'Gerard Dawson?'

She nodded. 'I always still thought of him as Brook.'

I wondered how best to approach what I wanted to ask next.

'During the post-mortem, the pathologist noted some historical injuries,' I said. 'I wondered if you knew about them, or remembered them, from when Brooklyn was growing up.'

She raised her chin interrogatively.

'Several of his limbs carried evidence of malunion. It's caused when a bone is broken and doesn't reset properly. He'd one on his leg which might have left him with a limp.'

Brenda nodded, her gaze dropping to where her hands were gathered together in her lap. 'He'd a limp from when he was no age.'

'What happened to him?'

She stared at me but did not speak.

'Brenda. Whatever happened, it's not going to change anything now for Brooklyn. It might help me understand him better, though.'

'I'm not worried about him,' she said, quietly. 'I don't want to have to go back through it all again. We shared that childhood.'

'I understand,' I said. 'I don't mean to upset you.'

We sat there for a moment, without speaking. I could see that the young woman's mind was somewhere else; at the mention of her brother's injury, that period had come to life for her once more. For not the first time in my career as a detective, I hated my job.

She took a slow, hissed inhalation, then straightened herself where she sat in the chair, as if readying herself for speech.

'My father broke his arms. If Brooklyn ever annoyed him, he'd lash out. I know one of the times was when he found out Brooklyn had stolen his fags. I think Brooklyn was only about six at the time and him and his mates were already smoking. I remember Dad giving him a Chinese burn as we called them then, twisting his arm up his back while he did it. Brook couldn't lift it for weeks afterwards. It swole up and turned purple. Mum sent him in a note to school excusing him from PE class and swimming so they wouldn't see it. He injured his leg being pushed down the stairs of our home.'

'I'm guessing it was never reported?'

'Who to? Who cared?'

'School? His teachers?'

'Brook was a little shit in school,' she said. 'He was my brother and at some stage I must have loved him, but Jesus, he was a nightmare in school. Telling teachers to eff off, setting off the fire alarms, stealing stuff out of the staff room. They were that glad to see the back of him every day that when he started scheming from school, I think they didn't want to tell anyone in case he was found and brought back into the place again.'

'And he didn't go to the hospital?'

She shook her head. 'The more he cried, the more my father would hit him. He thought it was toughening him up. The first time, with his arm, Dad twisted it harder every time Brooklyn complained it was sore.'

'What did your mother do?' I asked cautiously, aware that the two women still had some sort of relationship at least now.

'Nothing. She was afraid of him, too.'

'That must have been very difficult to have to grow up with,' I said.

She shrugged. 'Him and Brooklyn had a love–hate thing going on. He would let Brooklyn watch anything. He'd put on porn films – these tapes that he bought up in the shop in Belfast, down the markets. He'd stick it on and Brooklyn would sit on the floor next to him, watching it – and he'd shout out to my mother what he wanted to try with her later that night. Then he'd give Brook a wink, like it was all a big laugh. He'd even let him have the odd mouthful of his beer if Brooklyn ran out and got it for him from the fridge.'

I said nothing, waiting for her to continue, but she evidently misinterpreted my silence.

'Yes, Mum knew. She did nothing about it, though. She complained once or twice, but he hit her, too.'

I nodded. 'It was a difficult situation for everyone involved, I'm sure.'

She raised her head a little defiantly. 'He never touched me. I knew to keep clear of him when he was in his moods. But he never laid a finger on me.'

'Your dad?'

'Yes. Brooklyn chanced his arm. I'd be getting changed in my bedroom and realise the door was open a crack and Brooklyn'd be watching in. I found some of my underwear in his room a few times where he'd been, you know . . .'

'I'm sorry for bringing this up again,' I said. 'I understand how painful it must be.'

She shook herself free of her memory. 'It's no excuse, though. For what he did to Hannah. They tried to argue that at his trial, that his upbringing meant he couldn't control himself, that he'd an inappropriate understanding of sex because of all the shit Dad made him watch, that he'd a mental illness. Brook was a bad bastard from no age, like he knew the worse he was, the more attention he'd get.'

'You don't think it impacted him negatively in some way? That it did affect his mental health?'

She shook her head. 'It didn't leave me twisted. We both lived in that house.'

'So what do you think happened with Hannah?'

'He couldn't be told no. Dad hit him and all that, but he indulged him, whatever he wanted, so long as it didn't involve Dad having to do anything. Even when I told him that Brooklyn had been spying on me, he just hit him a clip on the head and laughed. "Don't shit where you eat,"' she added, puffing out her chest and pantomiming how her father must have sounded to her. 'No one ever told him no. Until Hannah. And look what that got her. The only thing is, Brook needed an audience. There was no point doing something bad if no one saw, no one knew.'

'Maybe Hannah Row was his audience?'

She shivered involuntarily. 'He's my brother and I'm sad that he's dead. Some part of me must die with him, the bit that makes me a sister. Now I'll carry those bad memories of our childhood alone. But I think I'm better able to carry them than Brook ever was. It was just a matter of time before he hurt someone again, himself or someone else. God rest him. But this is news that I've been expecting for twenty years.'

'Where is your father now?'

Brenda shrugged. 'He did a runner a while before the whole Hannah Row thing. I think someone might have warned him off or something, but he gave Brook the hiding of his life the night before he went. Woman's Aid helped us after he left. The last I heard, he'd headed to England, some-where. I don't even know if he's still alive and I don't want to know. If you do find him, don't come back to let me know. And if he's dead, well, that's what he is to me already, so there'd be no news there I'd need to hear, either way around.'

As I left the house, I thanked her for her help and apolo-gised once more for causing her to have to recall those events. 'You're not the first,' she said. 'We'd a journalist a few weeks back contacted us too, looking to talk to us about those days.'

'Why?'

'She's writing a book on children who kill and wanted to do a chapter on Brooklyn. I told her where to go.'

'Do you remember her name?'

'Cathy something. She left her card but I binned it. She worked for the *Sunday News*, she said.'

I nodded. 'I'll maybe follow that up,' I said. 'Thanks again and I am sorry for your loss.' As I moved down the driveway, past the people carrier, I could not easily shake the feeling that her upbringing had affected Brenda much more than she was willing, or able, to admit. And I was struck with a pang of sympathy, however misplaced, for Brooklyn Harris, that no one seemed to particularly mourn his leaving of this life.

Chapter Thirteen

That the first tears I subsequently saw shed for Harris came from Hannah Row's mother simply added to my confusion.

She had not moved home since Hannah's death and so still lived in one of the detached houses that sat on their own grounds on Hospital Road. The hospital itself – once the Tyrone County but now renamed Omagh Hospital – had been relocated a little out of town, so the original site was fenced off now, the old red-brick building seemingly abandoned. Despite the constant flow of traffic on the road below, it created a sense of stasis, of time stood still, this fine old Victorian building opposite, half hidden from view by the overgrown greenery of the grounds surrounding it.

That sense was not dispelled when Hannah Row's mother answered the door. I'd last seen the woman twenty years ago, in television appeals and news-story footage of the investigation into her daughter's death. Then, she had been an assertive force, straight-backed and confident in front of the cameras, even grief-stricken as she was at the time by her loss. The woman who answered the door still retained that assertive confidence, even if time had inevitably aged her.

She wore jeans and a fleece hooded top on her thinned frame and had cut her hair short, giving her a boyish appearance, offset by the shock of white her hair had turned in the interim. But she still stood straight-backed and confident as she asked me my business and hesitated a moment while deciding whether to allow me inside.

She didn't offer me tea as we sat, as most people in similar situations often do, as if attempting to postpone, even for a moment, the news that I had arrived to impart. Instead, she listened carefully as I told her about the discovery of Brooklyn Harris' body and explained that I felt it only fair to tell her before it became public knowledge, for undoubtedly some of the press might try to contact her for her response.

She nodded, as if I had confirmed something for her, but then raised her chin a little and I realised that she was attempting, without success, to stymie her tears. They ran, soundlessly, accompanied only with a sigh.

'Thank you,' she said, when I had finished speaking. 'And I'm sorry – you must think me foolish to cry.'

'Not at all,' I said. 'I understand this must bring up painful memories.'

'They're more than memories,' Mrs Row said. 'I live them every day. Every day I go into her room and open the blinds to let light onto a bed that's never slept in. I keep the window on tilt to air out the room. She's my first thought every morning and her name is the last word in my mouth every night. He took my life from me when he killed her; I'm not sure why I'm crying for him.'

I nodded, glancing around the room. Sure enough, the only pictures on display were of Hannah. I couldn't remember if the Rows had had other children, but if they did, their existence seemed to have been shadowed by Hannah's.

'Have you anyone here with you for company?' I asked. 'Is there anyone you'd like me to phone?'

She shook her head, wiping her eyes with the sleeve of her top, and in so doing seemed to regain herself.

'No,' she said. 'I'm fine now. Thank you. Would you like some tea?'

I didn't but felt I should stay with the woman for a little longer if, as it appeared, she was on her own.

'Please. Milk and sugar,' I added. 'I'll help you, sure.'

I followed her out to the kitchen, past the framed pictures of Hannah beaming for the camera in each image. Only one, towards the kitchen door, showed her standing next to a boy, slightly older than her with enough familial resemblance for me to ask who he was.

'That's my son, Aidan,' Mrs Row said, glancing at him as she passed. 'He's living in Derry now with his partner.'

'Do you see him often?' I wondered at how he felt in this home which had become a museum to his dead sister and from which he had been almost entirely expunged.

'Once in a while,' she said. 'We all went our separate ways a bit.'

'And is Mr Row . . .?'

She shook her head. 'He was the first to go. New Zealand. I heard a few years back that he'd died over there. He'd remarried so I had nothing to do with the funeral. After Hannah passed, we tried to keep things together, as a family, for Aidan. But it was too hard, too . . . artificial. Sean knew that first, I think. We just drifted apart, bit by bit. He said I reminded him too much of her, like that was a bad thing. Said it was too painful for him to see her in me.'

She offered this information without any sense of self-pity or recrimination, simply stating the facts of the dissolution of her marriage.

'We both changed when she died. I stopped being a mother the day that happened. It wasn't fair on Aidan, I know, but that was how I felt. Someone had taken the light from the sky from me and I knew I would never be the same. I couldn't be a mother so I couldn't be a wife either. Sean realised that. I wasn't the same person he married. He wasn't the same to me.'

I nodded, at a loss what to say.

'As if that was a bad thing,' she repeated. 'Seeing her in me. I was the opposite, looking for her everywhere I could, looking to find her smell on her clothes, her pillows. Once, about a year after she died, I was clearing out some boxes in the attic and found that.' She motioned across to the wall, where a framed fragment of paper hung. I moved across and read a short poem, written by a child, under the title 'Kangaroo':

Kangaroos are bouncy, and they like to jump
They hop around from place to place, bump, bump,
    bump.
They box and fight and play all day and the night-time
    too.
Sometimes I think it would be fun to be a kangaroo.
Joey the baby lives in the pouch of Mummy kangaroo.
I wish that, just like Joey, I could too.
I love you, Mummy.
Hannah Banana xx

Mrs Row watched me as I read, re-evaluating once more the worth of the scrap of paper based on my reaction.

'She wrote me that for Mother's Day when she was five. I've written the date on the back. She could have been so . . . could have given so much. That's what I couldn't forgive, in the end,' she said. 'The wasted potential. She might have done great things, cured things, written something extraordinary. He took that from her. From us, all of us.'

I nodded. 'It must have been very difficult,' I offered, aware that I'd used the same line half an hour previous with the sister of Hannah's killer. Different sides of the same coin, both women – both families – changed irrevocably by Brooklyn Harris' actions. Then, as now, the statement seemed insufficient to fully encapsulate the gravity of what had happened.

'You should see her room,' Mrs Row said, putting the kettle down, unplugged, and leading me back out and up the narrow staircase. At the top of the stairs, I could tell Hannah's room instantly from the small wooden plaque embossed with her name and a cartoon doll, which had clearly hung here for well over twenty years now, undisturbed.

The room, like a number I'd seen through my career, had not been altered, seemingly, since Hannah's death. Her things still graced the bookcases and desk surfaces, little trinkets, shells, pieces of rock which must have meant something to her but which, with her gone, had become simply pieces of stone again. Except to Mrs Row who lifted one – a rounded, shiny pebble – and stroked the surface as she regarded the room with maternal pride. I suspected she could see Hannah in each surface, could feel her touch on the pebble, smell her scent on the air. Each object here a talisman holding a piece of Hannah, inviolate, for ever.

On one wall hung a noticeboard, with an assortment of notes and pictures. One caught my eye; a cartoon of Hannah, done in a childish anime style on a scrap of paper that looked torn from a sketch pad. It reminded me not just of the image I'd seen in Harris' room but also the anime connection with the girls he'd been more recently grooming.

'Who did this?'

Mrs Row shrugged. 'Hannah collected these bits and pieces. They meant something to her. She touched each of them. Even the dental card. Isn't it silly to keep it?'

I looked at the card to which she gestured: a dental appointment that she never had the chance to keep, a marker of a life cut short, unfinished.

And I thought that I knew now why she had wept when I had told her of Harris' death. Not only was his death the end of sorts of that story, the coda on Hannah's life, but I also realised that, with his death, the last person to see her, to interact with her while she was still her, had now gone and, with him, so too had gone another fine thread that had tied her still to this world. Harris' passing had loosened the hold the quick held on the dead.

I stood for a moment beside the woman.

'It's silly keeping it all, I know,' she said. 'I know she's not

90

coming back to it. I donated some of her stuff to the charity shops, but these things I wanted to keep. Otherwise, I think she'd feel I'd forgotten her, betrayed her memory, if I cleared all this out too. The rest of the world never got a chance to know her, or remember her, so I have to, to make sure she's still a little bit alive, you know?'

'I understand entirely, Mrs Row,' I said.

She replaced the pebble, carefully, just so, on the book-case and I noticed for the first time a framed picture of the woman alongside a teenager underneath a banner emblazoned with 'Hannah Row 5K'. I assumed, by virtue of the event name, that the picture had been taken after Hannah's death, which made me wonder why it was here, among these chosen things.

'Who is this?' I asked, lifting the picture, an act which earned me a tut from Mrs Row as she took it from my hand and replaced it in its spot. The action was so swift, I found myself apologising for touching it.

'That's a life she saved,' Mrs Row said, pride evident in her tone and the warmth with which she regarded them. 'Maisie. Hannah had signed the donor card; picked it up one day at the dentist and insisted on signing it and telling us all. I remember agreeing with her, never expecting I would have to follow through with it. When she passed, they were able to successfully harvest her heart. Maisie is alive because of my Hannah.'

'Part of her remains always alive, then,' I said. 'And if this girl has her own family, Hannah's memory will always be alive for them, too.'

She smiled at me, laid her hand on my arm as I spoke.

91

'That's a comforting thought,' she said, though I suspected from the placement of the picture and the manner in which she had taken it from me that she'd had that same thought herself and consoled herself with it for years now. Who was I to deprive her of that comfort?

Chapter Fourteen

After I left Mrs Row, I called Joe McCready to see how he'd been managing. He'd arranged for uniforms to canvass the houses on the row along which we'd found Harris and had requested ANPR footage of all traffic along the road in both directions for that evening.

I asked him to follow up on the journalist who had contacted Brenda, to see if he could get a name and contact number for her; it seemed strange that her interest in Harris' case should so closely predate his death.

For myself, I wanted to speak with Hannah Row's brother and I also needed to follow up on Harris' previous address in the hope that someone there had stayed in contact with him. And, I needed to collect my father from the care home, which had promised to call when he was ready to be collected. Harris' address was in Dungannon, a run further down the A5. It made sense to do that now, having already completed half the journey from Lifford to there by coming as far as Omagh.

The road down was slow moving, the traffic heavy and the opportunities for passing limited at best. For years there had been discussions about upgrading what was the main arterial route from Dublin to the north west of the island. Despite various promises and budgets pledged, the road had not improved significantly from my childhood. Only from the Ballygawly roundabout onwards did it become dual carriageway, at least on the road towards Belfast. There was no doubt that the failure to invest in infrastructure was as markedly imbalanced in the north as the south.

I was happy though to sit at a steady speed as I reflected on the conversations with both the Harris and Row families. Death had visited both families, twice over now for the Row family, though in a different guise this time. Both had been changed by what that visit had wrought, how it had affected the relationships of those left behind. Mrs Row, in particular, saying she stopped being a mother the day her daughter died struck me.

I'd never really thought of myself as a police officer, not in terms of how I viewed myself. I was a father, a husband, a son. I realised that, as my father aged, that final definition would change too. Already he was relying on me more than ever. He'd been in a care home in Derry after taking sick. The growing coronavirus crisis across the globe had panicked me into worrying about the impact on him, particularly if we were locked down and barred from visiting, as was happening in other countries throughout Europe. But I was a little nervous too about what his living in my home would mean, how it would change the roles of father, son, husband, when I would have to fulfil all three simultaneously.

And, truth be told, I was concerned about the care my father would need; not because I begrudged looking after him, but because I knew that he would not be the man I imagined him to be any more. He would change with each show of vulnerability, change in a way that would be more difficult for him than me, I suspected, for he was a man who had always prided himself on his independence. I worried that his own sense of self would be damaged as my sense of him changed.

I had spent my adult life facing death, trying to make sense of it, to control it in some way and impose an ending to the narrative of each victim's life that would bring some sense of justice and meaning to it. Now, in the face of what was to come, I began to worry that that had been a façade, that the belief that meaning would somehow mitigate some of the grief had been wrong all along. I knew, even then, that however this case ended, whoever was brought to face justice, Hannah Row would still be dead, Brooklyn Harris would still be dead, and neither of their families would be able to go back to the point before that had happened and reclaim what once they were.

The sky darkened with my thoughts as I drove into Dungannon, the clouds scudding across from the west heavy with rain. When it came, it was as a fine mist which saturated everything and hung over the rooftops in the distance. The wipers did little more than smear the rain across the windscreen, which did nothing to improve my mood.

The address that Brenda had given me was one of a series of what appeared to be bedsits, four per house, running along a row of white pebble-dashed buildings at the centre of an old housing complex. The development was aged, worn, carrying architectural designs from the 1960s. The rivulets of algae that stained the gable walls of the rows facing me as I drove into the cul-de-sac on which Harris had lived suggested that maintenance was low on the priority list for most of the inhabitants. Only one house, at the end of the far row, looked freshly painted, window boxes of flowers in their final bloom still displayed outside. I suspected that if anyone would provide a source of information about the residents of the street, it would be the owner of that house.

And so it was to him that I turned when all other avenues failed. No one responded at the address Brenda had given me, nor did anyone answer the bells for the adjoining bedsits. Finally, I approached the house I'd noticed, pleased to see the owner already standing at the window, admiring his flowers and obliquely watching my progress down the street.

His front room reflected the same fastidious nature as the outside of the house had done. A row of paperback books sat on one shelf, organised by size. A few knick-knacks were dotted around the tables and on top of the china cabinet that dominated the room and housed two different types of Royal Albert tea sets, which rattled and clinked dangerously as I squeezed past the unit and took the seat to which the man had directed me.

'I remember him,' the man said, not hiding his disdain, after I'd shown him the picture of Harris I'd brought. 'He left before the summer. Sure your crowd were here the next day over it.'

'My crowd? An Garda?'

'No, the real police. The PSNI,' he said, then added, 'You know what I mean. No offence.'

I waved away the need for an apology. 'Did something happen?'

'Your man was driven out of his house, sure.'

He could tell from my expression that I had no knowledge of the event for he straightened a little, taking a breath as if in preparation for embarking on a lengthy disquisition.

'Last summer, a crew arrived over there just after seven p.m. one evening,' he said, gesturing towards Harris' house with a flick of his wrist. 'There must have been half a dozen of them, all standing shouting about him being a pervert and that. The young lad had to run out like he was coming out of court, with a blanket over his head.'

'When was this?'

'End of June,' the man replied. He'd told me his name though so quickly that I'd missed it, both times he'd said it. I didn't wish to ask a third time.

'Do you know who the people were who came to his house?'

He shook his head. 'I was just sitting watching the end of the news and I heard the commotion across the street. I looked out and saw them all standing, shouting at the house. I went out the front to see what was going on. They was shouting about him being a pervert and touching kids. They said he was a killer.'

'What happened? When did the police arrive?'

'Not until the next day.' He blinked at me, as if considering this for the first time. 'I don't think anyone thought to phone them that night; we were all out watching,' he said, finally. 'I suppose someone should have done.'

'So, what happened?'

'Like I say, his mate came running out first and got the car started, then that lad himself came out, with a blanket over him. They pulled it off him, started shouting at him and that. He was lucky he made it to the car.'

'Were they hitting him?'

The man considered the question. 'No. Not like that. They were shouting at him more than attacking him.'

'What happened when he made the car?'

'They drove off. The crowd that chased him stayed for a few minutes, standing up at his doorway. They dispersed not long after. I never saw them again. Or him.'

'He didn't come back?'

'His mate did. He must have lifted all his stuff for him. I saw him the next day moving everything out of the place and heading off with it. I don't know where the lad himself ended up.'

'Is this friend still about?'

'I've not seen him in a while.'

'Do you know his name?'

'Mellon, I think someone said. I don't know his first name.'

'Did you know the man who was chased?'

'He was that lad Harris, wasn't he? He killed that wee girl back a few years.'

'That's right,' I said. 'Did he call himself by that name or did someone tell you that's who he was?'

'I never spoke to him,' the man said. 'That row of houses is all young fellas that have done time and are coming out the other side. I tend to stay clear of them.'

'You don't worry living opposite them?'

'There's cops here most days about something or other. They'd need to be spectacularly stupid to rob houses in their own street,' he said, dismissing (ill advisedly, I thought) my concern.

'But they weren't here that night?'

He shook his head. 'Not till the next morning. They were out chatting with young Mellon. Then they headed off.'

'And Harris never came back?'

Another shake of the head. This did, at least, fit with Harris' pitching up in Limavady in early July. Clearly he'd been either relocated for his own safety, or had chosen to go into hiding himself. Though not so hidden that he wasn't targeting young girls online.

'Would you be able to describe the people who chased him?'

'It was months back, son,' the man said. 'The ringleader though, he'd be easy enough to identify.'

'Why?'

'Sure, didn't he put it on the computer? The whole neighbourhood saw it. That's how I knew who that wee fella Harris was.'

Chapter Fifteen

We met in the incident room again just before six that evening. Joe had been busy and had managed to track down the journalist, a woman called Cathy McCay, who had worked for the *Sunday News* at one stage but was now a freelancer. He'd managed to get a number for her from her former editor at the paper. She lived in Eglinton, which meant I could try to speak to her when I visited Aidan Row.

The uniforms had come up with nothing of any great value. A few people had complained about the house being used as an Airbnb as previous guests at the house had been noisy. There were no complaints about Harris, though. One neighbour said her dog had started barking around 2.30 a.m. the night of the killing, but she'd thought maybe there was a fox in the garden and had gone back to sleep. It did provide us with a possible timeframe for the killing.

Gerry Carter had been working on tracking down footage of the incident that Harris' neighbour in Dungannon claimed to have witnessed. He arrived in, just as McCready finished his update, to say that he'd managed to find something. He connected his tablet to the projector in the room and played the footage on screen for us.

The footage had clearly been filmed on someone's phone from the rear seats of a car. In front, the driver wore a hooded top with the hood pulled up. His passenger sat, twisted in the seat, speaking directly to the camera, which shook with the movements of the road as the person holding the phone swayed with the vehicle's momentum.

The speaker was also hooded and wore a Liverpool FC scarf across the lower half of his face, covering his mouth and nose. His accent was clearly Northern Irish.

'This is our first hunt, people,' he said. 'We're here today, standing up for the children of Northern Ireland who have been failed by the PSNI. Instead of keeping these scum bags targeting our kids off the streets, they're letting them out into our communities, into our estates, to do what they like. And worse than that, they're even helping them change their names and start over, giving them a clean sheet to reoffend without anyone doing anything to stop them. But we'll fucking stop them, won't we, lads?'

There was a cheer of agreement from the others in the car as the camera shifted briefly with the movement of the cameraman punching his fist in the air between them.

'We are Northern Justice,' the speaker continued. 'Remember that name, folks. Those of you who are good people, know that we're out patrolling the streets and the internet, protecting your kids. And any paedos who might be watching, thinking they're safe, know this: someday, when you're not expecting it, you'll hear us knocking at your door, just like this nonce this evening will, and you'll know what justice feels like. You'll be quaking in your fucking boots when you see my face, when you hear my voice. You'll know then what real power is. That day will be the day you face your reckoning.'

Another cheer greeted this. The language and tone had become increasingly self-aggrandising and I suspected that the speaker was getting a thrill from his perceived power.

'Tonight, we're going to confront someone who on this very day almost two decades ago raped and beat to death a child. He never fully accepted his guilt, never apologised to the wee girl's family, never admitted that he was a murdering, rapist, paedo bastard. Instead, he tried to hide behind some sob story because he'd been off his face. Now, what should happen to someone like that, do you think? Eh, Jake? What should the cops have done to him then?'

Jake was, presumably, the driver, for he muttered something, his hood trembling lightly as he spoke, but we could not hear his words. The speaker began to laugh, a strangely pitched giggle.

'You're fucking right, man!' he said, punching the driver lightly on the arm. 'Cut off his balls and tar the bastard, Jake says,' he explained for the camera.

'Fuckin' A.' The cameraman's voice was louder than the others.

The main speaker muttered something to the driver, presumably directions, for the car turned right and I recognised the entrance to the row of houses where Harris had lived, visible through the side window briefly during the manoeuvre.

'This guy we're going to see now was Brooklyn Harris. Google him, folks; he lived in Omagh and beat and raped a young girl in Strabane twenty years ago almost. And instead of keeping him locked up for the rest of his days, the cops not only let him out, but they gave him a new name so no one would know who he was. But we worked it out. Using a decoy, pretending one of us was a teenage girl, we were able to trap this bastard to the point that he started asking for dirty pictures of us. Now he did that thinking he was talking to a fourteen-year-old girl.'

'Dirty fucker,' the cameraman muttered.

'A-one,' the speaker said. 'But justice is coming for him this evening. Everyone will see him for who he is, will know his face and his new name. Gerard Dawson, living in Mourne Villas, Dungannon. Dawson is a name he was given by the courts to allow him to come back out of prison and prey on our kids. But that stops tonight.'

The car pulled to a halt and in a flurry of activity those inside climbed out, the camera tilting wildly for a second, offering us a view of the inside of the car and a glimpse of the main speaker exiting his side. He was squat and heavy set, seeming to struggle a little as his arm caught in the seat belt. Then they were off.

The image on the screen bounced as the cameraman ran up the driveway to Harris' house, his breathing quick and rasping. He coughed wetly, once or twice, with the exertion and I suspected he was a smoker; I recalled having such a cough myself, before I quit, any time I'd overly exerted myself.

The speaker from the car was more clearly visible now. He wore cargo pants and a fleeced hoodie with a skull on it. The hood remained up but he'd pulled it back from his face a little, perhaps to let him better see Harris. I could tell from his actions, the way in which he shifted his weight from one foot to the other and back, that he was running on adrenaline now. He banged on the door three times, then turned to the camera.

'This is what Northern justice looks like.'

The door opened a fraction and the sliver of a face appeared, which I knew not to be Harris'. I assumed this was the mate the old neighbour had mentioned.

'We're looking for Gerard Dawson, otherwise known as Brooklyn Harris,' the speaker shouted. 'We are Northern Justice.'

The friend muttered something and tried to close the door, but the man, empowered now, wedged his foot in the jamb, preventing him from closing it. There was inaudible dialogue between them and I assumed Harris' friend was asking them to let him close the door.

'We're not trespassing,' the speaker shouted for the bene-fit of the camera, holding his arms out open at his side, albeit with his foot still wedged in the doorway. 'Brooklyn Harris asked for this young girl to send him a picture of her naked,' he continued, holding up a sheet of paper he'd pulled from his pocket. 'He believed she was fourteen years old and he asked for naked pictures of her. Is he too much of a coward to come out to face us?'

The friend opened the door a little and, grabbing the sheet, balled it up and threw it in the driveway. The speaker turned to reach for it and shifted his feet, allowing the door to be closed. But in that moment, with the door more fully open, I recognised the friend from the photographs I'd seen pinned to the wall of Brooklyn's most recent flat, next to his bed.

With the door closed now, the excitement abated a little even as the men's frustration started to grow. They stood in the garden, shouting 'Big Man' and 'Nonce' in the window. Occasionally, the camera panned around the street to reveal the neighbours who had come out to watch what was happening, though not to intervene. Most were younger lads, though I spotted the old man with whom I had spoken, standing out at his door, watching up.

Finally, after about ten minutes, the front of the house was briefly illuminated by two quick orange flashes as someone remotely unlocked the car in the drive. Almost at the same moment, the door of the house opened, and two figures stepped out quickly. One was draped in a blanket, hunched over, the other I saw now was Harris' friend.

Northern Justice reacted as quickly as they could, rushing across. The speaker grabbed at the blanket and managed to pull it away enough that Harris' profile became visible. He looked askance in terror at the mobile phone filming his movements, which was now shoved towards his face.

'This is Brooklyn Harris, calling himself Gerard Dawson. He's a fucking paedo and a nonce.'

Harris had reached the car now and forsook the blanket, unbalancing the speaker who'd been pulling on it and giving himself time to get into the open vehicle. Too late, Northern Justice realised they should have parked across the entrance to the drive to prevent any exits. Now I saw the hooded driver lumbering down to his car, though he was too slow. The cameraman managed a final shot of Brooklyn Harris by pressing the phone against the car window, before the car reversed, causing him to drop the phone, which clattered to the ground and cut to black.

'That's all there is,' Carter said. 'They've deleted this footage off their Facebook page but have kept up videos of a number of other "hunts" since.'

'Have they got any better at it?' Joe McCready asked. 'That was a mess from start to finish.'

'I think we can be fairly sure that Sara Burke was the decoy they were talking about there,' I said. 'Can you use either this or the Burke account to see if you can identify anyone? I'm guessing they're not advertising their identities, based on what we've seen here.'

Carter nodded. 'I'm working on it,' he said.

'Good work, Gerry,' I said. 'Maybe they tracked him down again to Lifford.' A thought struck me. 'Can you see if there's any connection between them and Peter Shaw, too, Gerry?'

Just at that my own mobile started to ring. I thought it might be the home, calling to say I could collect my father, but it was Jim Hendry. I declined the call, planning to phone him back after our meeting but almost instantly he called back.

'Excuse me, folks,' I said, stepping out of the room. 'Jim,' I said, 'I'm in the middle of a briefing.'

'This can't really wait,' Hendry said. 'We've matched the blood sample you sent us from the Harris site. We've checked a few times in case there's a mistake but it seems the blood you found on the floor belongs to ... well, it belongs to Hannah Row.'

106

Chapter Sixteen

'How is that possible?' I asked. 'Did someone store it some-how since 2001?'

'We don't know,' Hendry said. 'It's fresh blood is all that I can tell you. What that means is beyond me.'

'Could it be a member of her family? She has a brother in Derry I was going to call with tomorrow.'

'He's not a twin, from what I remember,' Hendry said. 'Besides, I don't know if that would even work in terms of the blood match. I'm just telling you what's been passed on to me. I'll have the results emailed over and you can get some of the specialists over there to take a look.'

I was a little surprised. Hendry would usually go the extra mile, frequently so as to crow about how much better equipped were the PSNI compared to us, but also because I knew he genuinely wanted to help. I wondered whether, on some level, he was annoyed at the efforts being made to find Harris' killer, having been involved in bringing Harris to justice twenty years ago. Or, perhaps, it was simply a reflection of what he had already confided to me, that his enthusiasm for the job was waning.

'Thanks, Jim,' I said. 'I spoke with both the Harris and Row families earlier.'

'How's the mother?'

'Mrs Harris? She's—'

'No. Mrs Row. How'd she take the news?'

'She wept,' I said. 'And I don't think it was with relief or joy at Harris' death.'

'It wouldn't be. She was a good woman. I remember back then how she couldn't understand why this had happened to them. She kept asking over and over, asking us to help her make sense of it. Why Hannah? Not even why did Harris target her, but why did God or the universe or whoever let it happen. What had they done to deserve it? What could we say to her?'

'No one deserves it,' I agreed.

'Brooklyn Harris did.'

The silence grew across the line. Finally, I said, 'We've come across something else. A group called Northern Justice targeted Harris last year.'

'Remind me,' Hendry said.

'They seem to be paedophile-hunters.'

'That's right,' he said. 'I'd heard of them somewhere. I think some of the districts have managed to get people up before the courts on the strength of their evidence.'

'They outed Harris last year and drove him from his old house in Dungannon. Set up a decoy account to entrap him. Thing is, clearly there was no fallout from it. They've pulled the footage from their site and Harris got relocated to Limavady afterwards. Could you find out who'd have handled it?'

'Leave it with me,' Hendry said. 'I'll be in touch.'

By the time we got finished up, it was almost 8 p.m. I drove straight to Derry along the N13, coming up into the city via Coshquin where, at the height of the Troubles, a military installation commensurate in size with the Camel's Hump between Lifford and Strabane had stood. It was the target of a proxy bomb in 1990, when the IRA tied a local man, Patsy Gillespie, into his van with curtain ties taken from his house, packed the van with explosives and forced him to drive it to the checkpoint, whereupon they detonated it, killing him alongside five soldiers standing on duty. Those responsible had attempted to disprove the view that the poor man was a victim by letting it be know that he had worked in the local Army barracks and had continued to do so even after being warned to stop, as if this justified the cruelty of his killing.

Derry had expanded since then, housing and shopping complexes sprawling almost to the border now. I drove up through the town centre, the riverfront quieter than usual, due no doubt to the heavy slate-grey clouds that had draped themselves across the Foyle valley and portended rain before long.

Sure enough, as I drove up the Prehen Road, having collected my dad, the first thick drops exploded on the windscreen. As we passed through New Buildings, I could see where someone had spray-painted the British Army Parachute Regiment logo on the side of a phone box. A few miles further on, in a field abutting the main road, sat an old haulage container on which had been daubed the slogan 'I Stand with Soldier F' in reference to the aged soldier who, the previous year, had been charged with two counts of murder as part of the Bloody Sunday killings of thirteen civil rights demonstrators in the city in 1972. The case had caused consternation in Britain and in certain areas of the north where the feeling was that members of the security forces were being unfairly victimised in historical inquiries. In other parts of the north, the charges represented a welcome first step towards starting to hold someone to account for the shooting of unarmed civilians campaigning for their civil rights. The debate, as so many in the north seemed to at the moment, hung on how one defined the word 'victim'.

My father had dinner with us, then sat and watched the news, detailing the coronavirus horror unfolding in northern Italy. There was a news report on the issues of whether schools might shut, during which my dad took a walk out to the back garden. He'd been a keen gardener all his life and felt more comfortable outdoors. It was already dark out so I put on the light above the back door and joined him.

'That azalea will explode with colour when it opens,' he said, nodding at the plant nearest us which was, at this stage, still seemingly dormant.

We walked the confines of the garden, slowly, my father examining each plant, taking the thin tendrils of leaves between his thick fingers and gently rubbing their texture. He had to link arms with me for support.

'Are you sure I'm not putting you out staying up here?' he asked, apropos of nothing in particular.

'No, it'll be fine,' I said. 'I'd prefer knowing you were okay here than you getting locked in and none of us being able to come down to see you.'

'Is this lockdown thing definitely happening?'

'There are all kinds of rumours,' I said. 'Stuff about the army being drafted in, all kinds of things. We've been told nothing, but Debs said their school principal had heard the schools were going to shut soon. If that happens and things keep spiralling, it'll be hard to see how we won't go into a lockdown the same as they have in Europe.'

He nodded his head, though I could tell he wasn't quite listening to what I was saying, that his mind was already on something else.

'Your cherry tree is already budding,' he said, moving across to where the wide boughs spread. He reached out and gently touched one of the buds, the pink of the coming bloom already visible around the edges of the tightly packed shoots. 'That's the mild winter,' he said. 'It's playing havoc with the plants, flowering at all the wrong times.'

He stopped and, turning, looked down the garden towards the house. Through the rear window, I could see Debs sitting at the kitchen table watching the news and Shane moving about as he cleared the dishes over to the sink.

'You've a nice place here,' my father said. 'I always love it up here.'

I nodded agreement. The air was fresh, the earlier rain having cleared the sky.

'You need to look after this,' he said, taking in, not just the garden, but the house and those in it. I knew now where his thoughts had been since we'd stepped out onto the damp grass of the garden. 'Whatever happens, that's your job. I know you will anyway,' he added quickly. 'I just need to say it.'

'Of course,' I said. 'I've a good example to follow.'

He shook his head. 'I love cherry blossoms,' he said, turning again to the tree and lifting once more a bud between his finger and thumb. 'They're just stunning when they flower. Nothing like them. You see God in the beauty of them. But they don't last long enough. A week or so and the winds take them. And they're a mess to clean up.'

He held the bud a moment longer, then released it. 'But for that week or so, it's all worth it. You never think about the weeping of the leaves to come when you hold the bud.'

'That's true,' I agreed.

'I'm afraid, Ben,' he said, placing his hand on my arm again. 'I'm afraid of what's ahead.'

'Me too,' I said.

I wanted to say something else to him, something to comfort him. Or me. But I could find nothing that would suitably achieve either aim.

Day Three

11 March 2020

Chapter Seventeen

Joe McCready picked me up early the next morning and we drove back down to Derry, this time along the backroad from Lifford, bringing us in at the Brandywell. We'd two people I wanted to see: Cathy McCay, the journalist who had contacted the Harris family, and Hannah Row's brother, Aidan. I'd called McCay's number earlier and she agreed to meet us after 11 a.m. in a city-centre café. As a result, we headed on down to Eglinton, where Aidan Row now lived.

I recognised him from the one picture in his mother's house that I'd seen, as he came to the door and, as he showed no surprise when I introduced myself to him, I suspected his mother had contacted him to tell him of my visit with her. He was smaller than I was expecting, accentuated perhaps by the skinny jeans and slim-fit T-shirt he wore. Despite being indoors, he wore a beanie hat, which served to heighten the thinness and pallor of his face.

He brought us into the house, leading me into the living room where another young man was sitting in sweat shorts and a T-shirt, eating cereal as he watched a morning TV show. On the screen, Piers Morgan was angrily defending the postponement of a football match over coronavirus fears.

'This is my partner, Michael,' Aidan said.

I nodded in greeting as the young man stood, turning down the television as he did so. 'I never thought I'd see the day I'd be agreeing with Piers Morgan over things,' he said. 'I'll be in the kitchen if you need me.'

Aidan had not asked who we were, nor had given either myself or Joe the opportunity to introduce ourselves. I played my gut:

'I'm guessing your mum told you I'd been to see her.'

He looked for a moment as if he would feign some sort of denial, but finally nodded. 'She told me Harris is dead.'

'That's right,' I said.

He nodded. 'That's good,' he said.

I didn't react to the comment. 'I thought it best that you should know. It'll be released to the press later.'

I was surprised that it hadn't already leaked out. Clearly neither the Rows nor the Harrises had told anyone.

'So what do you want from me?'

'We're investigating his killing,' I explained. 'I wanted to just get a sense of things.'

'You wanted to know if I'd killed him,' Aidan Row said, laughing. 'What night did he die?'

'Saturday night into Sunday morning.'

'Michael,' he called.

A moment later, Michael appeared in the doorway.

'Where were we on Saturday night, Sunday morning?'

His partner thought for a moment before speaking. 'We were here. You weren't feeling great.'

'I was under the weather,' Aidan explained. 'I was in bed most of the weekend. Michael looked after me.'

'That's fine, Mr Row,' I said. I noted that, despite his youth, he did not tell me not to refer to him by his title. He was being deliberately veiled. Perhaps he'd been waiting since yesterday for me to call and, in the interim, had become defensive, expecting that I would be arriving with some form of accusation. Or perhaps his experience with the police had not been a positive one.

'Your mum seemed upset at what happened,' I said. 'I was sorry if it opened up old wounds again.'

'Have you seen that house?' Aidan asked. 'She keeps her wounds open every day. She only knows she's alive when she's walking that mausoleum.'

I noticed Michael's reaction and suspected he'd heard such comments before. 'Sorry,' Aidan said, to him.

'It can't have been easy, growing up with all that grief,' I offered.

He regarded me sceptically. 'I was always in Hannah's shadow,' he said. 'Beholden to her, even when she was alive. How could I compete with her once she died?'

'You weren't in her shadow,' Michael began in a manner that reflected how well rehearsed was the statement.

'I was. I'm okay to admit that. Hannah was brilliant at everything she did. She was a star for my mum and dad. When she died, the light went out for both of them. My dad eventually wanted to start living again. But living for him meant without me. My mother, as you saw yesterday, has no interest in life. She stopped being a mother the day Hannah died, as far as I can tell.'

'She suffered a huge loss,' I said, feeling the need to defend her, as a parent myself.

'We all lost Hannah. She was my friend. She was my sister, I know that, but we actually liked one another too. She wouldn't want what Mum has done. Hannah was the happiest person I knew. She wanted people to live: the last thing she'd have wanted was for the world to stop for Mum the way it did.'

'That must have been challenging for you,' I said.

He nodded, mollified a little.

I didn't blame him. When Penny was a teenager, she'd had an accident horse-riding that had left her with a head injury. For months afterwards, we'd treated her with kid gloves, focusing on her, inadvertently, to the exclusion of Shane. I remember how he'd resented it, resented the fact that an accident that had befallen her had impacted him so negatively. Initially, I'd thought he was being selfish and should have shared in our joy that his sister was recovering. But, over time, I'd realised that he was a child at heart. As Aidan Row was now. I thought, unbidden, of my father the previous evening, of his fear in the face of time and sickness. None of us stopped being children at heart.

'There is a complication which I'd not known about yesterday when I spoke with your mother,' I said. 'We found blood at the scene of Harris' murder. It's Hannah's.'

For the first time since my arrival, I could see Aidan Row was genuinely caught off-guard.

'But that's . . . that's not possible,' he said. 'You must have made a mistake.'

I shook my head. 'The PSNI confirmed it for us. We have our own technicians analysing their results at the moment.'

'How could that be? Hannah died. We saw her in the coffin.'

'I don't know,' I conceded. 'But it does suggest that his killing had something to do with Hannah's killing.'

Aidan looked at us askance, then glanced towards Michael who stood still in the doorway.

'You're not suggesting some of us killed him? I've already told you where I was.'

'We've no one to verify your alibi, sir,' Joe said. 'Except your partner, who presumably would have a conflict of interest.' He'd remained quiet until now as the conversation had focused on Aidan's mum, whom he'd not met. Joe's intervention seemed to formalise the tone of the discussion, for Aidan straightened a little in his chair, regarding Joe coolly.

'I'm afraid I didn't think I'd need an alibi this past weekend, otherwise I'd have arranged one.'

'We'll also need a DNA sample,' Joe said. 'To eliminate you as a suspect, of course.'

'You can take one now,' Aidan said.

Joe looked to me and I nodded, indicating he should go ahead. We'd a few spare cheek-swab kits in the car and he went out to get one. A review released the previous year had highlighted that over four fifths of gardai had taken DNA samples even though many of us hadn't been trained. Patterson, to his credit, had rectified that in our region.

Joe returned and, within a few moments, had the swab taken and labelled.

The certainty with which Row had agreed to it convinced me that his alibi was genuine and that he'd not been near Harris' house.

119

'Have you any other family near?' I asked. 'Apart from your mum?'

He shook his head. 'Dad went to the other side of the world. He put all of us behind him when he left. I heard rumours he had died, but who knows?'

'When did you last hear from him?'

'When did I come out?' Aidan asked Michael.

'Eleven years ago.'

'Eleven years ago,' Aidan repeated. 'Not a peep since.'

'He was certainly primed for our arrival,' I commented to Joe as we climbed back into the car.

'He'd all his bases covered. I'll get this sample submitted today, but I suspect it'll not be a match.'

'I'd say you're right; he gave it so willingly,' I said. 'He didn't ask how he died, though.'

'What?'

'Harris. He didn't ask how he died, if he suffered, anything like that.'

'Maybe his mother told him.'

'I don't think I told her. But she was upset when she heard he'd been killed. With Aidan there was nothing. No relief, no triumph, not even curiosity.'

'He was defensive from the start.'

'Without any need to be, if he has nothing to hide,' I said.

Chapter Eighteen

Cathy McCay was already waiting in the café on Bishop Street when we arrived. She had her phone sitting on the table in front of her and made it clear from the start that she would be recording what she referred to as 'our interview'.

'I assume Brooklyn told you what I'm working on,' she said, once we'd ordered three teas. She seemed to be under the misapprehension that we were meeting to discuss Brooklyn's attack on Hannah Row rather than his own killing. I decided not to disabuse her of that notion for a moment. Even when I had called her, I had simply said that I had been told she was looking again at the Row killing and wished to speak with her. Her opening question seemed to suggest that she had, as I'd suspected, been in touch with Brooklyn Harris before he died.

'What exactly are you working on?' I asked. 'The details are a little vague.'

She looked from me to Joe as if searching for the subtext in what I had said. She was younger than I expected, in her early forties, perhaps, with blonde hair cut into a long bob. She had been wearing glasses when I came in, but removed them when we sat, yet she had struggled a little to hit the right record button on her phone.

'I'd started looking at cases of young people who kill. My initial plan was to have a chapter on the killing of Hannah Row. Last year, Brooklyn was outed on social media. I was able to track him down and told him what I was doing. But the more I spoke to Brooklyn, and the more I read into the background details, the more convinced I was that there were flaws in the original investigation. That means the chapter is ballooning into a book all of its own.'

'Flaws in the investigation? You think Brooklyn Harris didn't kill Hannah Row?' I asked, incredulous. Brooklyn had pled guilt to manslaughter.

'I think he was there when she died. I'm not sure that was the full picture. What I'd hoped to speak to you about was what requests the RUC had made for footage from the nightclub they attended in Letterkenny.'

'I'm not sure I remember exactly,' I said. 'What flaws?'

'How about you answer my question before I answer yours?' McCay asked, smiling. 'Were the Guards asked for all footage from that night or was it specifically for footage of Brooklyn?'

Now that she had raised the question, I seemed to remember that we'd been instructed to look for Brooklyn Harris. Instead, I asked, 'Why do you think Brooklyn didn't kill Hannah Row?'

McCay shifted in her seat a little. 'Did Brooklyn ask you to . . . how did you know to contact me?'

'Brooklyn's sister told us that you'd been in touch with her, asking for an interview.'

She considered the implications of what I had said. 'Have you spoken with Brooklyn?'

'No,' I said. 'Not as such.'

She lifted her phone and stopped the recording. 'We've crossed wires here. I told Brooklyn that I wanted to chase down the Guards to ask about the footage. When you called to speak to me, I assumed he'd taken things into his own hands and contacted you directly.'

She put her phone into her bag and motioned as if to stand, then stopped. 'So why are you looking to speak to me? Did his sister make a complaint? But you're Guards so it wouldn't have gone to you anyway,' she concluded, articulating her thought process.

I was interested to know what angle she was investigating in Hannah Row's death and had only one thing to barter for that. I knew a press release was going out ahead of the noon bulletins anyway, so decided to use the information to my benefit.

'If I give you an exclusive, ahead of the main media outlets, I'll need something in return.'

'What?' she asked, her phone back on the table even as she spoke.

'I need you to tell me your concerns over the Hannah Row killing.'

'You can read the book when it's done,' she said. 'I don't work for free.'

'That's a pity,' I said.

She looked from Joe to me, as if trying to gauge if she was being played.

'I'll tell you the highlights,' she agreed. 'If the scoop is a big one.'

I looked to McCready who nodded.

'We're investigating a murder. The body of the man found in Lifford on Sunday evening.'

'Right,' McCay said, warily.

'Brooklyn Harris was the murder victim.'

This caught her. She sat back in her seat, absorbing the information, and I could already see her working out the angles, considering perhaps how this information impacted her planned book. Clearly she concluded that it could only help it, for she lifted her phone and began typing.

'Twitter?' I guessed.

She nodded. 'The rest of them will be running to catch up. When is the press release going out?'

I smiled. She was shrewder than I thought. 'You've about fifteen minutes head start on them.'

'That's enough,' she said. 'How did he die?'

I could tell the question, though couched in concern for the victim, was primarily harvesting more information for the inevitable calls she'd start getting.

'He was stabbed to death. You can add that Garda sources confirmed we were following a definite line of inquiry but we're keen to speak to anyone who may have had contact with Brooklyn Harris online or in person. We also want to trace anyone who may have had contact with Harris under his assumed name, Gerard Dawson.'

McCay nodded as I spoke, tweeting it seconds after I'd finished.

'What's that worth?'

She nodded her head. 'A bit. You'll need to give me a few minutes though.'

Her phone had already started buzzing as the first calls came through looking for her take on the scoop she'd released.

'We'll finish our tea,' I said, and she lifted the phone and stepped out onto the street to take the calls.

Thirty-five minutes and two more teas and a round of sandwiches later, she finally reappeared.

'So, what do you want to know?' she asked, lifting one of the triangles of bread and popping it in her mouth, leaving the filling on the tray.

'What's your angle in the book?'

She considered the question, though I knew she'd already decided how much she was going to give us and was enjoying the change in dynamic.

'Brooklyn never denied that he was there when Hannah Row was attacked. And he couldn't deny having assaulted her sexually, though he had no recollection of it. But he said that there had been someone else there, too.' She corrected herself. 'Actually, he said there were other people there. That there were shadows walking around him, trying to attack him. He said that Hannah was the one calling them, telling them to attack him. He claims he hit her to stop her calling them. He was afraid of what they would do to him. Then a voice told him he had to have sex with her or the shadows would get him. He said he could feel hands on him, pushing him down on her. When it was over someone told him he needed to stay quiet. That if he told anyone what he had done, the shadows would take him.'

'He claimed diminished responsibility at the time on the grounds of exacerbating an existing mental condition through drug use,' I said. 'This sounds like a hallucination.'

125

'It was,' McCay said. 'I've no doubt he had a psychotic episode. But that doesn't mean there wasn't someone else there.'

'Have you any evidence to support this, beyond Brooklyn Harris' own interpretation of his tripping?' McCready asked.

'There were discrepancies in the investigation,' McCay said. 'No one paid any heed to Brooklyn's home circumstances, or the fact he'd undiagnosed schizophrenia. He was sentenced to prison, not psychiatric support. No one looked at the abuse he suffered at his father's hands.'

'None of those were pertinent to the question of whether or not he attacked Hannah Row,' I said.

'The PM showed that Hannah Row had been raped. They found samples of Brooklyn's sperm in her body, but also traces of spermicide from a condom.'

'And?'

'Clearly Brooklyn wasn't wearing a condom, which meant someone else had sex with her that evening while wearing protection.'

'Maybe she had sex with someone at the nightclub.'

'Were the Guards asked to investigate that?' McCay asked.

'That hardly proves there was someone else involved.'

'Hannah's friends told the police at the time that they'd been with her all night until the bus stopped in Strabane. They lost sight of her for about twenty minutes when she said she was going down a side road to go to the toilet. I don't see how she could have had contact with anyone else until then.'

'It's tenuous,' I said. I wanted to know as much as I could about what she'd learned. By downplaying the significance of what she'd told us, I hoped it would compel her to offer us more in corroboration.

'There were inconsistencies in the witness statements from Brooklyn's two friends, Riley Mullan and Charlie McDaid. Neither were asked to give evidence because Brooklyn was encouraged into accepting a manslaughter plea with allowance for diminished responsibility.'

'That's still not particularly compelling.'

'The SIO running the case in Strabane at the time was apparently related to one of the boys in some way. This information was never revealed.'

'That seems unlikely,' I said. 'That type of conflict in interest would be revealed.'

'*Should* be,' McCay said. 'That doesn't mean it was.'

'Who was the SIO?' I asked. I knew Jim Hendry had worked the case.

'I think I've given you enough,' McCay said, and I realised I'd shown too much interest. 'I want first dibs on whatever you uncover.'

'What makes you think we're going to be looking at a twenty-year-old case?' McCready asked. 'The only thing we're interested in is finding out who killed Brooklyn Harris now.'

'I asked to speak to both Riley and Charlie about that night. Neither would speak to me. I got a rather threatening Cease and Desist letter from Charlie.'

'And?'

'They both still live near Omagh. Both of them were aware that I was looking into Brooklyn's conviction. Brooklyn had kept in touch with Riley even while he was inside. He'd told him his concerns.'

'And?' McCready repeated.

'You don't think it's strange that, once I start looking into who else might have been involved in Hannah Row's killing, someone murders the only other witness to the killing?'

Chapter Nineteen

We drove back up to Lifford, where Joe McCready dropped me off and headed on to Letterkenny. He had promised to check on Helen Shaw's alibi and had finally made contact with the mother of her friend, Ann.

I called into the house to check that my dad was doing okay. Shane was at school with Debbie. When I came in, I could see my dad out in the back garden, dead-heading hydrangeas from last year. For a moment, the familiarity of the scene, one straight from my childhood, took me back with such force it caught my breath. Then, just as quickly, the sense was gone, leaving me almost grasping at the air in a bid to reclaim it for just a moment longer. But like so much else, it was gone and could not be retrieved.

I made my dad's lunch, then, when he was sorted, I collected my car and, after a brief call to ensure he was available, headed back across the border to Strabane to meet Jim Hendry. He'd suggested that we meet at the area called the canal basin. At one stage, a canal had been built to run inland from the River Foyle (which divided Lifford and Strabane and ran down to Derry and beyond) to the centre of Strabane in the hope it would encourage more trade. The relative low depth of water the canal maintained, though, meant it eventually fell into disrepair due to lack of use and the canal now, in so much as it exists, ends far short of the town and has become an area for walkers and cyclists rather than serving any commercial purpose.

As a result, the canal basin is actually a concrete basin near the town centre, which is used more often now by skateboarders, sitting next to a car park. It was an open area, though a strange choice of place to meet Hendry. Except that it was where Hannah Row had been raped and beaten. I guessed it was no coincidence that Hendry suggested it.

'So what's the latest?' he asked without preamble when he arrived, sitting on the metal bench beside me. 'What did your team make of the blood?'

'I'm waiting for them to come back to me,' I said. 'But if your crew checked it a few times, I'm sure we won't find anything different.'

'So how does that happen?'

I shrugged. 'It beats me.'

'Maybe it's a ghost,' Hendry said.

'Ghosts don't bleed.'

'I was being facetious,' Hendry said.

'Maybe there's someone with Hannah's blood. Maybe someone stored it from back then,' I offered.

'Why? How would they even have it?'

'Beats me,' I repeated. 'We'll have to consider every possibility. Maybe even ghosts.'

'Are you sure it's worth all this hassle?' Hendry asked.

'I don't know. I met a journalist called Cathy McCay earlier,' I said. 'She was working on a book about Brooklyn Harris.'

'I heard,' Hendry said. 'She's been in touch with us a few times, looking for copies of statements, wanting to interview people. She's had no luck.'

'She's had some,' I said. 'She claims to know that there was spermicide found in Hannah's body even though Harris didn't use a condom. Was that true?'

Hendry looked at me a moment. 'Why are you doing this, Ben?' he asked.

'My job?'

'This. This here.' He emphasised his point with a jab at the seat on which we sat. 'Digging up a case that was closed years ago.'

'However Hannah's blood ended up on the floor of Harris' death site, it clearly connects his killing to hers,' I said. 'Whether by accident or design. I'm following what leads I can and seeing where it takes me. It's taken me back to Hannah Row's death. McCay is claiming there was someone else there. Is there any evidence of that?'

'Would it bring back Hannah Row?'

'No. But it might offer a reason why someone wanted Brooklyn Harris dead.'

'There are twenty reasons why people wanted Harris dead,' Hendry snapped. 'Ask half the people in this town who remember the Row killing and they'd gladly volunteer to be the one to make Harris pay – myself included, by the way.'

'But I'm only interested in the person who *did* kill him,' I said. 'And if that was because someone was trying to cover up their involvement in what happened to Hannah, they need to pay for both of those killings.'

'Do you honestly believe I'd have covered up a case?' Hendry asked. 'In all the time you've known me?'

'Of course not, Jim,' I said. 'That's why I'm asking. McCay claimed one of Harris' friends, Mullan or McDaid, was related in some way to the SIO on the case.'

'That's rubbish. The SIO was my team leader,' Hendry said. 'He retired fifteen years ago. The only one left from that investigation is me. The one who could be left carrying the can for anything you find will be me.'

'Jim, I . . . I know you're straight as an arrow. There'll be nothing.'

'But what if there is?' Hendry snapped. 'What then? I'm months from retiring. Can't you just leave things as they are?'

I stared at him. 'I'd never ask that from you.'

'You'd not need to, Ben. I'd know when things were best left alone. Did Hannah Row's mother ask for you to reopen this? Or Harris' own family?' He took my silence as confirmation of his suspicion. 'So who benefits from it, Ben? Who gains anything from this? Will Hannah Row be brought back? Will Harris be less dead?'

'If someone was involved in Hannah Row's death and got away with it, that needs to be fixed,' I said.

'I don't even think that anyone else was involved,' Hendry said. 'There wasn't enough evidence for us to think so at the time and nothing has changed my mind since.'

'Then what's your worry, Jim?'

'How many cases are perfect? How many shortcuts do you take every day? Chains of evidence disrupted? Every case we get to court gets there in spite of the legal system, not because of it. You know that. If you reopen this, who's to say some lawyer won't unpick the whole thing? What if they do find a shortcut? Something that allows them to claim an unsound conviction? That comes back on me now. Then they start investigating *me*. You do see that, don't you?'

'Jim,' I said. 'I have to do my job. But that job is to find out who killed Brooklyn Harris, not to double-check on work that you've done. I'm interested in who the possible other person at the scene might have been only in so far as if they knew Harris was speaking to a journalist about them, that gives them a motive for killing him. I'm not looking to put the spotlight on you.'

Hendry nodded, staring across at the rear of the library building, and to where Hannah Row had been attacked.

'You might not be looking to do that, Ben,' he said, 'but that doesn't mean it won't happen anyway.'

Chapter Twenty

I drove back across the border into Lifford but instead of heading on through to Letterkenny, I diverted in through the town to my old station. Lifford Garda Station sat opposite the old courthouse under which, in older times, recidivists were tried and imprisoned, and from the roof of which the worst of them were publicly hanged.

The station was originally a barracks house for the Royal Irish Constabulary through the 19th century right up until the dissolution of the RIC in 1922 and the formation of An Garda Siochana in the south and the Royal Ulster Constabulary in the north that would, almost eighty years later, change again into the Police Service of Northern Ireland following the Good Friday Agreement. Indeed, while it was the RUC in Strabane who investigated Hannah Row's death, by the time the case reached the courts it was PSNI officers who submitted their evidence.

I remembered the years of the changeover. In some ways it had been business as usual. The uniforms and emblems changed but some of the faces didn't: Jim Hendry being one such example. After its formation, there was a period of positive discrimination in practice in an attempt to bolster the number of Catholics serving in the newly established force to counter the predominantly Protestant make-up of the RUC, which had been viewed as a partisan force by the nationalist community in the north – and by many in the south too, truth be told.

2001 had marked a sense of change in the north and around the border regions. After the violence of the conflict, the peace process had been an uneasy time with frequent breaches of ceasefires and constant distrust over decommissioning of weapons. The marching season in the north, when the Orange Order process with bands through various towns and villages, had, through the late nineties, become increasingly fraught. Traditional Orange routes had been blocked by the newly formed Parades Commission, particularly where bands were marching through Catholic or Nationalist areas without the agreement or support of the residents who lived there. One such example led to an ongoing flashpoint at Drumcree Church in Portadown. The local Orange Lodge had wished to travel along the Nationalist Garvaghy Road on the return leg of their parade. The Commission had refused permission, partly due to the Lodge's refusal to meet and discuss the issue with the local residents. Over six years from 1995, the stand-off led to increased attacks, rioting and sectarian killings as the Army first blocked the parade for two years and then subsequently forced it through for two years before finally banning it from progressing along the contentious stretch. I remember reading that the stand-off and associated violence cost the Northern Irish economy in excess of £1 billion.

I recalled all this because 2001 was a turning point of sorts, the year that the violence began to abate. I recalled there had been several attacks in the months leading up to the July flashpoint, but ultimately, the parade passed relatively peacefully that year and continued to do so, even if an accommodation between the Lodge and residents has still to be reached.

And 2001 was an important year for me too when, after years of trying to have children, and several miscarriages, Debs became pregnant with our second, Shane, who was born in early 2002. Towards the end of that same year I was promoted to inspector. Thus, the improving situation in the north, while not perfect, was a welcome relief after years of conflict that frequently focused on the border regions specifically.

I found myself still thinking of the events of that year as I let myself into the station. It had been all but shut down for a few years now. While we still retained the building as a visible manifestation of An Garda in Lifford, residents looking for an officer who buzzed the intercom at the front door were automatically transferred to the switchboard in Letterkenny.

It was not simply nostalgia that drew me to my old office though. I knew that a lot of our records and evidence remained in the downstairs offices, locked away, waiting either disposal at some stage or the suggested digitisation programme. I suspected, based on the date of her killing, that any evidence we had gathered with regards to Hannah Row would have been stored there.

Cathy McCay had been astute in her question about the footage from the nightclub, which had been the primary involvement An Garda had had in the case as the attack occurred in Strabane and all those involved in it lived in the north. But I knew that, at the time, we'd been sent a picture of Brooklyn Harris and asked to look for footage of him interacting with Hannah Row. As a result, scrolling through five hours of tape for each camera, we'd identified fairly quickly what Harris had been wearing and had, as a consequence, only stopped forwarding the images when he was clearly visible on the screen.

Even now I remembered the ways in which our footage had challenged some of his claims. In his statement, he'd said that he and Hannah had danced during the 'slow set'. In fact, the only time we saw the two of them on the dance floor together, Hannah was dancing with her friends and Harris had danced behind her, turning every so often to watch her and, at one point, reaching out and touching the side of her buttock when he moved into close proximity. Hannah barely reacted beyond a glance in his direction, perhaps used to the bumps and knocks of a dance floor or else, more depressingly, already used to the sly touches and grim behaviour of some men, even at her young age.

I went down into the storerooms and began working backwards. I knew that we'd a significant amount of information stored on the Angela Cashell killing from December 2002. Once I located that, I moved down the shelves until I found a box from mid 2001. I'd not expected there to be much on the Hannah Row death beyond our DVDs of CCTV footage. There was, however, also a slim folder containing the original notes, which had been taken when the first request for information had come through, and a copy of our report, which had been sent back. The request, faxed through on headed RUC notepaper, had been signed by Detective Superintendent Jack Grimes.

I vaguely remembered Grimes as a heavy, florid-faced man, already, to my relative perception then, aged and nearing retirement. He'd been the SIO on the case, I realised, and that in itself gave me somewhere to start. My own boss at the time must have called Grimes for further information, for on the bottom of the fax were handwritten notes and I recognised the spidery scribble as that of Superintendent Ollie 'Elvis' Costello, whose departure had led, eventually, to Patterson taking over, heralding the slow abandonment of the Lifford station, which Costello had preferred as his base.

It was here that I saw 'Brooklyn Harris – wiry, 5'10 – blue T-shirt, jeans, white trainers' and next to it 'Hannah Row – 5' 4 – blonde, white skirt – short – peach/pink top'. Clearly either Costello had asked or Grimes had offered more specific instructions about who we were to look for. Beside this was the name 'Sean Row' highlighted in a box outlined several times in blue biro. There must have been some conversation about Row for Costello had underscored his name repeatedly.

I searched through the bottom of the box, where lay various items bagged from investigations in which we had not been the primary investigating team, until I found the bag containing the copies of footage, which I lifted out before returning the file to its rightful place.

As I locked up the station, I peered across at the bridge spanning the Foyle over which cross-border traffic rumbled between Lifford and Strabane 18,000 times every day. How

Brexit would affect it was something no one seemed to know. It seemed so normal as it was, so right. That change was being imposed on us by others living on a different island, claiming their motivation was to take back control, while denying us control of our own region, angered me more than I cared to admit.

But next to the bridge on the Lifford side, I could see the grounds of the community hospital and, just beyond that, Finnside Nursing Home, where Ollie Costello was now resident. I decided the quickest way to find out the significance of Sean Row was to pay my old boss a long-overdue visit.

Chapter Twenty-One

I'd not seen Costello in over a year, I realised. I'd meant to see him before now and indeed, following his moving into the care home five years previous, I had been a relatively frequent visitor. But my father's own deterioration had necessitated that whatever spare time I did have, I spent with him.

Finnside had had a facelift since last I'd been there, the colour scheme richer and warmer than I remembered, though the smell I had always associated with the place was still there, beneath the fresh paint and new carpeting.

I was met at the entrance by the manager, Louise McGowan, the daughter of the original proprietor who had overseen the investment in the place. Louise was solid, having moved into the business from nursing, which she'd practised in Derry for the past decade or more.

'Hey, Ben,' she said when she saw me. 'Everything okay?'

The familiarity of the greeting made me realise that I had spent the past few days interviewing people outside Lifford and I found myself grateful to be among my neighbours once more, to feel known for myself.

'I'm here to see Ollie,' I said.

She winced a little. 'He's not so good, Ben,' she said. 'Call down of course but keep it brief if you can. He's picked up a chest infection that's just not clearing.'

'I'll maybe leave it so,' I said, turning to go and feeling bad that the purpose of my visit had been for my own benefit and not his. 'I wanted to chat with him about an old case he worked.'

Louise patted my arm in the manner one might a child. 'Don't be silly. He loves seeing you. Just don't expect much from him.'

Costello's room was at the far end of the home. Louise had spared no expense, I thought. The carpet lining the corridor was thick and rich, the paintings on the wall not prints but original modern pieces. I knew the rooms too were spacious and bright, so it was a surprise, when I'd knocked and entered Costello's room, to see how dim it was. The blinds were pulled, the air heavy with heat and the funk of infection.

'Benedict,' he rasped when he saw me, his hand flailing ineffectually in the air as he reached out for my hand. Despite the passing years, he had not abandoned his habit of addressing me by my full name. 'Good to see you.'

'Hello, sir,' I said. 'I was passing and thought I'd call to say hello.'

He waggled a finger at me. 'You've something on your mind you need help with,' he said. 'It's the middle of the day.'

I laughed. 'You should have been a detective,' I joked, causing him to laugh before breaking into a prolonged cough.

Elvis had always been a big man, though in retirement and following the loss of his wife, he'd lost some of that weight more through neglecting himself than conscious effort. Still, I was not prepared for how frail he'd become. His forearm, visible due to the slackness of his pyjama sleeve, was wizened, the musculature gone, the skin loose and undefined. His face appeared narrow and sunken, due in part to the fact his dental plate sat in a glass of water beside his bed. He reminded me of my father. But then, even at his strongest as my boss, he'd always reminded me of my father. That time had taken the strength from both of them pained me more than I could say.

'How are you doing?' I asked, sitting in the armchair near his bed.

He rolled his eyes. 'I've this chest thing I can't shift,' he said. 'They spend their days prodding me with needles, sticking things into my back, drains and whatnot. It's not how I imagined things would be. Thank God Emily didn't live to see this.'

'How's Kate?' I asked. His daughter had moved to England to work.

'Good. She's hoping to get back over Easter,' he said. 'How are . . .?'

'Debbie?' I prompted.

He nodded his thanks. 'Debbie and the children?'

'Good,' I said. 'They're okay. Penny's at college now.'

'She's a smart one,' Costello offered.

We lapsed into silence and I could see him watching me, waiting. His head lay light on the pillow, his hair a thinning crown of white. I could see the effort it took to breathe, his head tilting as he gulped the air, the bedclothes rising abruptly with each strained inhalation.

'So, what have you got for me?' he asked.

'It's nothing,' I said. 'It's not important.'

'Benedict,' he said softly. 'Please.'

Using his elbows, he tried to move himself up in the bed. I moved across and helped him, gripping him under the armpits to lift him. I was surprised at the ease with which he moved. He'd gripped my shoulders in the movement and continued to do so.

'Please. I want to feel useful again. Do you know what it feels like, you've no dignity, no privacy. The girls come in here and change me, wash me. That's not right on those girls. They shouldn't have to clean me up.'

'I'm sure they don't mind, sir,' I said.

'They don't,' he replied. 'But I do. It's not right. I used to be able to do things. Now I can't even get out of bed to go to the toilet. So please. Let me be useful.'

I nodded and sat again, pulling the chair closer to the bed to save him having to raise his voice to be heard.

'Hannah Row,' I said. '2001. I found these notes in the office. That's your writing, isn't it?'

He took the sheet from me and held it a distance away from his face as he peered at it. Finally he nodded.

'Why have you marked out Sean Row separately?' I asked. 'He was her father, I know. But why have you underlined it? Can you remember?'

He thought for a second, sucking in his cheeks as he did so as a prelude to swallowing.

'She was the wee one died over at the canal basin, wasn't she? Around the powder keg.'

I nodded. 'Brooklyn Harris was done for her killing. Where was the powder keg?'

143

I must have misheard for he said, 'Here. Here was the powder keg. Everyone waiting for things to go off. All over.'

I wasn't sure if he meant that literally or metaphorically but he had already moved on.

'Sean was her father.'

'That's right,' I said. 'Why was he important?'

Costello lay back and closed his eyes and for a second I worried that the conversation was exhausting him.

'Are you okay, sir?' I asked, receiving, in reply, a raised index finger which I took to mean he was thinking.

Finally, he opened his eyes again and turned his head towards me. 'He was something to do with Drumcree. That's all I remember.'

'Drumcree? The Orange march?'

Costello nodded. 'I'm sorry, Benedict. I used to remember everything. Years of crosswords. But now? *Pfft!*'

He shook his head in frustration, though the movement was little more than a slight rolling within the indentation of the pillow.

'That's really helpful, sir,' I said, irrespective. 'Thank you.'

I sat with him for another ten minutes but could tell that his failure to remember exactly what Sean Row had done or why he was so significant had annoyed him.

As I stood to go, I extended my hand to say goodbye. He reached out and took it, clasping it with his other free hand. I was surprised at the coldness of his skin.

'I really appreciate you coming to see me, Benedict,' he said. 'It's good to see you.'

'I'll call again,' I said. And in that moment, I meant it.

But as I was leaving the room he called me back, coughing at the exertion of so doing.

'The Commission. The Parades Commission,' he said, snapping his fingers soundlessly. 'Row was one of them.' He tapped the side of his head, winking shrewdly. 'I've still got it,' he added.

'You were always the best, sir,' I said, earning in thanks the glint of his smile at having proved to himself that he was still of use.

As I stepped softly down the corridor, I was glad I'd said it.

Chapter Twenty-Two

I drove back up to Letterkenny, considering all I'd learned. Sean Row, according to Costello, had been a member of the Parade's Commission in 2001 when his daughter had died. Cathy McCay contended that her death had been caused by more than one person, but only one, Brooklyn Harris, had ever been charged, due to the supposed involvement of an alleged relative of the SIO of the case whom I now knew to be Jack Grimes.

Twenty years later, Brooklyn Harris is murdered and Hannah Row's blood appears at the scene of his killing. This happened shortly after Harris started working with a journalist and claimed someone else had been, in part, responsible for Hannah's death, and several months after being outed on social media by a paedophile-hunting group. It also happened the day after he'd arranged to meet with a young local girl whose parents had intercepted the messages. Either the girl, or her parents, had encouraged Harris to remain in the area an extra night, during which he was killed.

The range of possible suspects was, as Jim Hendry had suggested from the start, extensive. And, as Hendry had pointed out, there seemed little imperative from any of the families involved, including Harris' own family, to look too hard for his killer.

Joe McCready was checking on the alibi for Helen Shaw and I knew that Gerry Carter was attempting to trace back the account for the paedophile-hunter who had outed Harris to begin with. I could see two priorities for now - finding Harris' two friends and checking the CCTV footage for anything I might have missed when reviewing it twenty years earlier on the instructions sent by Jack Grimes. Before all that, I wanted to know a bit more about Sean Row and, several phone calls, multiple online searches, and one hour later, I did.

Row had indeed been on the Parades Commission in 2001, having been appointed two years earlier. His qualifications for the appointment were wide ranging: once a partner in an engineering company in Omagh, he'd given up his business and become a community activist in Omagh, working with youths in areas of social disadvantage for over a decade before becoming the CEO of Brighter Days, a charity to support families with sick children. He continued to advocate for the charity for a year after Hannah's death before resigning from it. There he vanished, registering only once more when he took a New Zealand passport. According to a report online in the *Otago Daily Times* from 2016, a man in his sixties called Sean Row died in a road traffic accident in Dunedin.

While I was reading that final story, my mobile rang. I recognised the number as the switchboard at FSI. Forensics Service Ireland handled all forensic analysis of samples we pulled from crime scenes and it was to them that I had faxed the report Hendry had sent me to support the samples that had been submitted from the scene the day we found Harris.

The lady on the phone introduced herself as Dr Jane Forbes. 'I've doubled-checked this information you sent me,' she said after we'd made our introductions. 'From the PSNI. It's definitely a match based on that information. What's the concern?'

'The person whose blood is being matched has been dead for twenty years,' I said.

'Oh!' she said. 'Are you sure?'

'She was killed when she was a teenager,' I said. 'In 2001.'

'There wouldn't have been a mistake?'

'Then or now?'

'Either?'

'The girl died,' I said. 'And the sample was taken by our own SOCOs. I can't see how there could have been cross contamination.'

'The matched sample results from 2001? Those came from the PSNI, is that right?'

'That's right.'

'Could they have made a mistake?'

'It's possible,' I said. 'But they did tell me they checked three times to be sure.'

'There's a mistake somewhere,' she said.

'Could the blood have been frozen? Could someone have kept it for twenty years?'

'In theory, yes, blood can be frozen without problems. It's the thawing causes the issue as it rips the cells apart and turns it into mush. There was a new technology developed in the past few years where you could add a polymer to stop that damage happening, but it needs to be added before freezing; you couldn't do it retrospectively. Having looked at the samples taken, there's no doubt in my mind that the blood you found is fresh.'

'How is that possible?'

'It's not really,' Forbes said.

'It couldn't be a relative? A twin, maybe?'

'Did the original deceased have a twin?'

'No,' I said. 'She has a brother a few years older. My sergeant has sent in a sample from him just today for comparison.'

'No,' Forbes said. 'That wouldn't account for it. Could you get the girl's original sample from the PSNI for me to test it against?'

'It's tricky,' I said. Jim Hendry was already opposed to my raising the Hannah Row killing at all. If he thought we were double-checking the work his team had done on the blood sample, I'd lose whatever co-operation I might have had from him. 'Could it be compared with anything else?'

'Is exhumation an option?'

'No.'

'Anything with several samples of the girl's DNA, then. Hair, maybe?'

I thought again of Hannah Row's room, essentially untouched since she had died. And on the bedside table, a hairbrush.

'There might be hair samples left on her hairbrush. Would that do?'

'So long as the follicles are in place,' she said. 'Cut hair is no good. Send me what you have and I'll do my best. At least it would confirm the samples are both accurate.'

'And if they are?'

'Then it gets complicated,' Forbes said. 'The chances of two people having the same DNA are infinitesimal. Unless you've a clone.'

'I'll see what I can do,' I said. 'Thanks for getting back to me.'

'You've me intrigued,' Forbes said. 'Stay in touch.'

After I hung up, I considered how best to ask Mrs Row for the brush. The objects in Hannah's room were clearly sacrosanct to the woman, as evidenced by her response when I lifted the picture from the shelf: I suspected getting her to part with a brush – or even a few strands of hair from it – would be difficult.

I knew too, though, that I could use my return trip to Omagh to track down the two friends who had been with Brooklyn the night Hannah died and who had refused to speak with Cathy McCay. To do so, it made sense to look afresh at the CCTV footage from the nightclub.

I knew from Costello's notes what both Brooklyn and Hannah had been wearing that evening, with the result I was able to identify them both fairly quickly. Thankfully, the footage from four cameras all appeared on the screen at one time, allowing me to scan across them to locate the two groups – Hannah and her friends and, likewise, Mullan and McDaid, the two youths who had spent the evening mostly in Brooklyn's company. Though I knew who they were as a pair, I could not tell them apart; one wore a white shirt and jeans, the other a wine-coloured top. I was able to fast forward through most of the footage, comprising, as it did, mostly images of Hannah and her friends dancing and Brooklyn and his friends, in a different camera feed, standing at the bar drinking. The feed was silent, obviously, and the footage of so low a resolution I could only identify people by the combinations of their clothing: their facial expressions were a blur.

At one point I did see Brooklyn and his mates moving out onto the floor and dancing near the girls. Brooklyn moved in behind Hannah and started gyrating, to the amusement of his friends. As he turned, as I had recalled from viewing this footage years back, he had touched her, for she turned her head towards him, but he was moving away from her.

I began to suspect that the original instructions to look only at Harris' movements had saved us a lot of wasted time, until towards the end of the night, focusing on Hannah alone, I saw something I didn't recall noticing before.

Harris was talking to a girl at the far end of the dance floor and Hannah had gone to the toilet. As she was waiting in the queue of girls snaking its way down the corridor, one of Harris' friends, the one in the wine-coloured top, came out of the boys' toilets and passed her. He said something to her as he passed, for she reacted, turning towards him as he went by her. She evidently replied for he stopped and returned. There followed an exchange of views that seemed to get more volatile, based on the body language and gestures used by the pair. One of Hannah's friends, who appeared to be staggering, came across and stood with her friend and, a moment later, the young man moved away and Hannah turned to her friend who hugged her.

I didn't recall ever reading about an altercation between Hannah and any of the other youths on the bus though, again, could understand that, when Harris presented himself as a suspect and admitted having followed Hannah down the roadway from the bus, the RUC team might have decided they had enough to secure a conviction without additional work.

McCay had mentioned that both Mullan and McDaid, Brooklyn's two childhood friends, had lawyered up when she'd contacted them. I wondered whether a different approach might encourage them to be more talkative. A quick online search on social media helped me find Riley Mullan who was oversharing on all media channels, from what I could see. In fact, just before Christmas, he'd posted a picture of himself and his work colleagues on their Christmas night out. He'd captioned it 'Shout out to all the Mullan Pharm fam!'

I picked up the phone and called Joe McCready who, by the ambient sounds on the call, was in the car.

'Joe. What was the name of the pharmacy where the prescription drugs I found in Harris' flat came from?'

'Mullan's in Omagh,' he said. 'I'm waiting for a call back from them. Why?'

'I think I've found our supplier.'

Chapter Twenty-Three

Joe drove as we headed back across the border yet again. While technically we should have contacted the PSNI to ask them to interview on our behalf, for years we'd been crossing the line on both sides to speak to witnesses or suspects. Only when we needed a formal trail of statements or an unbroken chain of evidence that could not be contested in court would we ask the PSNI to act on our behalf.

Thus, I didn't contact Jim Hendry or any of our colleagues in the north. Partly, it was also because I would have to explain to Jim what I was doing. Asking Mrs Row for Hannah's hairbrush, I told myself, would be okay as we'd not be using it as evidence in a case against anyone – it was simply being used for comparative purposes to confirm that the DNA sample we had been provided with for Hannah was genuine.

'I managed to sit down with Ann's mother,' Joe said as we passed the Tinneys, a huge art installation of traditional dancers and musicians that had earned the informal moniker by which everyone knew it due to the figures' metallic construction. 'Helen Shaw was with them for the whole evening. The Shaws had asked her to keep a close eye, so she'd checked on them at bedtime and then first thing in the morning when she woke. Helen was there the whole night. The only time the girls left the house was to go to the local chippy and they were driven there and back.'

'So, either Helen intended to meet Harris and didn't, or her parents sent the message.'

McCready nodded. 'Though that still doesn't explain how Hannah Row's blood ended up at the scene.'

'I still think it's a message,' I said. 'Someone wants us to connect this to Hannah. Which is why we need to double-check her DNA profile.'

While I called with Mrs Row, Joe stayed in the car and called through to Mullan's Pharmacy to see whether Riley Mullan was working.

Mrs Row looked surprised to see me again.

'I assumed everything was finished now,' she said. 'With Brooklyn Harris dead.'

'I'm afraid not, ma'am,' I said. 'We have to investigate Mr Harris' death. We found DNA samples at the scene of the killing and need to eliminate people from our inquiries. I spoke to your son already and he provided us with a sample.'

'I heard,' she said.

'I wanted to request the same from you, if I might.'

'You might not,' Mrs Row said.

I was a little surprised by the response and by the steeliness that had suddenly appeared in both her character and tone.

'Can I ask why?'

'We had nothing to do with Brooklyn Harris' death,' she said. 'Nor have we any interest in finding out who did.'

'Mrs Row, I don't want to upset you, but we found traces of—'

'Hannah's blood,' she said, her hand raised. 'I heard from Aidan. That makes this worse for us. I don't want to have to relive those days again.'

'Mrs Row,' I said. 'Can we speak inside, please?'

'I'd rather not, Inspector,' she said, her mouth tightening. 'I'm sorry. I can't talk about this any more. Aidan's unwell and I need to look after my son.'

'Mrs Row, I just need a sample—'

'Please don't call back at my home,' she said, then closed the door.

'Did you get it?' McCready asked when I got back into the car.

I shook my head. 'She's gone from weeping at Harris' death to stonewalling me in twenty-four hours,' I said.

'What changed?'

'Hannah's blood,' I said. 'What about you? Any luck with Riley Mullan?'

McCready nodded. 'Apparently he's out in the van doing prescription lifts all afternoon.'

We parked in the car park outside Mullan's and waited for the delivery van to arrive. About twenty minutes later, it did. We watched a man get out of the van and, after opening the rear door, lift out several clear plastic boxes of green prescription sheets he'd been collecting from the local health centres. It took a few return journeys in and out of the pharmacy before he'd got to the last one and, when I saw him balance it on his knee as he angled to pull the van door shut, I got out of the car and approached him.

'Riley Mullan?' I asked. I'd recognised him as both the man in the picture with Brooklyn Harris I'd seen pinned on his wall and the one who had escorted Harris out of his flat in Dungannon the previous summer. I recalled that the old neighbour had thought the friend was called Mellon. He'd not been far wrong.

He turned and smiled at me in the expectation of recognition. The smile changed to bemusement and confusion as he looked from me to Joe and back and realised he could place neither of us. A sixth sense seemed to tell him he was in trouble.

'Who wants him?' he asked, shifting the box to one side, and he clicked the lock button on the van key.

'I'm Inspector Devlin, this is Sergeant McCready. We're with An Garda in Donegal. We'd like a few minutes of your time.'

'You're way off your patch over here,' he said, laughing, and he turned to walk into the pharmacy.

'Is your boss in?'

'You mean my father?' he scoffed.

'Better still. We'll just follow you in and explain to your dad you've been illegally providing pregabalin and Viagra to Brooklyn Harris then,' I said, motioning to move. 'Mavis Holmes is one of the patients who uses here, yes?'

He held out his hand, wedging the box between his hip and the van side.

'Wait a minute,' he said. 'Just wait.'

I could tell he was weighing up his options. We'd not spoken to his dad yet, clearly, which told him that he could still avoid us doing so in return for the minute of his time we'd requested.

'I'm on my break in twenty minutes,' he said. 'There's a coffee place across the way. Meet me there.'

'If you're not there in twenty-five minutes . . .' I began.

'I'll be there,' Mullan said.

True to his word, he did appear twenty minutes later. He loped into the coffeehouse and, after ordering, came across and dropped into the seat opposite us. His face was soft, his frame fuller than Harris' had been. Despite his youthful appearance, his black hair was thinning, his cheeks shadowed with stubble.

'What do you want?'

'We wanted to speak to you about Brooklyn,' I said.

'What about him?' He knew we were aware of the prescription drugs he'd given Harris so clearly felt there was no point in pretence.

'I'm afraid he's dead,' I said.

He nodded. 'I saw that on Twitter. What's it to do with me?'

'You were his friend,' I said. 'We thought you might be able to help us.'

'I wasn't his friend,' Mullan said. 'We hung around together when we were kids. We met up once when he got out and he asked me for some stuff. That was it.'

'Why did he ask you? Why not his doctor?'

'He was on antipsychotics,' Mullan said. 'But they were leaving him jittery all the time. He couldn't sleep, couldn't do anything, he said. Someone inside had given him pregabalin to take the edge off and he needed some more.'

'And the Viagra?'

'The pregab meant he couldn't get it up.'

'How did you have it?'

Mullan shrugged.

'How did you end up with the drugs? Are you stealing patients' drugs?'

'No,' he said. 'Sometimes people order a monthly thing and by the time you go to deliver it, they're in hospital, or they've died or something and the stuff's lying spare. No one notices it's gone and it's not been taken off someone who needs it.'

'A victimless crime?' McCready offered.

Mullan nodded. 'Yeah. Victimless.'

'Did you see Brooklyn much?'

'Just that once or twice when he got out.'

'You were living with him in Dungannon when he got put out of his flat last year by Northern Justice,' I said.

'Who told you that?'

'We've seen the footage,' Joe McCready said. 'So, maybe we cut through all the bullshit and start again, eh?'

He nodded, glancing over at the counter, perhaps trying to work out some means of escape. 'What do you want to know?'

'Why was Brooklyn Harris in Lifford?'

Mullan shrugged but did not speak.

'When did you last see him?'

'A few weeks back,' he said, sullenly.

'Did he have any more run-ins with Northern Justice?'

'The crowd from Dungannon? No.'

'Why didn't he change his name when he moved?'

He shrugged again, but then said, 'I think he reckoned with Facebook and that, everyone would know who he was

158

anyway. The crowd that chased him, they were warned not to go near him again, so he thought he was safe.'

'Did he tell you that?'

Mullan nodded.

'But you don't know why he was in Lifford?'

'He was meeting someone is all I know,' he said. 'I don't know who.'

'Did you know that he was communicating with teenagers online?'

Mullan pantomimed revulsion. 'He was a freak about stuff,' he said.

'Are you an anime fan, too?' McCready asked, causing Mullan to regard him more coolly.

'You were contacted by an author, Cathy McCay, looking to write a book on Brooklyn, is that right?'

Mullan shrugged. 'Don't remember.'

'We know you were,' I said. 'She told us you and Charlie "lawyered up" was the phrase she used. Why?'

'She started going over shit about that night, about Hannah and Brook and that, you know?'

'And that?' McCready said. 'You mean the rape and killing of Hannah Row?'

'Yeah,' Mullan agreed.

'What kind of shit?'

'Asking what happened? Who was where when? Who else was with Brook and all that.'

'Anything else?'

Mullan shrugged.

'Can you remember what you were wearing the night of Hannah Row's attack?' I asked, changing tack.

'Why?'

'Just curious,' I said.

'Dunno,' he said again.

I took out two of the images I had printed off the CCTV footage. The first was of Brooklyn and his two friends standing at the bar. 'Can you tell me which of these is you?' I asked.

'The quality's shit,' he said. 'I don't remember what I was wearing,' he added. 'We'd all had a few that night.'

'So you don't know which of these two people is you?'

He shook his head. 'Nah.'

I took out the second image. This one was of the youth in the wine-coloured top standing, pointing angrily at Hannah Row during the altercation outside the toilets.

'So, is that you?'

Mullan looked at it and swallowed. His eyes flicked across the image, taking in Hannah Row, whom he clearly recognised. 'Nah. That's not me.'

'So it's Charlie McDaid then?'

'I dunno. It's not me is all I can say for sure,' he said.

We had even less luck with Charlie McDaid, who refused to speak with us at all. I called him at his office first; he worked as a solicitor just outside Omagh. I had barely explained why we wished to see him when he cut me off curtly: 'I've no wish to relive any of those days or experiences, Inspector,' he said. 'I've no reason, legal or moral, to speak to you about those days and I choose not to do so.'

'I just wanted some help with understanding Brooklyn,' I lied.

'I don't believe that but, even if that were the case, no one understood Brooklyn, not least himself. I lived through those horrific events once; I've no wish to do so again.'

'Can you even look at a picture for me?' I asked. 'It's taken from the nightclub you all—'

'I don't seem to be making myself clear, Inspector. I've no interest in speaking to you. You have no jurisdiction over here and should not be contacting me or anyone else touched by what happened twenty years ago.'

'I have footage of one of you arguing with Hannah Row on the night in question,' I said. 'Riley Mullan told me it was you in that picture.'

'No, he didn't,' McDaid said. 'He told you it wasn't him in the picture. Without even seeing it, I can tell you it wasn't me either. I've no recollection of the events of twenty years ago beyond those which the police have on file from my witness statement that evening. Anything further you require, I suggest you go through the correct channels and speak to the PSNI.'

He hung up before I could say anything else. Joe McCready looked at me, having been listening in on speaker. 'That's a dead end, then.'

I shook my head. 'They're hiding something. Mullan spoke to us five minutes ago and the first thing he did was contact McDaid to tell him what we'd been asking, including about the picture; he knew exactly what I was talking about there.'

Chapter Twenty-Four

I went back to my office to check for messages and to see Patterson who'd requested an update. I phoned FSI first and asked to speak to Dr Forbes.

'I've hit a brick wall with the DNA sample,' I said. 'The girl's mother is unwilling to support the investigation.'

'I'm afraid that is a brick wall,' Forbes said. 'I'm limited with how much more I can do.'

'Is there any way someone could have the same blood as Hannah Row? The same DNA and everything?'

Forbes was silent for a moment. 'It's possible,' she said. 'With a bone-marrow transplant.'

'What?' I remembered the picture in Hannah's room of Maisie, the transplant patient.

'Stem-cell donation turns the recipient into a chimera, essentially,' she said. 'Bone marrow contains blood stem cells. If someone is getting a bone-marrow transplant, their own cells are destroyed first before they receive the donor cells. As we constantly produce new blood cells, once the transplanted bone marrow starts producing new blood cells, those cells will contain the donor's blood cells and so their DNA, not the recipients'. The person would then have two DNA profiles – one in their blood and one everywhere else essentially. As I say, a chimera.'

'Hannah was definitely an organ donor after her death,' I said.

'Well, if part of that was a bone-marrow donation, there's a chance that would explain it.'

'Just bone marrow?'

'Yes. Any other organs would retain the donor's DNA but wouldn't change the recipient's DNA anywhere else in their body.'

'I'll be in touch,' I said, feeling for the first time as if I was making some progress forward in the investigation. Up until now, everything I had learned had simply widened the pool of those who might have killed Brooklyn Harris. But, following quickly on that thought, I considered whether there was any possibility of a positive outcome in this case where the distinction between victim and criminal had never been, for me, so blurred.

I called up with Gerry Carter before seeing Patterson. He'd been examining Shaw's computer and phones.

'I was about to call you,' he said as I stuck my head around the door of his office. 'I've news. Shaw's computer has been interesting.'

I recalled Debbie's words of support for the man and hoped desperately that we'd not uncover something that would force her to have to revaluate her view of him. One of the more depressing parts of the job was the requirement to unearth the failings and secret desires of others, particularly when they were known to you in civilian life, too. Inevitably there would be something, some aspect of their character they'd kept hidden from those closest to them, something that would change for ever the dynamic of every important relationship they had. It was an element of the job that never brought with it any sense of satisfaction.

'His computer is clean; nothing untoward in pictures and that beyond a few dodgy shots of his kids as babies sitting in the sink having a bath. There's a lot of pictures of sports teams – boys and girls – but nothing that rings any bells.'

'He coaches after-school clubs,' I said. 'I'd guess he's already been vetted for that anyway.'

'Social-media wise, he's looked up a few porn feeds, but nothing red flagging. He has, however, liked a number of posts from Northern Justice. I tracked them back and the first he liked was actually someone else's sharing of one of their videos, which he liked, and then he followed Northern Justice directly.'

'Okay.'

'This is where it gets a bit more murky,' Carter said. 'He sent a direct message to the NJ page last week, which he then deleted.'

'Can you retrieve it?'

'Eventually. This is it.'

He turned his screen towards me. I could see a brief message with a link attached. It read:

Hi. This creep has been contacting my daughter and wanted to meet her. He's staying in Lifford until tomorrow. Don't know where.

The attached link led to a page for 'George Day' whose profile picture was the anime-style cartoon of Brooklyn Harris I'd seen in his flat and which, by its nature, both made it hard to guess at his age and was generic enough to ensure he could not be recognised for who he really was.

'George Day was also the account that Helen Shaw was communicating with through her anime forum,' Carter said.

'So Shaw passed on details of Harris being in Lifford,' I said.

Carter nodded. 'Though he's not specific about the address, obviously. Maybe Northern Justice tracked him down anyway.'

I considered the information Shaw had sent. He hadn't made the connection that George Day was either Brooklyn Harris or someone with whom Northern Justice had already had dealings.

'Any chance we can identify who runs Northern Justice?' I asked.

Carter smiled. 'I knew you'd ask. I'm doing a bit of guesswork here, winging it from an informed position, so to speak, but I think I've worked out who one of them is.'

He opened Facebook and clicked on an account for a man called Bob Porter. His profile picture was clearly taken at his wedding. He knelt with his bride lying on her side in front of him, her head resting on her arm. Three friends stood behind them, the middle one leaning over, as if resting his folded arms on the groom's head, the two bridesmaids on either side standing with one hand resting on the groom's shoulder. It was absurdly posed.

'I worked on the assumption that those who started Northern Justice would be the ones to help spread the word about it until it got some traction. So I went back to its earliest posts and looked at who liked and shared them first. Porter here has been sharing their stuff from the start

– including the one on Harris that was deleted, eventually.'

'Maybe he's just an enthusiastic fan,' I suggested.

'Maybe,' Carter said. 'But check this out. He's friends with a guy called Frank Porter; his cousin. Here's something Frank posted last July.'

He brought up an image on screen of four people sitting in McDonald's. Porter was visible on the far side of the table. He wore a black fleeced hoodie with a skull logo on the front.

'The same top the gang leader in the Harris video was wearing,' Carter said. 'And this, too.'

He clicked to a different picture of Frank and Bob having pints at a barbeque. The two of them were raising their drinks in salute.

'Look at his watch,' Carter said.

It was a garish affair with a thick, metallic gold strap.

'So?'

Carter held up one finger in request for patience. He opened up a new screen and I recognised the video footage of Northern Justice's journey to Harris' house.

'Watch,' Carter said. 'I'll slow it.'

He moved through the frames as, in slow motion, the man in the passenger seat of the car unclicked his seat belt and motioned to get out of the car. I recalled this from the first viewing. I knew his arm got stuck in the spooling seat belt. Sure enough, that happened on screen and Carter paused as I saw, frozen on the screen, the same garish gold watch exposed for a second as his sleeve was pulled back by the belt.

'Good work, Gerry,' I said. 'I think you're bang on the money there.'

Carter smiled at the praise. 'I enjoyed doing it,' he said.

'Where's Porter from?'

'Derry,' Carter said, his smile widening. 'Wouldn't have taken him too long to make a run to Lifford after Shaw tipped them off.'

'True,' I said. 'Though, to date, his MO has been outing people, not offing them.'

'Maybe he was pissed after his first outing of Harris went wrong. They had to delete it and nothing happened to Harris after it anyway.'

'Maybe.'

Carter nodded. 'I'm done now with Shaw's things if you want to return them,' he said.

'I'll follow him up tomorrow,' I said. 'And Porter, too. Thanks again.'

As I left his office, I wondered at how the job had changed. When I'd first started, computers had barely featured in the crimes we investigated. Tracking someone down involved going door to door, hoping someone would talk. Now, people like Gerry Carter could track someone's movements, retrieve their lost messages and find connections from his chair in an afternoon. I understood why Jim Hendry was considering retiring. While I was a little young yet to consider it, the job had changed in ways none of us could have foreseen when we trained.

I was not wholly convinced that the changes were all positive either. The number of assault cases we'd investigated that traced their origins to a dispute on social media, the kids bullied into suicide attempts, or couples whose relationship soured through online interactions that had turned into something else had shown me a side of the technology that made we wish again for the days when we still needed phone boxes.

And worse, social media had opened up a world of predation where victims or their parents willingly and unwittingly posted the very information which, in years past, they'd have been warned to keep private.

I'd had arguments with my own kids about just that and they'd laughed at me for it. Theirs was a world built on such interactions. I thanked God it was not the one in which I'd had to grow up. But that offered me little comfort as I watched my own children having to navigate their way through it.

Still, for all my complaints, I relied on just such things to check each evening that Penny was safe and knew that, when Shane moved out to college, I would continue to do so.

Chapter Twenty-Five

'There are rumours we're going to be closing before the end of the week,' Debs said, over dinner.

'For Easter?'

She shrugged. 'Someone claimed it was discussed at a headteachers' conference yesterday, that everyone will be sent home and we'll be teaching online for a few weeks.'

'Nice one,' Shane offered.

'You'll still have to get up and do your classes every day at the usual time,' she said. 'Your teachers will still be teaching.'

'They will, right enough,' he said, laughing. 'I'll be in me bed until lunchtime! I must see if I can get extra hours at work.'

'If the schools close, shops might start closing down too,' I said. 'Work might not be quite the same.'

'Besides,' Debs said. 'Your Granda is living here with us. Might be best if you're not putting yourself at risk of catching coronavirus.'

'That's not fair,' Shane said.

'We'll talk about it later,' I said. My dad had been following the conversation, though had contributed nothing to it, eating his meal silently.

*   *   *

Later that evening, though, as I helped my dad up the stairs to his room, he did comment.

'I might be better back at the home,' he said. 'It's not fair on the young fella to have to stop working because of me.'

'It's not because of you,' I said. 'I don't want him catching anything himself. Or bringing anything into the house to the rest of us.'

'You'll still be working, though,' my father said, in such a way that I couldn't be sure whether it was a question or a statement.

'I'm sure they'll be taking whatever precautions they need to for us,' I said.

'You can't do one thing yourself and ask Shane to do the opposite. He'll resent it. And resent you for making him do it.'

'We'll see,' I said, a little rankled at the comment for reasons I could not fully recognise.

'I'm not telling you what to do,' he said. 'He's so like you at that age, I'm just thinking about how you'd have reacted to someone telling you what to do.'

'I always listened to good advice,' I said.

'You did?' Dad laughed and this time there was no confusion over the fact it was a question.

'If only I could have found someone to give me some!'

He laughed again, lightly, the sound rattling around his ribcage as he slipped his arm across my back to support himself. His grip was loose, his arm surprisingly light around my shoulder.

*   *   *

I woke at around 3 a.m. with my dad calling for me. When I went into the room, he lay on the floor, one leg still caught in the sheets on the bed, where he'd fallen out.

I rushed across to him, as he protested that he was okay. But, even as he did, I could see that he was unable to lift himself, his arms ineffectually pushing against the ground, one hand twisted in the duvet that had fallen off with him.

I knelt down next to him and recognised his fear.

'Are you hurt?'

He shook his head. 'I shocked myself, I think,' he said. 'I wasn't expecting to fall. I've a rail around my bed in the home.'

'You ready?' I asked.

'Do you need a hand?'

I looked up and saw Shane standing in the doorway, staring in disbelief at the sight in front of him.

'Give me a hand with your Granda's legs,' I said.

'I can get up myself,' Dad complained. 'I'm not completely useless.'

'We've got it, Dad,' I said, putting one arm under his back and cupping him beneath his armpit on the far side while I stretched my other arm across his chest. I lifted him, cradling him the way I had once cradled Penny and Shane, while Shane helped disentangle his foot from the sheet and pulled back the covers to allow me to place him in bed.

'Are you okay?' I asked him as I set him down, laying his head on the pillow.

He shook his head, his eyes wet with tears that I knew to be in shame and which threatened my own resolution.

'I shouldn't be doing this to you,' he said. 'Not to any of you.'

'You're not doing anything, Dad,' I said. 'It's my job to look after you. You looked after me for long enough.'

But I could tell the reversal in roles hurt him. And, if I'm honest, mixed along with a sense of privilege in being able to help him, it hurt me a little, too.

After we got him settled, I went back into my room.

'I don't know how he'd feel about it,' Debs said, sitting at the edge of the bed now, all chance of a return to sleep gone, 'but we have the bed guard upstairs from Shane's old bed. It's still in the attic.'

I knew what she was talking about. When both Penny and Shane first moved from cot to bed, we'd bought a guard that slipped under the mattress and sat up on the outside of the bed a foot or so to prevent children from falling out. Rather than dumping any of the children's things, we'd stored them all in case they should prove useful at some later date. Seemingly, that date was now.

And so, at just after 4 a.m., I found myself sitting in our attic. I located the guard easily enough, in the corner alongside the panels of the dismantled cot and a folded playpen. There were boxes too, of toys and games, of books, and piles of photographs from before we used a digital camera or our phones to record our family memories. I sat among the dust and looked through them. Penny as a baby, with Debs, the latter's face still swollen a little from pregnancy, her smile ablaze with this newfound joy the child had brought us both. Then of Shane, sitting in a walker, his small fist raised in a salute of seeming defiance to the camera even as his grin suggested he was playing.

There were pictures too of Frank, our old Bassett, staring

dolefully at the children, his tail raised in a mixture of joy at the attention he received and annoyance that his place in our affections might have been usurped by them.

And there were Christening pictures, including ones of my mother and father holding first Penny and then, a few years later, Shane. They hadn't changed much between the two images, despite the gap in years between the events. It was a shock then to realise how much things had changed since; the loss of my mother, my father's illness. It all seemed so sudden.

For years, we had seemed to be in some sort of happy stasis. As I recovered objects we'd once used to protect our children to now protect my parent, I felt as if I might suffocate with the relentlessness with which time was passing and longed, just for a few moments, for time to set itself in abeyance and give me a chance to catch my breath.

Day Four

12 March 2020

Chapter Twenty-Six

The following morning, my dad was quiet over breakfast. I sensed something had shifted between us, the plates of our relationship had moved irrevocably. I could see it in the way he slumped slightly as he sat, the way his spirit seemed defeated, the way that, as I looked at him, I felt ineffably saddened.

'I'd be best being at the home,' my dad said, finally.

'I think you'd be better here,' I said. 'If the schools are closing, there won't be too long to wait for a lockdown. If that does happen, you'd be stuck in the home. We'll not be able to get down to you and you'll not be able to come out.'

'I'm fine,' he grumbled. 'I don't need fuss.'

He did not look at me, his gaze settling towards the middle of the table in a show of recalcitrance I'd not seen since Shane hit his early teens.

'It's not fuss,' I said. 'It's trying to keep you safe.'

'You can't keep everyone safe,' he said. 'Can't wrap the world in cotton wool and hope it doesn't break.'

I looked at my father, briefly, and felt something crack inside my chest. 'I know it's going to break,' I said. 'I'd just rather not speed up that process.'

'It's cool having you up,' Shane said, coming into the kitchen and lifting a slice of toast. He'd clearly been listening outside of the room. 'You should stay up with us. I'll set you up a Netflix subaccount and get you some good movies to watch. Something with plenty of blood and killing!' He winked at my dad who responded with a light nod of his own and the briefest smile.

'That's that decided then,' Shane said. 'I'll tell the boss I'll have to stop work when the lockdown starts, too,' he said. 'See youse later.'

'He's a good lad,' my dad said as we heard the front door closing.

'He is,' I agreed.

'Apples don't fall far from trees,' he added.

'Is it me or you who's the tree in that analogy?'

'Aye,' my dad said, continuing to sip his tea.

Peter Shaw was just leaving the house when I arrived with his equipment.

'Come in off the street,' he said, clearly concerned at how his neighbours would react to seeing us speaking outside.

He led me into the kitchen but did not invite me to sit.

'We've finished with your stuff,' I said. 'And Helen's, too. Is she here?'

He shook his head. 'She's at school already.'

I laid the bag containing their effects on the table. 'Did you ask Harris to stay for an extra night, or did she?' I asked.

He pantomimed bewilderment for a moment, then seemed to realise it was a waste of time for I'd clearly seen the message on Helen's phone suggesting that she would find some way of making it to Lifford if only the man she knew to be George would stay.

'She did,' he said, and for the briefest moment I was disheartened that he would so quickly blame his daughter rather than shield her.

'When did you find out?'

'That same evening. It was one of the reasons we arranged for her to stay with Ann the following night. We knew she'd be okay there and Ann's mum is a good friend; she'd keep a close eye without Helen feeling she wasn't trusted.'

I nodded. 'And then you contacted Northern Justice?'

Again, Shaw's initial instinct was to feign confusion.

'Please don't,' I said. 'You sent a message to the Facebook account for Northern Justice then deleted it. Our IT specialist was able to recover it.'

Shaw took a second, then sat. I took the gesture to be an invitation for me to do the same and so joined him at the table.

'We found the messages between them and told her she couldn't go,' Shaw said. 'I wanted to go down and confront him straight away but Mags wouldn't let me.'

'That's your wife?'

He nodded. 'She said we just had to keep an eye on things.'

'You didn't consider calling the police?'

'We did,' he said. 'But I didn't want all this coming out. Or Helen being asked about sending topless pictures of herself. I didn't want anyone else knowing about that. What does it say about us as parents? Or her, for that matter?'

'Nothing,' I said. 'It says she was duped by someone who had a lot of experience duping people. There's no shame in that.'

'Yeah right,' Shaw said. 'What kind of a father would I look?'

'The type of father you *look* is irrelevant. All that matters is the type of father you *are*. You should have contacted us.'

'I couldn't put Helen through that. Through court cases and giving evidence. Having to make statements and having people judging her.'

I was going to argue with him but, on some level, understood what he meant and, to an extent, agreed with his analysis.

'So what did you do instead?'

'Mags checked her phone again later that evening, when she wasn't looking, and saw the second message. That was when we decided to send her to Ann's the next night.'

'But you didn't take her phone from her?'

He shook his head. 'I know we should have, but we wanted her to know we trusted her. She'd not think that if we went in too heavy-handed. It's a bloody balancing act, isn't it?'

I nodded, aware the appeal was to my paternal nature rather than my professional role.

'I'd seen that crowd online a few times. I agreed with what they were doing. Back in the day, the perverts would have been tarred and feathered. You remember that?'

'That doesn't mean I agree with it.'

'You think they should be allowed to wander free?'

'I didn't say that. But summary justice is dangerous. There have been cases of people being falsely accused. Once that happens, the damage is done. People will always assume there's no smoke without fire.'

'For every one they get wrong they get plenty right.'

'So you contacted them,' I said, keen to keep him on subject, rather than debating the merits of paedophile-hunting.

He nodded. 'I didn't give them any information about where he was or anything. I didn't even know myself. Just that he was in the area. But you know that if you saw the message.'

'Did they respond?'

He shook his head. 'But they read the message. You know the way it changes from a tick to the other person's profile picture when they've seen it; it did that.'

'Why did you delete the message afterwards?'

Shaw shrugged. 'I suppose I worried that maybe we had done something wrong.'

I nodded.

'Have we?'

'I don't know,' I admitted. 'If it transpires that Northern Justice were involved in his death, then, yes, you could be facing charges. If they had nothing to do with it, then I'd guess not.'

'Have you spoken to them?' he asked, his face blanching as he realised the situation in which he had put himself.

'Not yet,' I said. 'I will be shortly.'

'Will you let me know what happens?' he asked.

'I'll do my best to keep you updated,' I said. 'My priority though is finding who killed Brooklyn Harris first.'

As we walked out to the front door he asked, 'Does it rest easy with you? Standing up for people like Harris?'

'Who said I'm standing up for him?'

'You're going through all this for him,' Shaw said, not in an accusatory way, but seemingly with genuine curiosity.

'Harris served his time for what he did to Hannah Row. If we'd been contacted, I would have had a chance to try to hold him to account for what he tried to do to Helen. I didn't get that chance.'

'But as a father, how can you go through all this for a killer and a paedophile?'

I considered the question. 'Because Brooklyn Harris was someone's son. At one stage he was a kid, just like our kids. And now, he's a victim, whether you agree with that term or not. The fact is, he's a victim of a crime and that fact doesn't care about your, mine, or anyone else's opinion.'

Shaw stared at me but said nothing.

'So that's the crime I have to investigate. And when I find who killed him, whether I like it or not, I'll have to arrest them and see them brought before the courts. Otherwise, we're just savages.'

Chapter Twenty-Seven

Porter's address was listed in one of the newly built estates in the Waterside area of Derry, part of the continuous expansion of the city. The houses backed onto an out-of-town retail park so the traffic getting in was slow-moving.

Porter's house was semi-detached, red brick, newly built in the past few years, with a small walled garden and tarmac driveway. I parked on the street outside and went up to knock on the front door.

Rather than opening the door, I heard a male voice respond from just inside a moment later.

'Yes?'

'I'd like to speak to Mr Porter, please,' I said.

'Why?'

'Could you open the door, please, sir?' I asked, bending slightly and opening the letter box to be better heard and hoping to get some sense of whether it was Porter behind the door, but with no success. Through the narrow, frosted-glass panel in the door I could see movement.

'What do you want?'

'I'd like to speak with Mr Porter, please,' I repeated. 'My name is Garda Inspector Ben Devlin.'

'What do you want to talk to him about?'

'Is he there?' I asked, the use of the third person in the speaker's response making me question now whether this was Porter himself. 'It's best if we speak inside.'

'I'm not letting you in,' the voice said. 'You're a Guard. You've no authority over here.'

'I'm not looking for trouble, sir,' I said. 'I want to speak to Mr Porter about Northern Justice. Are you Mr Porter?'

The figure behind the door moved away but remained in the hallway. I hunkered down and opened the letter box again, trying to peer in.

'Mr Porter,' I said. 'It would be very helpful to talk to you. I'm investigating the killing of Brooklyn Harris. Your organisation outed him last year on one of your videos.'

'The fuck are you doing at my door?' a voice shouted behind me and I turned to see Bob Porter lumbering up the driveway towards me, his phone held aloft, followed by a second man, slim and agitated, also holding up a mobile phone, presumably both recording all that was happening. Porter wore a T-shirt and grey sweat bottoms, but no shoes or socks. Across the road I could see a woman standing at her door, still wearing a housecoat and bed clothes and I guessed Porter had just come from hers.

'Mr Porter?' I asked, trying to stand up and losing my balance a little in so doing. I eventually righted myself and stood to face the man. 'I'm Garda Inspector Ben Devlin—'

'I heard,' Porter snapped. 'What are you doing at my house?'

The door behind me opened and I glanced around, guessing now that the occupant had phoned Porter when I'd arrived and relayed everything that I'd said to him. Sure enough,

Frank Porter, Bob's cousin, according to Gerry Carter, stood in the doorway, also with a mobile phone trained on me.

'I'd like you to turn off the cameras, sir,' I said. 'I just want to talk with you about a case I'm investigating.'

'The cameras are for my insurance,' Porter said. 'They'll not go live unless you do something you shouldn't.'

I wasn't hugely convinced by the assurance. 'I'd like you to stop recording, sir,' I repeated.

'You've no jurisdiction here,' Porter said. 'You're shouting in my letter box at eleven in the morning, acting the big man. What do you want?'

'I want to speak to you about the death of Brooklyn Harris,' I said.

'Who?'

'You outed him as Gerard Dawson almost a year ago. He was murdered in Lifford several nights ago. I want to know what your involvement was.'

'My involvement?' Porter snapped. 'Fuck you, coming to my house and shouting this shit about me.'

'I know you were contacted about Harris' arrival in Lifford,' I said. 'I'll need to speak to you privately about that, sir. Without the cameras and the lackeys.'

'You don't come here speaking shit about me.'

'Did Northern Justice target Harris a second time?'

'Northern Justice does what people like you can't do,' Porter snapped. 'We take the power back to the people and away from institutions—'

I motioned to move past Porter and back towards my car. 'I've heard the sales pitch before,' I said. 'Vigilantes are vigilantes. We'll continue this conversation later.'

'We'll continue it now,' Porter said, positioning himself in front of me so that, to pass, I would have to push past him. 'You're not in control here, bitch,' he said. 'This is my patch you're on.'

'Let me past, please, Mr Porter,' I said, standing still, aware of the mobile phones trained on me from both front and back.

'Do you feel in control?' Porter sneered. 'This is what power feels like. You come here, throw around your rank like you're the shit, the cock of the walk. This is my town, son.'

The fact that Porter was, possibly, in his thirties, made his comment all the more absurd.

'You'll need to let me past, Mr Porter,' I said.

'I don't need to do anything I don't want to do,' Porter snapped.

I decided to try a different tack. 'That's true. Shall we talk instead about what Northern Justice has achieved?'

'Achieved? We do what the cops are afraid to do!' Porter shouted, looking up to his cousin for the benefit of the camera the latter still held. 'We expose the filth for what they are.'

The vehemence with which he pronounced the word 'filth' made me question exactly to whom it referred. 'Do you?' I asked. 'What about Brooklyn Harris?'

'What about him?' Porter said, turning on me. 'He should never have been allowed out of his cell.'

'Yet, you outed him last summer and what? He moved on somewhere else? That was some result – chasing people into the shadows. That's sterling work. You must be proud.'

Porter moved closer to me, his face inches from mine. 'I am proud. We told the cops about Harris and they did nothing. We told them again afterwards and they warned us to take down the video. Us? Do nothing about Harris but warn law-abiding citizens?'

'You need to step back from me, sir,' I said.

'Or what?' Porter moved closer again and I could smell the coffee and cigarettes off his breath.

'Step back, Mr Porter,' I said. 'I'm warning you.'

'You're on my property,' Porter began, gripping my left arm with his free hand, as if to move me.

I reacted instinctively, punching him quickly, full on the face. He staggered backwards from me, his phone skittering across the tarmac driveway, his mouth already bloodied, his face twisting with rage. I could tell he was preparing to lunge and tried to move away but my size and his proximity made it almost impossible to avoid him. He drove me back into Frank Porter who was still behind me and we, all three, ended up on the ground.

We traded restricted jabs, each trying to get the advantage on the other and get back to our feet. Frank Porter was sprawled still beneath us, scrabbling at me and pulling at my hair.

I rolled, getting Bob Porter onto his back and tussling to get free from me and used the change in position to lean my weight on the knee currently on top of cousin Frank's groin, beneath us, something which put an end to his involvement for the moment.

Bob continued to flail at me, aiming for any sort of contact so, gripping one hand in the other, I drove my elbow into his solar plexus, hard enough to incapacitate him but not so hard as to do lasting damage, I hoped.

'Don't touch me,' I said, standing now. I was aware of the taste of blood in my own mouth and when I spat onto the ground, my saliva was thick and red; one of Porter's punches must have landed.

'Now do you feel in control?' I snapped, then turned to see the thin man who'd accompanied him still standing, camera aimed at my face.

'Do *you*?' he asked, twitching the phone slightly to remind me I was being filmed.

Across the way, the woman stood still in her doorway, her phone to her ear as a PSNI car pulled up outside the house, blues flashing.

Chapter Twenty-Eight

The officers who arrived, though courteous, had no interest in my explanation as to why I'd been at Porter's front door, nor to my protests that he had started it by laying his hand on me. Perhaps unsurprisingly, though still to my shame, the first officer on the scene handcuffed me, despite my assurances that I had no intention of being violent; a claim undermined by the fact Porter was still bleeding from his mouth and nose and I suspected I had dislodged one of his teeth.

Almost instantly, his witnesses took over, including the woman I had seen from across the street. I had attacked him, they said; I'd thrown the first punch when Porter had asked me to get off his property. The thin man showed them footage of the scuffle and, I guessed, Porter putting his hand on me was either not visible or had been edited out already, for while I remained in cuffs, Porter was assisted into the squad car, in which he would be taken to Strand Road, unrestrained.

The two officers in the car with me were friendly, but neither seemed convinced by my story that I was a Garda inspector. I knew better than to say too much for now, waiting until I had a chance to make a statement once my head was clearer and my heart rate settled; I'd lost count of the number of people who, once arrested, compounded their own situation by senselessly ranting from the back seat of the police car.

It was not until we reached the Strand Road and the custody sergeant recognised me almost immediately that they took off the cuffs as I was processed and asked the obligatory questions about whether I'd taken drugs or alcohol and whether I required medical assistance. Rather than asking for a solicitor, I asked the custody officer to contact Jim Hendry for me.

I was taken into one of the interview rooms to give a statement. It was no different from ours in Letterkenny, no less dispiriting: a narrow room with felt boards on the walls to suggest comfort; four plastic chairs – two per side – facing off across something no larger than a school desk; recording equipment and a camera. Viewing all this from the other side of the table was surreal and I could see how the banality of the process, the mundane administration of criminal investigation, was designed to intimidate those at its mercy; nothing frightened most people more than a well-oiled machine bearing down on them.

I gave my statement to the younger of the two constables who introduced herself but whose name I forgot, not deliberately but because my brain seemed to be catching up on processing what had just transpired.

Porter hadn't set me up as such, but he certainly had played me, goading me into hitting him. It was my own fault – I was under no misapprehension about that – but he'd known what to do, what buttons to press, and I guessed

190

that a year of door-stepping people and videoing the results had helped him become more proficient in the act. It was a far cry from the fumbling attempt he'd made on Harris the year before. And that thought brought with it a question over what he'd said, about the PSNI warning him to take down the Harris footage. As far as I could tell, his Facebook page was still running plenty of other outings – why had Harris' been different and who had told him to remove it, I wondered.

They left me in the interview room as, I suspected, a professional courtesy, rather than taking me to the custody suite, and I was still sitting there when the door opened and Jim Hendry came in.

'The people you meet when you're out without a gun,' he said, with a Scottish lilt.

'Great movie,' I said. 'Thanks for coming down.'

'What the hell happened, Ben?'

'Porter runs Northern Justice, the crowd who targeted Brooklyn Harris last year.'

At the mention of Harris' name, Hendry groaned and, pulling out the plastic seat opposite me, sat down.

'Fucking Brooklyn Harris,' he said.

'Porter outed Harris in his old house, and that meant he had to relocate. I told you that the night Harris died, he'd arranged to meet a young girl from Letterkenny. Her parents prevented her visiting him, but the father contacted Northern Justice and told them that Harris was in Lifford that night.'

'Do you think this Porter guy had something to do with Harris' killing?'

I shrugged. 'I didn't get a chance to find out. He was film-ing me from the start. He got in my face, grabbed my arm. I saw red. My own fault entirely.'

'Mea culpa, mea culpa,' Hendry said.

'Something like that. The speed that the PSNI officers arrived, mind you, I think they were called before anything even kicked off. When I called at the door, it wasn't Porter inside but his cousin who called Porter and told him who I was and what I wanted. He'd been across the street with a female neighbour, by the looks of it.'

'You think they called us first and then came out and what?'

'He goaded me,' I said. 'That's not my blaming anyone else; but he laid hands on me, he got in my face, cameras filming everything.'

'You should have known better.'

'I should.'

Hendry sat, legs splayed, his arms folded, watching me.

'What about Harris now?'

I shrugged. 'All I'm finding are new problems,' I said. 'Hannah Row's blood was at the scene. Our forensic scien-tist has suggested that if one of the organ donations taken from Hannah was her bone marrow, that might account for how someone would have her blood. I can't see how or even if that connects with Porter.'

'And what about the Hannah Row killing? How's that cold case reopening going?'

'I went back and looked at the footage from the club that night. Hannah got into a row with one of Harris' friends – either Riley Mullan or Charlie McDaid. Mullan denies it's him, McDaid wouldn't even answer any questions. One of Hannah's friends was with her when it happened but I don't have access to the files so I can't follow that up. But at the moment, I've three possible scenarios for what happened to Harris. Either Northern Justice got involved and finished what they started a year ago and were warned off by one of your officers in the north, or Hannah Row's family had something to do with it, or either Mullan or McDaid felt they had something to hide and were worried that Harris was talking to a journalist about what happened back then and might implicate one of them. All three possibilities have motive, Northern Justice and either McDaid or Mullan have means, as they'd stayed in touch with Harris after he got back out, but Hannah's blood ties her death to the scene and so, possibly, her family.'

Hendry listened quietly to all that I had said, seeming to weigh up each possibility.

'Ben, Harris was a dirtbag no matter which way you look. Not just the death of Hannah Row, but this contacting young girls now, drawing porno cartoons of them, taking stolen prescription drugs, selling his story to some hack; none of that recommends him as someone worthy of you landing yourself in a custody cell, you know that, don't you?'

I nodded my head. 'I'm tired of being told what to think of him, Jim. I can make up my own mind.'

'This isn't even about reopening the Row case and what that means for me if something untoward is found; this is about you, about all the shit you have going on outside of this, with your dad and that. And I mean that sincerely.

Give yourself a break on this one. You're going to need it with what's coming at you.'

I glanced up at him. 'I know what's coming,' I said.

He shook his head. 'No, you don't. You think you do. You think you're ready but ... I know when my dad died, it didn't hit me right away but after a while? It's like your anchor's been cut loose.'

'I'm sorry, Jim,' I said. It was the first time he'd spoken about his father to me since the man's passing.

He shrugged, his arms still folded across his chest. 'It is what it is. It's shit.'

'Is that why you're thinking about leaving?'

Another shrug. When he spoke, his voice was huskier.

'You wonder what you've managed to do,' he said. 'What difference any of it makes in the grand scheme of things. My old man worked in the shipbuilders', painting parts. He used spray paint all his life and it was only in the last decade or so before he retired that he got a face mask to stop him breathing in all the shit that was being sprayed. He ended up carting an oxygen bottle around after him most days. Who's to blame for that? What did he achieve for the loss of a lung? You find yourself asking those questions and, I guess, inevitably, asking the same questions of yourself. It's like a cosmic stocktake.'

He said the last line with a laugh, though I knew the sentiment was genuine.

'That's why I'm still trying to find out who killed Brooklyn Harris,' I said. 'I know he maybe wasn't the most deserving of victims, but it's not up to me to decide the worthiness of the dead. Everything is changing – Penny's gone, Shane is going to be going soon, Lifford station is gone, you're going, my dad – everything's changing and I need something stable to hold on to. And the idea that there's a victim and a criminal and those two things are clear and distinct is something stable. I can't control what's happening in my life, but I can control what I do here, in this case. I already feel like I'm cut loose, and this is that anchor, the only anchor, that I have.'

'That's not a good thing, Ben,' Hendry said. 'The job can't be the only thing.'

'It's not the only thing,' I said. 'But it's stable at a time when everything else is not. It's a way for me to feel in control of things.'

Hendry gestured around the room. 'Do you still feel in control of things?'

I laughed joylessly. 'Honestly, if I was in the same situation again, I'd hit him twice as hard, the prick.'

Hendry laughed at that. 'That's the old Ben I know,' he said. 'Lucky we're not recording this; it hardly smacks of remorse now, does it?'

'I know no one cares,' I said. 'But there's a story there, about why Brooklyn Harris died and even about why Brooklyn Harris killed and I need to know the truth of both those things. I need to know his story, even if no one else does.'

'You know that sounds mad, don't you?'

I shrugged. 'Maybe. But it is what it is.'

We sat in silence a moment as Hendry pulled at the corner of his moustache.

'So what happens now?' I asked.

'I'd a chat with the custody sergeant out there before I came in. Porter is keen to press charges, but if we can push the fact that he touched you first, that might be enough to put him in his box. You shouldn't have been over here interviewing and they'll want to make something of that, I've no doubt.'

'That's not quite what I meant,' I said.

'I know,' Hendry said, standing. 'I'll pull our files on Hannah Row's death and see what we have. I'll be able to get the medical notes too and find out about the transplant. As for Riley Mullan and Charlie McDaid? You'll have a chance to hear one of them sooner than you might have hoped.'

'Why?'

'McDaid is in the building; he's Bob Porter's solicitor.'

Chapter Twenty-Nine

Ten minutes later, I found myself sitting in a small viewing room, watching on the CCTV screen while Jim Hendry went in to speak to Bob Porter.

'This isn't about the assault, is that right?' McDaid said after Hendry had introduced himself and explained the reason for his being there.

'Tangentially,' Hendry said. 'You run the site called Northern Justice, is that right?'

Porter looked to McDaid who shook his head lightly.

'If you've not broken the law, you've no reason not to admit to that,' Hendry said.

'We support the PSNI,' Porter offered. I suspected his own narcissism was of such a level that he felt compelled to be credited for his action, even at a possible cost. 'Several of the people we've caught have been arrested.'

'So I understand,' Hendry said. 'And that's invaluable to us. How does it work?'

Porter sat up a little straighter in his seat, Hendry's morsel of praise baiting him. 'We establish a decoy,' he said. 'An account that looks like it's from a child. We target their interests to those of someone we're following who we suspect of being a paedophile and then we introduce the account into a forum frequented by the suspect. Then we wait to see if they make contact. We never make first contact as that might be seen as entrapment. Once they make contact with our decoy, we monitor the situation and wait until the suspect asks the "child" to do something we know to be illegal. We keep screenshots of everything we do and we pass those to the police.'

'But not before you door-step the suspects, is that right?'

Porter shrugged. 'It's part of our process.'

'My client isn't admitting to any wrongdoing in this. Such groups have provided evidence in almost half of the successful prosecutions of online grooming cases in the UK,' McDaid said. 'Northern Justice have done nothing wrong in that regard. If you have no specific charges for my client to face in relation to this, I suggest we're finished with this line of discussion now.'

'I'm just chatting,' Hendry said. 'I'm interested in how this works. Especially the door-stepping part. I don't get that. Isn't that just you getting your moment in the sun, looking for credit for your work?'

He'd pegged the question properly; Porter would never leave the room without justifying the importance of what he did. And, of course, he would want his moment in the sun.

'It's not about me,' he said.

'Frequently the first ten minutes of your videos is you talking,' Hendry said. 'You're the focus.'

'No,' Porter said, even as McDaid put his hand in front of him in a gesture meant to suggest they were done. 'The shaming of the paedophile is a key part of our organisational strategy.'

The verbosity of his language in an attempt to legitimise what he was doing did not change the fact for me that he was a vainglorious vigilante, but it seemed to enflame him further with the righteousness of his actions.

'Public shaming has a place in society whether we like it or not,' he said. 'We put people in the stocks centuries ago; now we put them on social media. They're lucky insults are all that's being thrown at them nowadays.'

'So the public shaming is the key element?'

'It takes the paedos out of the shadows, lets people see their faces, recognise them in their communities. Keep our children safe.'

'Do you have children, Mr Porter?'

There was a pause. 'No,' Porter said. 'Hopefully someday.'

'What happened with the Brooklyn Harris outing then?' Hendry asked.

'That's it; we're finished,' McDaid said.

'Your client was contacted the day Mr Harris died,' Hendry said. 'He was informed that Mr Harris was in the Lifford area. We know he read the message that was sent. There are questions to be answered, Mr Porter, and it's best if you answer them now and let us eliminate you from the enquiries.'

'This is an An Garda investigation,' McDaid said. 'Headed by the man who has just assaulted my client. We don't have to answer anything here.'

'Our colleagues across the border requested earlier today that we would take a statement from Mr Porter about the involvement or otherwise of Northern Justice with Brooklyn

Harris, to save him having to travel into Donegal to provide same. I'm ticking boxes here, but would still like that box to be ticked so I can move on with my day.'

'I didn't go anywhere near Harris that night,' Porter said. 'I have an alibi for the whole night. My car never left my drive.'

'That's perfect,' Hendry said. 'But going back to the first time you confronted Harris, last year. That footage has vanished from your site and, unlike those other investigations you supported, that one didn't do anything except drive Harris to another area where he continued contacting young girls. Did you make mistakes?'

'What we did was perfect. Only afterwards, we were told that the PSNI wouldn't agree with some of the methods we'd chosen. We were told they might consider it entrapment.'

'Sara Burke was the name of the decoy?'

'I believe so.'

'And she sent images to Harris.'

'Mr Porter—' McDaid cautioned.

'They were stock images from porn sites,' Porter said. 'None of them were of kids.'

'I can see why the officer you dealt with had issues with it. Who was the officer?'

McDaid moved to protest again but Porter had already said, 'Someone Fleming in the PPU.'

Hendry nodded. 'And he told you that he didn't think your evidence would support prosecution.'

Porter nodded.

'Why did you take the footage down?'

'This has nothing to do with your initial request for a statement,' McDaid said, standing. 'If An Garda wish for a statement, they'll have to go through all the relevant channels and we'll be complying with nothing that puts my client in a room with his assaulter.'

'My colleague from across the border says that Mr Porter laid hands on him first. Footage put online by Northern Justice which I've just reviewed supports that. It can clearly be heard that Mr Porter is asked to remove his hands on several occasions,' Hendry continued. 'That's a textbook example of assault right there. You may wish to take further advice on how you choose to proceed, Mr Porter, if you don't want another assault charge levelled at you as a counterclaim.'

'Another?' Porter asked, suddenly defiant.

'I've seen your records, Mr Porter,' Hendry said. 'I'd think carefully before you move forward with this. I'm surprised you've not been counselled in that regard.'

McDaid stood at that point. 'We're clearly finished here,' he said.

'I don't believe so,' Hendry said. 'Inspector Devlin has made it clear that he will press charges regarding your client's physical assault on him. The footage, which your client's own phone and friends' phones provided us, corroborates that narrative. If you choose to pursue charges, we will be charging Mr Porter here with assault: a charge that, with his colourful history, he can well be doing without.'

'I need to consult with my solicitor,' Porter said.

'I imagined you would,' Hendry said, standing now as McDaid reluctantly retook his own seat. 'One last thing;

how did you know where Gerard Dawson was, the first time you targeted him?'

'He engaged with one of our decoys.'

'Sara Burke?'

'We've already established all this,' McDaid said.

'But how did you know that Gerard Dawson was Brooklyn Harris?'

Porter glanced across at McDaid. 'I'd seen his picture,' he said. 'I recognised him.'

Hendry shook his head. 'Harris' picture wasn't released at the time he was sentenced, because of the age of his victim. He had no social-media presence. There were no public photographs. Someone told you who he was, didn't they?'

'I don't . . . no, I must have seen his picture somewhere. Who'd have known who he was otherwise?'

'Who indeed?' Hendry said. 'Were you still in contact with him after his release, Mr McDaid?'

'That's an absurd inference,' McDaid barked.

'I didn't infer anything,' Hendry said. 'I implied it. You inferred it.'

Chapter Thirty

By the time Porter left the Strand Road, he was undecided on whether to press charges and, despite Hendry's suggestion to the contrary, so was I – not that I'd had any intention to do so in the first place. I'd lost my temper; I accepted I'd acted inappropriately.

I also knew though that, as Porter had already commented in his interview with Hendry, public shaming was one of the tools he most relished using and I had no doubt the footage of what happened would be online imminently.

'I need to call up and collect my car,' I said.

'We'll take a ride first,' Hendry said.

He drove us down through the city and across the arching Foyle Bridge to Gransha Hospital, which had housed the city's psychiatric units for years. We continued on down the dual carriageway past it and the city's rugby club before hitting Maydown roundabout, off which sat a massive PSNI complex. It was into here that Hendry manoeuvred the car.

Inside the barricaded walls, the space was more redolent of a training college, partly because of the cohort of trainee officers currently jogging round the grounds. Hendry parked up outside a small block to the far end of the compound and led me up the pathway to the Public Protection Unit, the entrance to which was marked by a closed door with reflective foil on the glass, preventing me from seeing inside. Hendry rang the bell and, a few moments later, the door was opened by a young female officer, fine featured with short cropped hair.

'Lucy!' Jim Hendry said. 'This is Garda Inspector Ben Devlin. Ben, this is Sergeant Lucy Black.'

'Inspector Devlin,' she replied. 'Good to meet you.'

'Ben,' I said. 'Nice to meet you, too.'

'I'll not shake hands, what with coronavirus and that,' Lucy said. 'But please, come in.'

'We're looking for Tom,' Hendry explained.

'He's in the office,' Lucy said, stepping back and gesturing that I should follow Hendry where he was already disappearing up the corridor.

Tom Fleming sat behind his desk, already joking with Hendry when I knocked and entered his office. He stood immediately and offered his hand, which I thought it rude not to shake in spite of the advice to social distance. I looked at Lucy Black who shrugged in a 'what can you do?' manner.

'Ben's investigating the killing of Brooklyn Harris,' Hendry explained. 'We've just spoken to Bob Porter.'

'Him?' Lucy said. 'He's a piece of work.'

'Mr Porter certainly has his own ideas about the justice system,' Hendry explained.

'We've had to speak to him a few times,' Lucy added.

'He said you warned him off the first time he targeted Brooklyn Harris,' I said.

Fleming nodded. 'We were contacted by Harris' parole officer. He'd been given a new identity when he left prison,

204

set up with a new address, the whole nine yards. Then Porter outed him on the internet.'

'We took a look at the footage,' Lucy said. 'They'd entrapped him for a start, from what I remember.'

Fleming nodded. 'Yeah. The decoy contacted him. And they had shared footage themselves through their decoy that we had issues about.'

'Porter claimed it was all legal.'

Lucy laughed derisively. 'We couldn't prove some of it was underage, but I was pretty sure that it was. Porter is one of those ones you think is protesting too much, you know?'

I nodded. 'He has no kids himself but he's talking about protecting children.'

'He had a seventeen-year-old girlfriend there for a while,' Lucy said. 'He's twenty-five now. He used to pick her up from school. The school principal contacted Gateway and they referred it through to us as a child-protection issue. She was overage, just about, though, so we couldn't do anything.'

'I took a look through his record,' Hendry said. 'He'd a caution and a suspended sentence for assault a few years back too.'

Fleming nodded. 'He's not the nicest character you'll encounter,' he offered with some understatement.

'Ben here just hit him a smack,' Hendry said, laughing.

'Seriously?'

I blushed with shame. 'I lost my cool. He grabbed me by the arm.'

'I'd love to smack him,' Lucy said. 'Good for you.'

I nodded, grateful for her show of solidarity rather than in agreement with the sentiment. I knew that when the footage came out, I'd have questions to answer, first with Patterson and then, more importantly, with Debbie.

'Who helped relocate Harris?' I asked.

'We'd a hand in it,' Fleming said. 'He refused to change his name again. Said he saw no point, if he'd already been found once. We wondered whether some of his friends or former cellmates had identified him, to be honest, though we could see no reason for them to do so.'

'Should he even have kept contact with them?'

'He said they supported him when he was inside, more than his own family did. They knew he was getting out so he thought there'd be no point not telling them.'

'Which friends?'

'That solicitor, McDaid, was one,' Lucy said. 'The other was a nervous fella.'

'Riley Mullan?'

'That could be it,' Lucy said.

'Jack Grimes' protege,' Fleming said.

'Riley Mullan is Grime's son?'

Fleming nodded. 'Not quite; I don't remember the exact connection, but Grimes had a soft spot for him. For all of them.'

'Including Harris?'

Fleming nodded. 'I was involved a little in the Hannah Row case when I was working with vulnerables in Omagh before this was set up here. Grimes knew the three boys from before the case; I think he coached or taught them at some stage. Something like that.'

I could tell from the flicker of annoyance that this was news to Hendry.

'Anything else you remember from back then?'

Fleming shook his head. 'Not much of value, I suspect. Harris was a sad case. The home life had been fairly abusive, by all accounts, although by the time we got involved, the father had walked and things had settled a little. Mind you, by that stage, the damage was done. Harris was already broken. I remember sitting in on one of the interviews as his appropriate adult just before he turned eighteen; he was all over the place. His witness statement was like a fever dream.'

'The copy I saw was fairly coherent,' I said, glancing at Hendry who had provided it to me.

'Then it was cobbled together from various interviews. It was like panning for gold, trying to find a nugget of information in the stuff he was saying; shadows chasing him, telling him what to do, worms crawling under his skin, bursting out through his stomach like something out of *Alien*. Voices telling him to rape that wee girl. Telling him they'd kill him if he didn't. He was off his head when he did it and seemed to remain off his head in some fashion for months afterwards.'

'He was using in custody?'

Fleming shook his head. 'It was almost like he opened something in his own head that night that didn't close again afterwards. He never really came back from it. Truth be told, I felt sorry for him a bit. Not for the attack on Hannah,' he quickly added, sensing perhaps Hendry's tensing. 'But he'd suffered such levels of abuse and neglect at home, he'd rather have been living in a world where he was being chased by shadows and had worms crawling in his muscles than this one.'

'I feel sorry for Hannah Row,' Hendry said.

'Undoubtedly,' Fleming said. 'As do I, primarily. But by that stage, Harris was already a monster. We got a glimpse into what made him that monster to begin with. I always thought it's a pity we couldn't put Brooklyn's father on trial for what happened to Hannah Row because, in many ways, he was most responsible for that child's death. Context is important.'

'Harris was eighteen by the time it came to trial,' Hendry said. 'He'd reached the age of responsibility.'

'And it was right that he was held to account,' Fleming said. 'Who's looking likely for his killing?'

'No one yet,' I said. 'But we found traces of Hannah Row's blood at the scene of his murder.'

'Fresh blood?'

I nodded.

'That's freaky,' Lucy said. 'Almost like she came back to avenge her own killing.'

'The thought had struck me,' I agreed.

I felt my mobile buzz in my pocket and, taking it out, saw a message from Shane. It read:

WTF, Dad???' followed by a laughing emoji and a link to a YouTube video. I knew, even before I clicked on it, what I would see.

'The video's online now,' I said.

Four minutes later, Patterson called.

Chapter Thirty-One

'You can't stay on as lead,' Patterson said, simply. 'It's all over the place. People are talking about police brutality; I've had the local press on the line almost constantly.'

'I'm sorry,' I said. 'He laid hands on me, I told him to remove them; he didn't. That's not justification; it's an explanation.'

'Ben, I'd have broken his arm if it was me,' Patterson said. 'I don't care about you smacking him; it's the fact it was being filmed.'

'I know.'

'Is he pressing charges?'

I shook my head. 'I suspect not. Hendry was able to pull up his own record for assault and told him I'd press charges if he did. I have a feeling he knows he'd not win his day in court.'

'So, he's taken it to the court of public opinion instead,' Patterson said, grimly, though seemingly pleased with the bon mot.

'He has a better chance of winning there,' I said.

'Do we release details of his own record?' Patterson said. 'Leak it to a friendly journalist?'

'I suspect we just ride it out,' I said. 'See what happens.'

'Times have changed, Ben,' Patterson said. The frequent use of my first name unnerved me. 'Back in the day you could give someone a shoeing, a bit of summary justice, and they were happy to accept that. Easier than being tied up in courts and solicitors for months. But, unfortunately, things have changed.'

'I know, sir,' I said, not surprised that Patterson might think the advent of accountability in policing was both a recent development and one to be regretted. 'I accept I lost my temper. I'm prepared to accept whatever is required.'

'You'll have to step down as lead,' he said again. 'The optics aren't good for us otherwise. You've not got anywhere with it anyway, have you? So much the better for that,' he added with an upraised hand as he saw me prepare to disagree with his assessment.

'I've been making some progress,' I said, and filled him in on the various strands within the investigation.

'So forensics think there's a connection with a transplant donation,' Patterson said. 'That should be the focus.'

'There is something odd about the Hannah Row investigation, too,' I said.

'That's neither our investigation to begin with nor ours now to reopen,' Patterson said. 'The focus is on who killed Harris, though to be honest, I don't care if we never find out. I'm going to move McCready up to SIO on it. You can offer support from behind, especially with your contacts across the way.'

He nodded his head towards the north, as if it were in the next room and not fifteen miles away.

'What happens next will depend on whether Porter makes a complaint to us,' Patterson said. 'It might be wise to have the Ombudsman take a look at it, anyway, but I

210

don't see that you've anything to worry about. You were surrounded, being hounded under pressure with cameras and that and he touched you first.'

I nodded.

'On the minus side, you were there alone and carrying out an investigation in the north. If you'd had your mate Hendry with you, we'd have been covered.'

'He was unhappy about the fact I was looking into the Hannah Row killing again.'

'I can understand why,' Patterson said. 'But that notwithstanding, you shouldn't have been there on your own and that's the only thing the Ombudsman might take issue with. That and your history for lifting your fist, though you're hardly alone in that regard.'

'Am I suspended?'

'What's the point in that?' Patterson said. 'This isn't shooting an unarmed suspect. You defended yourself in a volatile situation.'

'Context is important,' I said, echoing Tom Fleming's comment.

'Indeed,' Patterson said. 'Now get this Harris thing off our board, for the love of Christ, will you?'

I sat with McCready and got him up to speed on what I'd found. Like Patterson, he focused on the transplant issue, wisely, I realised now with the benefit of some distance from the case. I began to doubt the path I'd taken, lost among the trees and not seeing for looking.

'I'll request information regarding the recipient of her donation,' McCready said. 'And contact forensics about it.'

211

'Mrs Row mentioned a girl called Maisie. But I think she was a heart transplant. It needs to be bone marrow,' I said. 'Anything else won't have affected the DNA in the blood. Jim Hendry is looking to see what he can find at their end, too.'

McCready nodded.

'What do you need me to do?' I asked.

McCready blushed, clearly already finding it awkward to be issuing orders to his own superior officer.

'Whatever you think best, sir,' he said.

'Whatever you need me to do, Joe,' I said. 'I'm supporting *you* here. What do you need?'

'What would you do?'

'Honestly? I want to talk to Jack Grimes,' I said. 'There's something not right about the killing of Hannah Row. The blood at Harris' killing ties his death to hers – that's something I'm sure about.'

'You think Grimes covered up the involvement of some of the others?'

I shrugged. 'I don't know. But if Grimes was related in some way to Riley Mullan, that's a conflict of interest. McDaid is Porter's solicitor; it wouldn't surprise me if we find that McDaid was the one who directed Porter to Harris' house last year, though I can't work out why he would do so.'

'Maybe he was worried about the book Harris was contributing to?'

'That only happened as a result of Harris being outed. McCay tracked him down because of that.'

'Do you want me to request an interview with Grimes then?' McCready asked.

'Before that, I think we need to see the RUC's investigation file on Hannah Row's death.' I'd resisted asking for it because of Hendry and my wish not to alienate someone who had proven to be a good friend over my time working in Lifford. I realised now that the request coming from Joe McCready would be seen as less of a personal slight. I did feel a little ashamed using Joe McCready as cover in that way.

'Okay,' McCready said. 'I'll put in a request for it. You'll know better than me what to look for, so I'd like you to work through it, seeing what shakes. I'll chase up the transplant angle.'

'Thanks, Joe,' I said. 'I should have kept you better informed about what I was doing. I'm sorry.'

McCready shrugged. 'Things will have to change now that I'm the boss,' he joked. Or at least, I think he was joking.

Chapter Thirty-Two

I was finishing up in the office when Penny phoned. It was a rare occurrence; mostly she would call her mother and I'd be an addendum to the call.

'Hi, love,' I said when I answered.

'You know you're online,' she said, without preamble.

'I know. I meant to—'

'Everyone here has seen it . . .'

'I'm sorry,' I said. 'I hope it didn't embarrass you.'

'Embarrass?' she snorted. 'You just don't get it, do you? Still going round throwing your fists about like that'll solve the things your brain can't.'

'Wait a minute, Penny,' I began.

'Do you know over seventy people were killed by the police in the US last month? In one month!'

'It's a different situation, Penny. He grabbed me.'

'He grabbed you? Do you know how childish that sounds? You're not in the playground, Dad. All my friends have seen it now. Do you know how ashamed I am?'

'Wait a second,' I said, trying again to explain myself, but I realised there was no point.

'You're all over Twitter,' she said. 'You want to see what people are saying.'

'No, I don't,' I said.

'We're campaigning down here for equal treatment for all, for accountability in public office, and my own father is filmed brawling on the street with a suspect.'

'Apart from that, how's the rest of your day going?' I asked, aiming for levity and missing.

She hung up.

'Everything okay?' McCready asked, having, presumably, overheard my half of the conversation.

'I think I've just been parented by my daughter,' I said.

The one benefit of Penny's call was that Debbie's disapprobation was, by comparison, relatively mild. As Penny had suggested, it was not the first time I'd lifted my hand to someone while investigating a case, though by the time I got home, Debs had watched it a sufficient number of times to begin to convince herself that, if I wasn't justified, at the very least my actions were understandable.

'I'm going to be tortured with kids asking me about it,' she said, over dinner. 'That's the worst bit. I already had classes this afternoon asking if I ever use YouTube. Like I'm some kind of pre-digital dinosaur.'

'That's not going to be a problem,' Shane crowed with a cheer. 'They've just closed the schools.'

'What?'

Shane held up his phone where a breaking-news banner confirmed that schools were to close for two weeks as a precaution due to the coronavirus outbreak.

'There you go,' Debs said. 'Hopefully it'll be tomorrow's chip wrapper by the time we go back.'

'That's not how the internet works, Mum,' Shane said.

'You know what I mean,' Debs said. 'Don't be clever.'

'What happened?' my father asked.

'They've closed the schools over this virus,' I explained, grateful for the change in subject.

'Not that,' my dad said, undeterred. 'What happened with you?'

I blushed a little as I told him, then again when Shane produced his iPad – the screen being bigger and so easier to see – and played the footage for him.

'You've twenty-eight thousand views,' he said. 'That's not bad going.'

My father watched it in silence. Even though I could not see the screen, I could tell whereabouts they were in the incident from the snatches of dialogue alone, something confirmed by my father's lips pursing as he reached the part where I threw the first punch at Porter.

'Benedict,' was all he said when it was finished.

Before bedtime, he asked me to help him have a shower. I'd bought a small stool for the bathroom which allowed him to sit while he washed and, having helped him change and get into the shower, I put down the toilet seat and sat, my head averted, waiting for him to wash yet unwilling to leave the room lest he fell again.

My hand hurt, now that the adrenaline of the earlier events had dissipated completely. Porter's tooth had split the skin on one knuckle and, as I flexed my hand to try to dispel the stiffness, the cut opened again. I wadded some toilet paper and dabbed it.

'That was some smack you hit that young fella,' Dad said,

and I realised that he'd seen what I was doing through the glass front of the shower.

'Yeah,' I agreed. 'Not hard enough though.'

'Shane's secretly proud,' he said. 'He must have showed me the film a half dozen times before you came home.'

'I thought you only saw it at teatime.'

He laughed. 'Just make sure he doesn't think it's the way to deal with all his problems.'

'I know that, Dad,' I said, rankling a little at being told how to parent my own son. 'Penny's already phoned to scold me.'

'Boys and girls are different, though,' my father said. 'I remember you and Tom fighting all the time when you were kids.'

My brother Tom lived down the country. To my mind, beyond the usual sibling arguments when we were younger, we'd got on well as children. I didn't remember us fighting.

'Tom knew how to wind me up.'

'You knew how to be wound up,' Dad said. 'You still do by the looks of it.'

'You think I shouldn't have hit yer man today?'

'I didn't say that. Someone crosses a line, they have to expect they're going to get a reaction, you know?'

I nodded my head, then unsure whether he could see me through the rising steam, I grunted, 'Yes.'

'But you need to think about Shane, too. About the example you set him.'

'I know, Dad,' I said.

'He's a good lad. He's a whizz with that iPad. He's set me up a Netflix account, set up some films for me to watch.'

'Yeah, he said he was going to,' I said. 'He is a good fella. He must take after his granda.'

There was silence for a moment, then he added, 'I hope I set you a good example.'

The words hung in air already thick with the humidity of the shower and, beyond that, the context of what we both knew lay ahead, just out of sight.

'You did, Pops,' I said. 'The best.'

'Because family is all that matters,' he added.

'I know,' I said, understanding that I'd want to remember every word he said but keen for the conversation to be over, too. 'Are you done?'

I opened the door and turned off the water before handing him a towel to start drying himself. He had his back to me as he hunched over. His skin, despite his age, was still young and supple and it surprised me: his youthfulness, despite his age, his vulnerability in that moment, the manner in which our roles had changed, as Penny's seemingly had with me just hours earlier. I felt my vision blur a little and had to grip the shower door to steady myself, but even that shifted a little on its mechanism.

'When I think of all the things I've done, the jobs I've done, the time spent on so many things,' he said, 'in the end, here I am, with you and your family. Everything else is gone now; your mother especially. All I have left is what's left of our family. You and Tom.'

'That's all we need, Dad,' I said, drying his hair and draping the towel across his shoulders as I used to do with Shane and Penny when they were young.

'Blood is the only tie that matters, Ben,' he said. 'Family is all that matters.'

I helped him out of the shower and held him steadily while he dressed. He had to hug in close to me while we pulled up the back of his pyjama trousers and as he clung to me, he whispered, 'You two boys will stick together, won't you? You and Tom?'

'Of course,' I said, turning my head a little to the side so he would not see the tears the comment tore from me.

But as he clasped me again, a second time, his own cheeks were wet against my neck, and this time we stayed in that embrace for a moment, both of us lingering as if to fix it in our memories.

Day Five

13 March 2020

Chapter Thirty-Three

I dreamt of my father that night. When I was a child, I had pestered him to take me to a stunt show that was performing in the grounds of Templemore Sports Complex on the outskirts of Derry. One of the drivers had been the man responsible for driving the car on two wheels up an alleyway in the movie *Diamonds Are Forever*, though possibly not to blame for the car exiting the alley on the opposite two wheels due to a continuity error. I'd imagined, in my childishness, that being in close proximity with the stunt driver would be almost as good as meeting Bond himself.

My dad, more in sufferance than enthusiasm, had taken me along on my own, Tom being still too young to go to such things. We'd bought candyfloss – an unprecedented treat – and spent the evening together, watching the stunt drivers, getting carried away in the faux tension of whether the motorcyclist driving through a ring of flame would make it out alive.

When it came time for the two-wheeled stunt, the crowd had moved forward, blocking my view. My father, without words, had lifted me and hoisted me onto his shoulders, so that I could see. Marvelling at the stunt being performed, at one stage I glanced down to see if he shared my sense of amazement, only to see his head bowed, the crowd in front of him so populous that he could not see with the added burden of me on his shoulders weighing him down. I had thought often on that moment of selflessness when, as a new parent myself, following the birth of my own children, I struggled through night feeds and broken sleep.

In my dream, we were once more at the stunt show. I was sitting on his shoulders, watching the cars careening around the showgrounds. I could feel the heat of the Ring of Death, could smell the acridity of the plumes of black smoke drifting from it through the crowd, mingling with the exhaust fumes that lay heavy on the breeze.

Yet, when I looked down, I realised that I was standing alone, that my father was not there. I knew I had to find him and, though an adult, pushed my way through the crowd as a child might, earning from other spectators, first glances of annoyance and then sympathy as they understood I was lost.

I made my way to the Lost and Found area, which was, inexplicably, in the centre of town, and I knew that I would not find him, for the crowds now were too populous, the area too extensive. I told the paramedic who was stationed there that I was lost and could not find my father. He spoke to me as one might speak to an infant, putting his arm around my shoulder and telling me that we'd find him and I realised in that moment that it was not me, but my father, who was lost.

Someone told me that he'd been seen in the bus station and I wondered why he'd abandoned me, why he would have left me alone at the sports ground, watching the cars. I ran down to the station, the sky the colour of old bones, the sun's glare so brilliant it hurt my eyes and seemed to bleach my vision of colour. The gates to the station were shut and, beyond, I could see a bus pulling out onto the road and I knew my father was there and that, try as I might, I could not reach it. He looked out of the window as the bus drove off, but made no effort to disembark, merely raising his hand in a silent salute of farewell. The sunlight caught the window and I lost sight of him in its glare.

I woke in tears, a migraine aura already blooming behind my eyes, and just made it to the toilet before being sick. Afterwards, I crept into his room to prove to myself that he was still there, still breathing.

As I was awake anyway, I went to early Mass, calling with our old parish priest, Fr Brennan, afterwards to ask him to offer Mass that weekend for my father. The church had already emptied all the water fonts and the doors were left open through the service as part of the coronavirus social-distancing measures.

Brennan was struggling with his vestments when I called into the sacristy and I could hear his breath catching in his chest from the exertion of simply removing the ceremonial garments.

'How's he doing?' he asked, when I explained the purpose of my calling.

'Not good,' I said. 'The lockdown, when it comes, will complicate things even further.'

'For us all,' Fr Brennan said. 'They're shutting the churches, I believe. Suspending the Sunday obligation to attend Mass.'

I was taken aback by the news and, on reflection, strangely saddened at the thought. For all its other failings, the Church had defied persecution through history to maintain Mass, even in Penal times. This acknowledgement now of our powerlessness in the face of something we could not see and could not prevent, connected with me at a visceral level.

'Things are going to get bad,' he said. 'I don't envy you your job.'

'Nor I yours,' I said.

'Are you working the young Harris killing?'

I nodded. 'It's proving tricky getting to the truth.'

'The truth is always tricky,' Brennan said. 'You know that. All we can do is our best. Everything else is beyond our control anyway. I'll be praying for your father.'

The station was quiet when I went in, possibly as many of the officers who were also parents were trying to find alternative childcare arrangements with the schools' closure.

I was earlier than usual; Debs and Shane were both staying at home and Debbie had contacted Penny telling her to come back to Lifford from college, which had, likewise, been closed down, classes moved online for the foreseeable future.

The muted conversation in the station was around what might happen next. Rumours were building of checkpoints on the border to stop travel across the frontier. Someone had heard the army were being recalled to barracks in Dublin in order to assist us in case of civil unrest and one of the custody sergeants swore that his wife, who worked in a supermarket, had been told already that they would be introducing purchase limits to avoid the stockpiling of pasta and toilet paper which had been seen in other parts of the world but which everyone had vainly hoped we'd been too sensible to mimic here.

For all the joking, there was a palpable sense of rising anxiety, an awareness that things were about to change in ways none of us could predict and that we would be policing that change with little guidance on how to do so, this being an event that no one had really believed might actually happen outside of novels and TV shows.

'What if we end up being the ones who close the border?' a uniform was posing to his colleagues as I walked down to the canteen. 'Between Brexit and this, what if we impose the border instead of them? Are you going to be the one to set up the barriers?'

'It'll not come to that,' someone else said.

'They wanted to take back control of their borders,' the first speaker said, jabbing a finger in the general direction of the north.

'They didn't vote for Brexit,' someone else said. 'England did.'

'I'll not be policing Britain's border,' the initial speaker said. 'They can fire me first.'

A few grunts of agreement greeted this proclamation.

'Unless it gets bad over there and people are trying to come across here with the virus,' he added, laughing. 'Then I'm going to *Walking Dead* that shit. I'll be there with my trusty staff, aiming for the brains!'

'We'll have a tough time searching if we have to find yours,' his friend replied.

The lady at the till, a Polish woman whose name was Magda, rolled her eyes as she handed me my change. I could only imagine the conversations the day ahead held for her.

Chapter Thirty-Four

The murder file appeared just after midday. Joe and I split it and worked together through it. It had been pieced together in chronological order of the investigation, starting with the report from the initial call-out and the discovery of Hannah Row's injured body.

Hannah had been found in the canal basin, where Hendry had met me a few days earlier. She was lying behind one of the high walls that enclosed the basin itself. This had meant she was hidden from the view of anyone passing, or of those who'd disembarked the bus in the town square to buy food.

Pictures taken of the scene showed blood, hair and skin tissue on the wall, which forensics had confirmed to be Hannah's. This suggested, the report said, that she had been standing when someone had banged the back of her head, repeatedly, against the wall with sufficient force to fracture her skull and to incapacitate her. She'd then fallen to the ground where the bulk of samples were found. There, she was subjected to a brutal sexual assault, based on tears found on her body. Samples of Brooklyn Harris' DNA were found both inside her and on the ground beneath her.

The forensics report further stated that though there were other DNA samples found at the scene, they were of insufficient quality or quantity to allow further investigation, for both the public nature of the space and the rain that had fallen during the time between the attack and Hannah being found would compromise any samples.

Reading the report, I found whatever sympathy I'd had for Brooklyn Harris quickly disappear. The assault on Hannah Row, from first to last, had been violent and animalistic. He had shown no regard for her or her dignity and, though she was still alive when he returned to the bus, had offered no assistance in trying to get help for her. He took what he wanted and left her to die. It was hard for me to see the child Harris – the victim of assault and abuse himself – in those actions.

And there was no doubt that he had assaulted her. His DNA was found as I had already noted. Hair samples were found on Hannah's body. Even days later, after his arrest, traces of her blood, found on his trainers, tied him to the scene. And then there was his statement, a copy of which Hendry had already sent me after he'd first been found. He did not deny assaulting her, though in his addled mind, she had acquiesced to his advances rather than being knocked unconscious and raped.

The more I read, the more I was convinced by Hendry, and Patterson, and all who had said so, that I was wasting my time investigating too closely the killing of Brooklyn Harris.

And yet, there were notes in the file that caused confusion. The pathologist report did, as McCay had claimed, say there was significant evidence of spermicidal lubricant found, consistent with the use of a condom during sex. Clearly from the other evidence, this was unlikely to have been from Brooklyn Harris who did not use protection. The tears present inside Hannah's body and scouring on her legs suggested the possibility that more than one person had had sex with her.

I waited until Joe had finished reading the report.

'What do you think?'

'Someone else could have been involved?'

I shrugged. 'Or she had sex with someone at an earlier stage in the evening. It says there is evidence that might suggest more than one person had sex with her; it doesn't specify whether that activity had been non-consensual or if it had happened around the same time as Harris' attack on her.'

'We need to speak to some of her friends. They'll know what she was doing in the nightclub.'

'There's no mention of bone marrow either,' McCready said. 'The PM report mentions that her heart was removed but no mention of bone marrow.'

'We need to double-check that,' I said.

McCready nodded.

We continued moving through the file. There were various reports and diagrams of the scene of Hannah's attack. Pictures of her clothes, each labelled, and stains circled and numbered: her top and coat, her bra, her shirt, her socks and shoes.

'No underwear,' I noted. 'Her pants aren't mentioned here.'

There was a series of short statements taken from people who had been on the bus but all had that vague quality of those who did not remember much about the night and who simply confirmed that Hannah had been on the bus at one stage and then wasn't once the bus left. I suspected many of the kids interviewed had been drinking and when they had to afterwards give a statement to the police in front of their parents, kept what they had to say as non-committal as possible. The only statement that had a little more detail was that of a girl called Leah Walsh.

Walsh was clearly the one who had been closest to Hannah and the friend who had spent most time with her the evening of the attack, for she ran through the events of the night from their first meeting at her house to get ready, right through until the discovery of Hannah's body.

It was Leah's birthday that the girls were celebrating that evening as well as the start of the summer break. They'd managed to buy two bottles of West Coast Cooler, which they'd poured into lemonade bottles to disguise. Hannah hadn't really drunk alcohol before; her parents, the statement implied, were strict and she was a little afraid. One line which stood out in the statement in this regard was: 'The drink seemed to help Hannah lose her inhibitions'.

I'd written statements with teenaged witnesses before and that line read as one an adult might put into the mouth of a child. I could imagine that the person who'd taken Leah's statement might have proposed that as a more concise way of wording whatever had been suggested about Hannah's behaviour that evening through their conversation. It made me wonder why Hannah's conduct had been discussed at all in a crime where she was the victim. But of course, I was well aware of why.

It was also clear from the section when the bus reached Strabane that Leah was not being wholly honest either. After reams of detail, she skirted over the stop in town with a simple statement of, 'Without my noticing, Hannah disappeared, and I didn't realise until the bus was leaving again and she wasn't there. This was about twenty minutes later'. I wondered what she'd been doing for that time and why, having spent the evening at Hannah's side, the two friends seemed to have parted for that period.

I glanced at the end of the statement: it had been taken by Jack Grimes. I knew that at some stage, I'd need to speak to him.

More than that, I wondered why Leah hadn't mentioned the argument I'd witnessed on the nightclub CCTV footage. I had a fair idea how to find out, for I thought I knew where Leah Walsh worked now.

Chapter Thirty-Five

A few years ago, Patterson had organised training for us on domestic abuse, led by a Woman's Aid group in Donegal that offered shelter to women escaping abusive situations. The woman who had led the talk – and impressed everyone there with her honesty and sincerity – had been called Leah Walsh. I remembered her especially because of how useful the talk had been: in-service training days can be spectacular wastes of time on occasion. But Walsh had struck the right level of being informative without being either patronising or boring. And I recalled that part of the reason for that had been that she had shared her own story, as a survivor of domestic abuse.

One phone call had been enough to confirm that Leah Walsh was indeed the same person I had thought, she had indeed been Hannah's friend and that she would indeed be happy to talk with us.

She was based in Buncrana, a small seaside resort about a half-hour drive from Letterkenny, on the Inishowen peninsula. We'd gone to Buncrana frequently when we were children on Sunday afternoons for a 'run' which, in a country as damp as Ireland, meant a drive in the rain with a speculative stop at the beach for a brisk walk and a sprint into the local shop for ice cream, eaten with shivering hands. If that sounds like a disappointing day, it wasn't. As kids we loved these jaunts, Tom and I, in a car rich with the smell of our father's pipe tobacco and my mother singing softly to herself as we drove.

I'd always, therefore, had a fondness for Buncrana. It hit a gold mine in the early nineties with the arrival of Fruit of the Loom, which employed a vast bulk of the townsfolk and allowed prosperity to thrive and new shops to open. However, as is always the case, when the company pulled out of the town two decades later to relocate closer to cheaper labour, it gutted the local economy, closing businesses and causing the younger residents to immigrate in search of work. It was, in microcosm, the story of Ireland's economy at the start of the millennium, except banks had brought it down rather than a textile company. And in the same way the region's overreliance on a single player had decimated the economy eventually, I did wonder what would happen nationally when all the digital companies, more recently drawn to the country on the promise of tax deals, eventually relocated too when someone else offered to take even less tax. Though less than zero was, admittedly, hard to imagine.

Walsh's office was on the main street of the town, next to a now-abandoned department store that had been there when I was young. Her office was, in fact, a shop unit that had been converted through the use of free-standing dividers which allowed people sitting at one of the four desks in the room some privacy from passers-by on the street beyond.

When we went in, one desk was occupied, a hushed, tearful conversation in full flow. On hearing the door open, the speaker glanced nervously past the grey felt partition that obscured her from sight and, when she saw us, reacted with panic. Someone from a different desk moved forward quickly but without fuss and, leaning over the woman's shoulder, whispered something which I took to be reassurance before standing and moving down to meet us. This was Leah Walsh.

She was in her mid-thirties now, with black hair tied back. She wore jeans and a smart blouse with the sleeves rolled up and, after greeting us and turning to take us somewhere more private, I noticed a pen twisted into the bun of her hair.

She led us through into the kitchen of the office, which was little more than a narrow corridor with a sink and a few desultory cupboards on one side. A small fridge hummed noisily in one corner.

'No offence, but you'll scare off our clients,' she said.

'Understandable,' Joe McCready said. 'Thank you for agreeing to see us.'

'I'm only surprised it took this long,' Walsh said. 'I expected someone to come looking to speak to me years ago.'

'Why?' I asked.

'You said on the phone that you'd read my witness statement?'

I nodded.

'Then you've read my statement,' she added, as if this was response enough. Which it was.

'Why didn't you come to anyone sooner?' Joe asked, and I could see him wince almost as he said it. 'That's not what I meant—'

'I know what you meant,' Walsh said. 'I was a child. We've adult women who come in here, intelligent, professional women, who go through an interview process like that and don't see that they were being led from start to finish.'

'Why would someone have led you?' I asked. 'In your opinion?'

'Brooklyn had already admitted he'd done it. They'd found blood on his shoes. They already had him, why look any further?'

'And should they have looked further?'

'All three of those boys were missing the whole time we were in Strabane that night. And all three of them were interested in Hannah.'

'Was she interested in them?'

'A little,' Walsh said. 'Some more than others. Hannah was a butterfly, you know. She drifted from group to group but didn't stay too long with anyone. She was like that with boys too. She flirted a bit with them, but you got the sense she really wasn't interested.'

'Too young?'

'Looking back now, I'd say she possibly would have preferred girls,' Walsh said. 'I'm not sure if she knew that then or not.'

'So what happened that night?'

'Pretty much as my statement said,' Walsh said. 'Except, it wasn't all about Brooklyn. Hannah started off the evening in our house. We'd had a few drinks, nothing too strong, just something to make us happy, you know? We got the bus and straight away Brooklyn was down at us, chatting to

Hannah. She was always polite with him, more than any of the rest of us, even then. He was odd, you know?'

'In what way?'

She shook her head. 'He was different and you know what kids are like about people who are different. Even then, you could tell there was something broken inside him – I don't mean morally or anything, though there was, but something in him, his spirit or his sense of himself. He was like someone looking at himself in a broken mirror, constantly shifting, trying to find a better reflection. One minute he was charming, the next disgusting, the next morose, the next bouncing around like Tigger on speed.'

She paused, lifting a glass and pouring herself a water. 'I didn't ask if you wanted tea,' she stated.

'We're fine,' McCready said. 'Thank you. So Hannah had time for Brooklyn?'

'Yeah, I guess,' Walsh said. 'She humoured him a little, talked to him, like he was an injured bird she'd found at the side of the road. She was gentle with him. Ironic really when you think what he did to her.'

I nodded but did not speak.

'The other two were different. Riley was a nice boy, but again, he was odd. His family were poor and his dad was sleeping with his aunt who lived two doors down from him, so he had all kinds of shit going on in his life. He was a bit of a weeb and Hannah was too, so they got on.'

'What's a weeb?' I asked.

'Anime,' she said. 'They both liked *Pokémon* and all that kind of crap.'

I didn't look to McCready but could sense that he'd glanced at me at the mention of anime.

'They got on okay,' Walsh had continued. 'So, on the bus, he was chatting with Hannah about that and doing a cartoon for her on her arm, like a tattoo. McDaid got jealous because of it, I think, because he got into a real strop that evening. He was one of those fellas who thought being aggressive would impress Hannah, like she'd want to earn his approval the bigger an asshole he was.'

'Did she?'

Walsh shrugged. 'Not so much. Hannah wanted people to like her, I guess. She'd always been told she was special; her father especially just doted on everything she said and did, so she was used to people liking her. I think she got upset when she thought McDaid didn't.'

I could sense her dislike of Charlie McDaid even as a teenager. 'Was there a row that night outside the toilets?' I asked. 'I spotted something when I was reviewing the security footage from the nightclub.'

'That was him,' Walsh said. 'Charlie.'

'What was it about?'

'What it was really about was jealousy. Hannah had been talking with Riley and Charlie had his nose put out of joint. We'd gone to the toilet and he'd followed us there. Obviously, he was able to get right into the gents when we were standing in a queue outside ours. When he came back out, he started on Hannah about Drumcree of all things.'

'Drumcree?'

Walsh nodded. 'Yeah; you know the Orange march?'

'What had that to do with him?'

239

'His dad was a member of our local Lodge. We all mixed then; Omagh was a mixed town, you know. It was why the bombing was so bad there, because we mostly all got on okay with things. Hannah's dad was on the parade's panel and Charlie started on her about her father stopping the parades. He was off his head by that stage, but still . . .'

'How did Hannah react?'

'I don't remember the details,' she said. 'She apologised; I remember that, even though I told her she had nothing to apologise for. It was mostly drunk crying by that time of the night. But it put a real dampener on things.'

'Did you report this at the time?'

Walsh nodded. 'I told the cop. He said it wasn't relevant to Brooklyn so there was no need to include it on the statement. It would just complicate things. My mum was with me and she agreed. You know what parents were like then, giving in to the first sign of authority to avoid "trouble". Well, that's what my mum was like at least.'

'Things have changed since then,' I said, wondering if perhaps it had gone too far in the other direction now.

'So, after the argument, what happened?'

'We went back dancing and I met someone. Hannah was sitting with Riley and seemed okay and the boy I met wanted to go outside for a bit so I checked she was all right and headed outside.'

She folded her arms and stared at me, as if willing me to make some comment on her choice. I had none to make.

'Did anything else happen in the club?'

She shook her head. 'No, that was it. Harris and McDaid were out dancing with people, Riley and Hannah were sitting talking *Pokémon*. That was it. We all got back on the bus and I thought that was the evening over. Then we got to Strabane.'

She paused a moment while she took another drink of water. 'I'm parched today,' she said, by way of explanation, though I suspected she'd reached the part of the story she'd not wanted to retell.

'Take your time,' I said. 'I know it's difficult going back over bad memories.'

She nodded. 'It's fine,' she said. 'We got on the bus. I'd met a boy I knew, Aaron Gilmore,' she added, laughing mirthlessly at the memory. 'We were together on the bus and Hannah was sitting in the row in front. Riley was sitting with her, chatting about their comics and things. Charlie McDaid was in the seat in front again and Brooklyn, though by that stage he was bouncing around the inside of the bus. The driver had to warn him to settle a couple of times even on the drive from Letterkenny to Strabane or he said he'd throw him off. You kind of wonder what would have happened if he had, you know?'

McCready nodded lightly, though neither of us spoke.

'So, someone asks to stop in Strabane for a pee stop. People wanted food and for some of us it was a chance to get a last shift before we got home. The driver got off every week and stood with some of the other bus drivers having a smoke or something to eat from the chippie. So they got off. Brooklyn was over at us then, over round Hannah. Even Riley was getting fed up with him at that stage. Riley and Hannah got off the bus and stood outside, just at the doorway, like. I remember looking out and seeing her standing there with him, the two of them laughing and joking. I thought she was cold because she'd only this wee belly-cut top on her and a skirt. I told Aaron I needed to get off to speak to her but he asked me to stay on with him, you know?'

Her timbre changed as she spoke and I could tell the thought of her choice still continued to haunt her.

'So I stayed on. You know? I was fifteen with a hot boyfriend, or so I thought. I'd been babysitting her all evening and I wanted fifteen minutes to myself.'

She raised her head a little as she regarded both of us, almost defiant.

'That's totally understandable,' I said.

'It was a mistake, obviously,' she said. 'Next time I looked out, the two of them had gone. Aaron said he saw them going to get food, but then afterwards, after everything happened, he said he'd just told me that because he wanted to stay on the bus with me. Then, a while later, the driver got on and announced that we were leaving. I shouted to him that Hannah wasn't there, that there was someone missing, but he said he didn't have time to wait.'

'Were the three boys back on the bus at this stage?'

Walsh nodded. 'They'd sat somewhere else, down the back. I went down and asked Riley where she was and he shrugged. He said he'd been talking to her and she'd walked off to use the toilet. McDaid was sitting with Brooklyn who was like a ball of energy being contained. He was gathered in on himself but his knees were pumping like he'd too much adrenaline in his legs and needed to keep moving. I thought Riley looked like he'd taken a whitey and I thought

242

the three of them had been smoking something. Hannah had no interest in anything like that, so it would have explained why she'd ditched them.'

I nodded, encouraging her to continue.

'I got off the bus to look for her; the bus driver said he'd give me a few minutes. We checked all the chippies and down around the square but she wasn't about and no one had seen her. Then someone said we should check over at the car park across the way, just past the canal basin, that a lot of people driving tended to park up there at night. But she wasn't there either. In the end the bus driver left and Aaron and two of the other girls who were in our class offered to stay with me to keep looking. I phoned my dad and he came driving straight down to collect us. While we were waiting, we walked back across to the car park and then through the canal basin to come back to where Dad was to be. It was then that I saw her shoe. She'd been wearing these wedge sandals she loved, with the soles decorated with a straw weave. There was one, lying at the bottom of the steps coming down into the basin. I picked it up and moved over towards the corner of the basin, where there were two big pillars and a raised flower-bed-like thing, that was all overgrown with trees and stuff. I saw her legs there – sticking out through the shrubs. Aaron was with me and he climbed up and pulled her out from the bushes but we could already tell she wasn't well. She seemed to be breathing really fast and shallow and her face was pale white. Aaron got covered in her blood from holding her head and her skirt was only half covering her. She wasn't wearing her pants. I knew then what had happened.'

She stood glassy eyed and I knew she was there now, still fifteen, still watching her friend dying on waste ground in a strange town with a boy she would probably not see again, with nothing to bring her the comfort of familiarity or recognition.

'What happened then?' Joe asked.

'The others ran for the police; there was always some of them hanging around the town square as if they were expecting trouble or something. Me and Aaron waited with Hannah, talking to her, telling her things were going to be okay. But her breathing was so weird. It was like it was mechanical, like she was on a ventilator or something. It hurt to listen to it, like it sounded like it must have hurt her, you know. I wanted it to stop, for her breathing to change rhythm or something, just to show she was okay, that she was still in control. But she wasn't by then.'

She looked at me, her eyes brimming with tears.

'It's tough, you know, watching someone you love being like that,' she said simply. 'Watching them going through it and you wanting to be able to be with them so they're not alone, but knowing that you're not. Even standing beside them, you're still not *there*, with them, you know?'

I nodded, feeling my own eyes well a little.

'So, then the police arrive. And my dad arrives around the same time. And then we're taken up to the station in Strabane and asked what happened. I told them about the boys and about Brooklyn. The police said they were going to try to stop the bus but I think by that stage it had already reached Omagh and everyone had gone. The next day, I heard that Brooklyn had been arrested. They'd found her blood on him or something.'

244

'What about the other boys?'

'They were all spoken to – we all were who'd been with her that evening. But after a day or two, it came out that Brooklyn had confessed to it and that was that. Then we heard they'd turned off the machine and taken Hannah's heart and that opened it all up again, you know?'

Another nod.

'It's strange, like the last I saw her was lying in that corner of the canal basin there, with all the police around her while we were being pulled away. The ambulance crew were working with her so all I could see were her two legs sticking out and all these people in their high-viz jackets all working around her. Just her legs and that one stupid wedge that she loved wearing. That was the last time I saw my friend.'

'I'm sorry,' I said.

She shrugged. 'What can you do? I didn't spend her last half hour with her because of Aaron Gilmore wanting a wank on the bus. I still see him sometimes, with his wife and his kids. His life just moved on. Or maybe it didn't,' she added. 'Maybe he still feels the stickiness of her blood on his hands at times too.'

She shook herself free of her thoughts. 'I freaked out last week, the first time I had to use the hand sanitiser in here. It's that aloe vera stuff that dries a bit slower and leaves your hands all tacky. The first time I used it, I was right back there again, beside her. But then, working here, in a place like this, the stories you hear and people you see going through the most horrendous abuse, I hope that I'm beside her every day.'

Chapter Thirty-Six

We sat in the car after leaving Walsh.

'So, what do we have now?' McCready asked.

'We need to speak to Riley Mullan again,' I said. 'As soon as possible.'

'And Charlie McDaid.'

I nodded. 'McDaid won't help us,' I said. 'He wouldn't before we lifted Porter and I suspect he'll be even less helpful now.'

'We need to speak to the cop, Jack Grimes, too.'

'I'll get on to Jim Hendry,' I said.

'I've also tracked down the transplant recipient from Hannah Row,' McCready said. 'The woman who got Hannah's heart. She lives in Letterkenny.'

Maisie Logan wept as we spoke to her. She was in her thirties, a fine-framed young woman who looked younger than her age. I half recognised her from the picture in Hannah Row's bedroom, though was aware that I might have been retrospectively remembering her.

'I'm sorry,' she said, sniffling. 'I know it's stupid.'

'Not at all,' Joe said. 'There's no telling how people respond to these things.'

Joe had explained to her on the phone about the blood profile found at the scene of the crime and she had agreed to offer a sample of blood without hesitation, something which I took to suggest she was sure that it was not her who had been at the scene of Harris' death, irrespective of whatever vagaries her DNA profile might throw up.

'It's funny,' she explained, 'I felt so guilty afterwards. I'd been sick for over a year; my heart was failing and we knew I needed a transplant. My mum and dad were praying for it every day, lighting candles, getting Mass said, the whole bit. When I heard we'd got one, it was like this amazing exhilaration. And then the whole focus was on the surgery and recovering from it and everything. You were too busy to think, you know? Then, afterwards, it hits you. Someone died for me to live.'

Joe nodded. 'That must be tough to get your head around, right enough.'

'It's like, how did God decide whose prayer to answer? Like, I'm sure Hannah's family were praying she'd recover. And my folks were praying that I'd recover. How did he choose? Why me over her? That's hard to reconcile yourself with.'

'I can see why,' I said.

'It's shit. They don't tell you that, but it is shit. You start feeling really unworthy, like unless I cure cancer or something, will I have wasted two lives instead of just one?'

'I'm sure you've not wasted anything,' I said.

She laughed lightly. 'You don't even know me. But thank you.'

'You've met Hannah's mum since, haven't you?'

She nodded. 'They ask you afterwards if you want to write to the family. You don't have to, and they don't have to read it either if they don't want to. It's hard, like so one-sided. I wrote to them because I thought it was the right thing to do, to say thanks and I'm sorry and I won't waste what you've given me and I'm sorry someone died for me to live. It was probably rambling nonsense, but then the hospital contacted me saying Mrs Row wanted to meet me and how would I feel about it. It was a tricky one: what if she expected something from me? Or wanted a say in what I did? Like, not like I'd smoke, but if I wanted to, would she have a right to say, "No, you can't do that to my daughter's heart" or something? For a year or two, I'd been a victim of illness, had been the one people were gentle with. You start feeling that you're not the victim any more – not that you want to be – but you're almost like the aggressor or something instead, like it's your fault in some way that this other person died, like there's some cosmic plan that choose you over them. But then I met her and she was lovely. She just wanted to hug me and she put her head against my chest and listened. Then she started to cry and I was in bits and that was that. She held my hand the whole time we met and I realised the whole time she was there, me just being alive was enough for her to convince herself that Hannah's death had had some meaning.'

'I'm not sure she ever got over it,' I said.

'She hasn't,' Maisie said. 'She organised runs and charity events and I always do them because, well, you'd be an arsehole to say no, wouldn't you? But it's like there's a hole that's never been refilled, like someone tore something in her and she's trying to find different ways to heal it, but nothing's working. For a while, I think hearing Hannah's heart helped her, but that's not enough either, is it? I just feel so sorry for her.'

'Have you had any complications?' Joe asked. 'With your blood or that?'

'Thankfully nothing too extreme,' Maisie said. 'For a while afterwards you're walking on like bubble wrap, thinking you're going to break something that's not yours. Then you start to relax. I'm still on medication, though not as much, and I will always be. But there's been no issues with DNA tests or anything, if that's what you mean? No crime scenes where I've been a suspect.'

'Until now,' I said.

She laughed. 'That's true.'

'Did Mrs Row ever explain why they donated Hannah's organ?' Joe asked.

'She wanted them to, apparently,' Maisie said. 'Her mum said she'd told them for years before anything happened to her that she wanted to donate her organs. Even when she was a kid.'

'Remarkable,' Joe said.

'It wasn't her first time,' Maisie explained. 'She'd given a living donation when she was younger and wanted to do it again.'

'What kind of living donation?' I asked.

Chapter Thirty-Seven

I called Jim Hendry after we left Maisie's, in the hope that he might have had some success with Hannah Row's medical records to find out to whom she had made a living donation.

'I'm pushing,' he said. 'But we need the mum's permission and without that, I don't hold out much hope. I'll keep trying. In other news, our technical team have got back to me. When you and Porter were brought in, we took his phone to check for footage of the incident. They took the time to check his records from the night of Harris' death, too. He did get a message from Peter Shaw, as you knew. We ran his GPS record and matched it with his calls that evening. He didn't leave Derry.'

'Could he have left his phone at home?'

'He was texting and calling through to midnight and then on social media until around 2.30. According to his health app, he was then sleeping. It wasn't him, unless he had someone else using his phone for him.'

'Thanks, Jim,' I said. I wasn't hugely surprised; the blood at the scene was the key to Harris' killer no matter how I looked at it and Porter didn't connect to that, as far as I could see.

'On the plus side,' he said, 'one of the calls he made that evening was to his solicitor, Charlie McDaid.'

'In his line of business, it's maybe not surprising he has his brief on speed dial.'

Hendry grunted agreement. 'McDaid took the call too. It lasted a minute and thirty-two seconds.'

'It might be worth having another word with Porter,' I commented, more thinking out loud than anything more concrete.

Still, Hendry replied. 'Someone else other than you having a word with him, maybe.'

'Thanks for that, Jim.'

'I have other news, too. Jack Grimes has agreed to have a chat. When are you free to meet?'

Grimes was still an imposing figure, even now in his seventies. He was well over six feet and I guessed nearing twenty stone, but carried it well. He sat in his armchair, his thick paws of hands resting on his knees, his legs firmly planted. I imagined how Leah Walsh, or any child, might have felt, sitting opposite him, how readily they might accede to his suggestions.

'You're wondering about Hannah Row,' he said as I sat. Hendry had suggested that the best approach was to say we were looking for background, rather than immediately flagging up concerns over some of the details of the case.

'Brooklyn Harris, really,' I said.

'I heard he bought it in Lifford a few days back,' Grimes said, nodding his head. His hair was thick and white, his complexion ruddy, but he had a habit of clearing his throat each time before he spoke. He did so now.

'Brooklyn was a sad case. He was always going to end up that way, but I kind of hoped he'd come out the other side of all of this with something.'

'Did you know Brooklyn before the Hannah Row killing?'

Grimes nodded. 'I knew the three lads,' he said, as if pre-empting my next question. 'I was doing a line years back with Riley's mum when I was in Omagh. The wee lad was a good fella, lacking a bit of something because his old man had fucked off to Liverpool with their neighbour and then never came back. Riley was too used to being around women all the time. I did a spot of coaching with the local rugby club and suggested his mum send him along, build his confidence up a bit. He brought along his two mates, Charlie and Brooklyn. That was the first time I met them.'

'When was this?'

Grimes glanced to the ceiling, one eye shut in a panto-mime of thought. 'Must have been the mid nineties. I moved from Omagh just after the bomb in '98.'

'Were you there for that?'

He nodded, solemnly. 'That was a nightmare. Carnage doesn't describe it. There are things that change you as a person. That day was one of those things. It's like JFK.'

I nodded. Anyone in this country over a certain age could tell you what they were doing when they heard about Omagh.

'I was glad to move to Strabane,' Grimes said. 'Then this case came up and the three lads reappeared on my radar.'

'Sorry,' I said. 'Did you say you coached them?'

Grimes looked to the ground, as if the thread of his story might be found there. 'Coached? Yes, I brought them along to the rugby. The three lads came and they couldn't have been more different if they tried. Riley, Lord love him, was never built for it. He was there because his mother told him to go, but he'd no interest. He was afraid of tackles, couldn't carry without shit flinging any time anyone came near him when he'd the ball. He told the other kids I was his stepfather in the hope they'd be nice to him, but sure that just put a target on his back. Charlie was the opposite in that he came in thinking he knew it all already and no one could tell him different. He'd be the one challenging you with every drill you did: Why this? Why that? His old man used to come down and watch and tell me where I should be playing the young fella and who I should be taking off. But Brooklyn? He was something else entirely. He knew nothing about the game and had no discipline at all, but he was fearless. He'd have tackled a pillar if you asked him to do it. He was the first into every ruck, the last to give up a chase on someone. But he'd also be the first to lift his boot if someone beat him to the line and some of the racist shit he came out with had to be heard to be believed. But, you know, if he could have got out of his own way, he'd have made a decent centre. He was scrappy and strong, vicious in his own way. But he was strange too. I lost count of the days he had to wear the kit home because he forgot his change of clothes or his T-shirt had got wet or whatever. Then, one day, I noticed the bruises on him. His back and chest were thick with them; his dad had lost it because Brooklyn had lifted a few cans of his beer from the fridge for a party and he left him black and blue. I asked him had it happened before, but you could tell it had. Under the edges of the fresh bruising you could see the yellowing of old bruises still healing? So I visited the Harris' home. It was a shithole. His mother was just turning a blind eye to everything, pretending it was normal. His sister looked like a rabbit in headlights, all the time. She spent the whole time I was there skulking around doorways, watching, like she was waiting for the next explosion to go off. Brooklyn wasn't there: I knew he was out with the other two boys somewhere. Me and his old man had words.'

'How did that go?'

'He started with the crap about it being his boy and none of my business. Then I was a nonce 'cause I was coaching kids and he knew what I really wanted to do. Then he was going to report me for police brutality. Then he'd have the Provos on me; I'd wake up some morning and get into the car and not know what hit me. The usual crap. I explained to him the error of his ways and showed him what would happen if he laid another finger on anyone in the house. The whole time, I see the mother standing in the kitchen doing her ironing. Standing folding tea towels, like someone polishing the deck of the *Titanic* as it's going down.'

'What happened?'

'He hung around for a while, for his own sense of self-worth, showing that he wouldn't do what someone else told him to. A bit of posturing, but that was all. At least that was as much as I ever heard.'

I suspected there was a bigger price paid by the Harris family. Some colleagues and I had carried out a similar intervention with the abusive husband of my old partner, Caroline Williams, after she turned up at work bruised. We'd congratulated ourselves on our efforts even as he set into beating her once more, worse than before, his already fragile ego wounded by our behaviour.

'Did things improve after that?' Hendry asked.

Grimes shrugged. 'Myself and the woman broke up and Riley stopped coming to the training. Once he stopped, the other two lads gave it up as well. I never saw them again. Then I transferred down to Strabane and packed it in myself. The next time I saw them was when Brooklyn's name came up after that poor Row girl was found.'

'Brooklyn's name or all three names?'

Grimes considered the question, good-naturedly, though I knew he'd already made his mind up on his response. 'Definitely Brooklyn's. One of the kids mentioned him specifically, that he'd been hassling Hannah through the evening. The others were mentioned as satellites to him. I'd an idea as soon as I heard his name anyway. That viciousness that I'd seen him display on the field, that anger spilling over when things didn't go his way: I recognised that the moment I saw that wee girl's head and heard his name. We tried to stop the bus to get him before he got off and got changed, but there was too long a gap. Someone called at the house around six a.m. and he was in bed, but his clothes were already washed. Like what kid, off his head, comes in at three a.m. and washes his clothes?'

'What teenage boy washes his clothes at all?' I asked, wondering whether Shane would know how to operate our washing machine without instructions from Debs.

Grimes grunted agreement. 'Well, his clothes were washed: nothing on them of any use. But his trainers were different. They'd looked clean, but he'd stepped in the wee girl's blood and got some just on the edge of the sole of one shoe. Walking home after the bus in the rain had cleaned quite a bit of it off, so he mustn't have noticed it, but there were blood traces all along the grooves of the grip, tying him to the scene. Once we had that, the rest just came tumbling. He was still half off his head, talking about shadows and voices and everything else. Some of the other lads on my team thought he was faking it, trying to play up for a diminished responsibility plea, but I knew Brooklyn and he wasn't that smart.'

'What about the other two?' Hendry asked. 'McDaid and Mullan?'

'You were there, Jim. You should know,' Grimes said.

'For Ben's benefit,' Hendry explained. 'I remember some of the investigation, but I wasn't directing things so I'm not over the order in which things happened.'

Grimes nodded, though his avuncular demeanour was growing forced, his clearing of the throat as a precursor to speech somehow now more aggressive. 'Well, the two boys confirmed what we'd heard from other witnesses. Brooklyn had had a thing for the wee girl and had been following her around all night. He'd taken speed as well as drinking and had lost it. After they got off the bus in Strabane, they wanted food, but he went off somewhere, off his head, bouncing around the place like he was still listening to dance music. They saw him again when he got back to the bus and by that stage he'd become more paranoid than energetic, they said.'

'Both of them said this?' I asked. 'The same statement?'

'I can't remember,' Grime said. 'You'd need to check.'

'I did,' I said. 'Both of them said something similar.'

'There you are then.'

It was strange that both boys had commented on the same change in similar language. Mullan, now, didn't strike me as the most articulate, especially in comparison with McDaid. I wondered what he'd have been like at seventeen.

'Were their clothes checked?'

Grimes feigned thought yet again, then cleared his throat dryly. 'I don't think they were. By that stage, we'd tied Brooklyn to the scene and he'd confessed that he went down the street after her and that he'd attacked her. He told us he was on his own and we'd no reason to doubt his confession.'

'You didn't feel compelled to double-check? Cross every T and all that?'

Grimes straightened in his seat, his chest rising as he pushed back his shoulders. Even in age, his physique was still intimidating.

'Are you saying I was sloppy?'

'No,' I said. 'I'm just wondering if their clothes were checked. Hannah's friend, Walsh, told us that the three boys were around Hannah that evening. She suggested there had been an argument in the club between Hannah and Charlie McDaid. She also suggested that Riley Mullan was friendlier with Hannah than all the rest of them that evening. The PM suggested evidence of sexual activity that involved a condom, but we know Brooklyn didn't use condoms. You didn't think at some point that there might have been other people involved?'

Grimes stared at Hendry, clearly now realising that his former colleague had not been straight with him about the purpose of my visit.

'What is this shit?' he asked Hendry.

'Brooklyn Harris' killing is tied to what happened to Hannah Row,' I explained. 'Forensically tied. Blood tied.'

Grimes turned to regard me now, his expression inscrutable.

'I need to know who killed Hannah Row if I'm to know who killed Brooklyn Harris.'

'Harris killed Hannah Row,' Grimes snapped without a cough this time. 'He confessed to it, the blood *tied* him to it, the witness statements supported it. He never disputed that he'd done it, ever. Even when he came back out, he accepted that he'd killed her.'

'But were other people involved?'

Grimes shifted his weight in his chair. 'Have you a daughter?'

'That's not relevant.'

'Have you a daughter?'

Reluctantly, I nodded.

'Say something happened to her,' he said. 'You get that knock at the door at four a.m., the one that makes your stomach heave, where you know the face at the door isn't smiling, isn't bringing you good news. You go through that. You lose your child, just a child too. Then you learn that she was raped before she died. You lose all of those things, all you have left is your sense of who they were, what they

258

were to you and to the rest of the world. Your teenaged kid. Then those same people who tell you that they're going to treat her with respect and dignity, honour her memory, those same people start muck-raking, bringing up all the things she'd been doing. That perfect child you had? She wasn't so perfect. She'd been shagging some kid in a night-club. So now your memory of her, her identity, for you is gone for ever. Harris took her body, but then we'd come along and take her, the person you thought you knew. Would that be a job well done?'

'They deserve the truth.'

'They got the truth. Their daughter was killed by Harris. Whatever else she got up to before that didn't matter.'

'They needed to know what happened to their daughter.'

'They needed to know their daughter was who they thought she was,' Grimes said. 'They needed to keep who she was inviolate and pure. Who was I to come along and tell them different? They hero worshipped that kid. Do you think they'd have thanked me?'

'Did she have sex with someone prior to Harris' attack on her?' I asked.

Grimes looked at Hendry who said nothing.

'Sometimes, knowing when to draw a line in something is a greater gift than bludgeoning on, through some personal crusade that does no one any good,' Grimes said, turning to me.

'Surely it came out at the inquest?'

'It was handled in the right way,' Grimes said.

'You asked how I'd feel if it was my daughter?' I said. 'Nothing you could tell me would change the reality of her

259

loss. But I'd want to know that the people tasked with bringing her justice did everything in their power to make sure that that happened and that everyone involved, everyone . . .' I struggled to find the right thing to say and, unbidden, Debbie's comments at that play came to mind. 'That everyone touched by that original act, that corruption, paid the price that was due. That's what I would want, if it were me.'

'They got justice,' Grimes said. 'Now more than ever, with Harris gone. We did the job right,' he added, looking to Hendry for agreement. 'I've no regrets about anything I did. Anything we did.'

Chapter Thirty-Eight

I relayed all that had happened back to Joe McCready when I got back to the station. Hendry had agreed to come back to me if he had any luck with Hannah's medical records, but I had a feeling that he was annoyed at how the interview with Grimes had gone. Whether his annoyance was with me or with his old boss, I couldn't tell, though I suspected the former.

'Maybe he's right,' Joe said, when I explained Grimes' viewpoint. 'Even if she did have sex with someone earlier in the evening, what bearing does that have on what happened at the end of the night? If Harris was tied to the scene and confessed to the killing, what else is there?'

'Clearly Harris changed his tune, though,' I said. 'He must have told the reporter, McCay, that someone else was there that night.'

'Maybe she's just trying to sell her book,' Joe said. 'Pick any old case and you'll find issues with it, avenues that could have been explored more fully. But if it gets you to the same place in the end, what difference does it make?'

'Riley Mullan is the key to this,' I said. 'One way or the other. He was the one Hannah connected with most that evening, the one who spent time with her, according to Walsh. He's the one who likes anime; I'd bet money he was

261

doing those pictures for Harris to send to people. He was providing Harris with prescription drugs. He's been risking his job for Harris. Why? What does he owe him? McDaid will stonewall us all day. Mullan is the one with the answers.'

'Let's go and ask him, then,' Joe said.

Mullan wasn't working that day so we went straight to his father and asked for his home address. We had to knock four or five times before he eventually appeared at the door, opening it as far as the security chain would allow. He was clearly just out of bed, his hair standing on end, the white T-shirt and sweat shorts he wore in disarray. He visibly paled when he saw us.

'I've nothing to say to you,' he said, before we could speak. 'I've no comment to make.'

'Did Charlie tell you to say that?' I asked, guessing from whom he'd been given such legal advice.

A dry swallow confirmed my suspicion. 'I've no comment.'

'We need to talk to you about Hannah,' Joe McCready said. 'We know you liked her and we know more importantly that she liked you. We know you were with her the night she died.'

'I've no comment,' Mullan stammered, pushing the door closed.

McCready had wedged his foot at the jamb. 'Leah Walsh told us that Hannah really liked you, Riley. She said you were the one Hannah liked most.'

'She told us about the anime,' I said. 'That you and Hannah shared a love of that.'

262

Joe nodded lightly, a sign, I assumed, that he could feel the tension of the closing door lessen. Mullan was listening to us.

'We just want to get to the bottom of what happened to her,' I said. 'We owe that to her. To get to the truth.'

'Brooklyn attacked her,' Mullan said. 'He killed her. That's the truth.'

'That's *a* truth,' I said. 'But we know there's more than that. Please talk to us.'

'I'm not allowed to,' Mullan said.

'Not allowed?' Joe echoed. 'Who doesn't allow you?'

'That's not what I meant,' Mullan stammered. 'You're confusing me. Move your foot, please.'

'Why were you providing Brooklyn with anime drawings of girls he was meeting online?' I asked. 'That was you, wasn't it?'

There was a moment of silence. Then Mullan started pushing the door all the harder. 'Move your foot,' he shouted. 'I'll call the police. The real police.'

McCready, sensing our chance was missed, stepped back and the door slammed shut.

Before we left, I opened the letter box and slipped my card through. 'Riley? Hannah deserves the truth of her story to be heard. All of it. If you know something about what happened, you owe it to her to tell us. Forget Charlie and Brooklyn and whomever else. The only person who matters here is Hannah. And whatever you felt for her then, you owe this to her now.'

I was walking back to the car when I felt my mobile buzz in my pocket and, for a moment, I hoped my words had

had some impact and Mullan was willing to talk. Instead it was Debs.

'How's day one of lockdown going?' I asked.

'You need to come home, Ben. Your dad's taken a turn. The ambulance is here.'

In fact, by the time we made it across the border, he'd already been taken to Letterkenny General.

My dad had lain in bed late that morning, something that was unusual for him, but Shane and Debs had just allowed him to sleep on. By mid morning, when he'd still not woken, Shane had gone up to him. He'd been groggy, he said, complaining he felt as if he had something stuck in his throat, almost like a chunk of bread he'd not been able to swallow. He ate breakfast, hoping that the act of eating would dislodge the blockage, but it hadn't. Soon after, he felt sick and only just made it to the toilet in time. He complained that he felt dizzy, the room unsteady around him. Debs thought he was taking a panic attack and (having talked not just some of her pupils but also, on occasion, me through such an event) tried to calm my father. It was she who decided to phone our local GP who, in turn, had a paramedic team at the house within ten minutes.

When I reached the hospital, I was initially told I would not be allowed in. The lockdown which had closed schools had also meant a restriction on hospital visitations. I showed the porter my warrant card and explained the situation. He agreed to allow me alone up to the ward, providing I put on a surgical mask and sanitised my hands.

264

I got no further than the main doors of the ward before I was met by the ward sister.

'I'm afraid you can't come in, Inspector,' she said, the use of my title making it clear that my rank meant nothing in this particular scenario.

'My father's on his own,' I explained.

'We're with him,' she said. 'He'll have someone with him all the time. Don't worry.'

'It's difficult not to,' I said. 'It's my father.'

'I understand that,' the sister said. 'I do. But we have to think about everyone on the ward. We have to be careful with visitors.'

'Is he okay, at least?'

'He's had a cardiac event,' she said. 'We're trying to find out how much damage has been done.'

'But there is damage?'

She nodded. 'I'm sorry, Inspector. I understand how hard this is for you. We're looking after him and we'll be in touch as soon as we know anything. But we can't risk bringing anything onto the ward that might cause harm to any of our patients, your dad included.'

She glanced around, then said, 'Look, I can let you come up the corridor and look in the window to let him see you. That's the best I can do until we have everything checked.'

I thanked her for even that small allowance. But, as I stood at the door of my father's room, looking in through the window at where he lay, surrounded by staff and attached to various machines bleeping discordantly, for a moment I regretted the gift she had given me. My father turned and looked out at me, offering me a weak thumbs up. But in his eyes, I could see only terror. And I suspected that, despite my own ineffectual return of his positive gesture, he could see that same thing reflected in mine, too.

Chapter Thirty-Nine

It felt strange to be sitting at home while my father lay in the hospital. My instinct was to be with him, or near at hand should anything happen. But the staff nurse had been adamant that I could not remain on the ward until they had tested him for the coronavirus and I reasoned that the worst thing I could do for my father was to distract the very team working to help him. I had called my brother Tom and suggested he come up and stay with us to be near at hand, just in case, so I gave Debs a hand to change the bedclothes in the room where my father had been sleeping, so Tom could stay, if he wished.

I had called back to the station after I'd left my father to explain to Patterson what had happened. He was more understanding than I might have expected.

'You're on leave,' he said. 'Force majeure, so you'll be on pay.'

'I'm okay working,' I said. 'I can't get into the hospital much anyway with this virus thing until my dad is tested.'

'It's going to get worse before it gets better,' Patterson said. 'Once people start having to take off with that, we'll be too tight. Take the leave now, while you can. You've already handed over the Harris case to McCready so that'll be a smooth enough swap over to him.'

I thanked him and shook his hand out of habit, then, thinking of my father, regretted that I had done it and went straight down to the staff toilet to wash my hands.

While watching the news on TV as I ate dinner, though, I began to understand the ulterior motive behind Patterson's altruism. The local press had picked up on the online response to my scuffle with Porter and had learned from someone that this was not the first time I'd been involved in such an incident. Accordingly, a reporter had been posted at the doors of our station, as if the sight of my place of work would be sufficient to create a sense of me to their viewers. In a way, of course, they were right. All that I was to those watching and listening was a Garda officer and nothing else. It didn't matter that I had kids, a wife, a sick father: my identity, in that moment, was condensed down to a Guard who had hit someone, the aggressor, authority run rampant, all simplified through the refractive prism of social media.

'This afternoon, Chief Superintendent Patterson issued the following statement: Pending an internal review of the incident in collaboration with our colleagues in the PSNI, the Garda officer in question has been placed on leave. We will await the outcome of that review before making any comment.'

Debs looked at me, her mouth open, her fork clattering to the plate. 'Did he just hang you out to dry?'

I shrugged. 'Perhaps he's using the situation to his advantage,' I said.

'That's unusually charitable of you when it comes to Patterson.'

I nodded. 'He's given me time off. I can't complain.'

*   *   *

Penny arrived back around 7.30 p.m., calling for me to collect her from the bus stop down on the border where the Customs post had once stood. From where I sat, waiting for her bus, I could see the lights of Finnside Nursing Home, turned on early against the coming gloom. The sky was still pale, the spring light strengthening. In a few weeks, the clocks would change and the summer lay ahead. And yet, I felt none of the joy that thought usually elicited, and the clouds overhead hung heavy and leaden.

Still, Penny's arrival brought me momentary joy. She opened the rear door and flung her bag onto the seat, then climbed in beside me, bringing with her the stale smell of the bus.

'Well, that was a nightmare,' she said as she pulled on her seat belt. 'Some sleazebag sat behind me coughing and sneezing the whole time. He kept leaning in between the seats, trying to talk to me. He wouldn't take fuck off for an answer. Then they're talking about you on the evening news getting suspended or something. So thanks for that.'

I struggled to know where to start. 'Good to have you home, love,' I said.

She grunted. 'Shane says you've been spying on me with Find My iPhone. Well, now I'm home, you'll know where I am all the time. I'm sure you're delighted.'

'Do you want to get out and start again?' I asked. 'Or walk? I'm the only taxi man I know who gets abuse instead of payment.'

'You shouldn't be watching me.'

'I wasn't watching: I was worried. I—' I looked at the set of her jaw, her stubborn nature, a nature I'd imbued in her, reflected in the fold of her arms. 'You're right. I need to let go. I've not done this before, and it takes some getting used to. I'll not do it again.'

'I've turned it off anyway,' she said.

I didn't mention that I'd noticed that already.

'Your granda's in hospital,' I said. We'd not told her, seeing no point in unduly worrying her when she was coming up that evening anyway.

'Shit. Is he okay?'

I shrugged. 'He's had a cardiac event, they're calling it.'

'Are we going up to see him?'

'We can't,' I said. 'Covid-19 and that. They're not allowing many visitors. I'm hoping to get in myself later.'

She looked at me a moment, then laid her arm across my shoulder and hugged me lightly. 'I'm sorry, Dad. It's been a bit of a shit day.'

I nodded, not trusting myself to speak, the simple comfort of contact almost more than I could bear. 'The shittiest.'

'And I've made it worse,' she said, straightening.

'Not that much worse,' I said, starting the engine. 'It's good to have you home, love. I missed you.'

To pass the time while I waited for word from the hospital, I searched online for more information on Sean Row. I knew, as part of his résumé, that he'd been CEO of Brighter Days, though admittedly knew little about the charity. Its website explained that it was for families of children with life-threatening illnesses, particularly childhood cancers. It had been founded in 1992 and, even in the earliest images from the site, Sean Row featured prominently. Finally, I found an interview with Row from an old health newsletter just after his appointment as CEO. One part in particular stood out. Row was asked how he had first become involved with the charity.

'I guess, like everyone else involved with Brighter Days, it was because of a family illness. If one of your children takes sick and you're totally lost, it's important to feel that there are other like-minded parents who've been through what you're going through and who understand the whole complexity of emotions you feel as a parent, especially: loss of hope; your sense of yourself; impotence; frustration; and, of course, most of all, fear and, sadly, at times grief. Brighter Times helped me and my family when we were going through our dark days and I think it's important to pay that forward and to be here now for other parents taking the first steps on a journey that my family, thankfully, have already taken.'

One of Row's children had been ill when younger. The article didn't clarify whether it had been Hannah or her brother, Aidan, who had been sick. Maisie had told us that Hannah had been involved in a previous living donation, though again, that didn't help identify whether she had been the donor or recipient. I knew I needed to speak to Mrs Row again, but I also knew that her attitude on my last visit made it unlikely she would talk to me. I had to hope Hendry would have some luck on Hannah's medical notes.

Around 8.30 p.m., my mobile rang. I snatched it up, expecting it to be the hospital, but instead there was a number I didn't recognise. I answered it anxiously, my mind already creating scenarios where this was my father's consultant, calling at such an hour with only one type of news.

Instead it was Cathy McCay, the journalist.

'Riley Mullan is ready to talk,' she said, after introducing herself. 'This evening.'

'I can't,' I said. 'I'm on leave.'

'I heard about that,' she said. 'He's saying he'll only talk to you. You left your card with him. Tonight or not at all. At the canal basin.'

I called McCready after I'd hung up, hopeful that he might either accompany me or indeed go himself to see Mullan, but I couldn't get an answer. Reluctantly, I called McCay back and agreed to meet them at the basin at 9 p.m.

Chapter Forty

There was no one there when I arrived and I used that as an opportunity to call the hospital to check how my father was doing.

As I waited for the ward to answer, I took a look around the canal basin itself. It was an oval structure comprised of a series of walls, of perhaps twelve feet width, with similar-sized gaps between each around the circumference, where there were steps to allow people to walk down into the bed of the basin itself. Only the four corners were more structured, with a curved wall between two thick pillars. The space inside the bow of the curve had been filled with a flower bed and a retaining wall, though the beds had long since become overgrown with trees and shrubs that shielded the basin from view for those on the outside of the wall. It was in one such space that Hannah Row had been found and, instinctively, I was drawn to that corner. When the nurse answered the phone, I sat up on the wall to talk.

There was no update beyond that they had carried out a series of tests and were waiting for the results. He was comfortable, they said. I decided to pick up a new phone in the morning and leave it up to him, in the hopes the staff might be able to show him how to Facetime so I could speak to him face to face if the restrictions tightened.

I was just hanging up when Cathy McCay's car pulled up and she got out.

'No sign of him yet?' she asked.

I shook my head. 'If he's not here soon, I'm leaving,' I said. 'My dad's sick. Besides, I'm not even meant to be working.'

'Yet you're here anyway,' McCay said. 'Why?'

I shrugged. 'Because I want to know the truth.'

'Doesn't everyone?'

'I'm not so sure,' I said. 'Take your book. If you find out that Harris killed Hannah, that there was nothing else to it, nothing more, will you still write it?'

McCay considered the question. 'I'll still research it.'

'But will you write it?' I asked. 'Will anyone want to read a story they already know?'

'People are endlessly fascinated with death,' McCay said. 'You should know that, in your line of work.'

'But if there's no mystery to it? No conspiracy? What if it is what it is? Just grubby and unpleasant. Will you still tell that story?'

'Probably not,' McCay agreed.

'Yet most death is just that. Grubby and unpleasant. Someone stabbing someone because of something they said, or because they can't take being controlled any more, or because they need a fix, or because they don't like the football scarf they're wearing.'

'You're in the wrong job by the sounds of it,' she said.

'No,' I said. 'Those stories need to be heard too. Even if no one wants to hear them very much.'

'What's the point?'

I looked across the canal basin, bleak in the bleached-out glow of the street lamps. 'Everyone dies before their story is done,' I said. 'Everyone leaves something unfinished, something undone, something unsaid. The best that we can do as Guards is to write the final chapter for them, round their story off as best we can.'

'The detective as ghostwriter?'

'Literally and metaphorically,' I agreed. 'But sometimes, it doesn't end the way you hope.'

McCay glanced over my shoulder and nodded. 'He's here,' she said.

Riley Mullan came stepping lightly down towards us. He was visibly agitated, his jaw shivering, seemingly with cold that certainly I could not feel.

'All right?' he asked, nodding at us but not quite catching our eyes.

'Riley,' I said, standing.

'Sit down,' he said. 'This won't take long. I didn't want to speak to you on the phone, and I don't want to have to tell this twice, so this was the easiest thing to do.'

'Okay,' I said.

Cathy McCay already had her phone out and I guessed she was recording.

'You want to know who killed Hannah,' Riley said. 'It was Brooklyn. That's all there is to it. He killed her. He hit her head off that wall, just behind you,' he said, nodding over my shoulder towards the pillar. 'Then he raped her while she was unconscious.'

I glanced at McCay, aware from the drop of her shoulders that she was disappointed with the confession.

I stood up again. 'It needed no ghost from the grave to tell us this,' I said, aware that Debs' literary allusions were rubbing off on me.

'But that's not the full story of what happened that evening,' Mullan added quickly, his hands raised in a manner that suggested he wanted me to sit, yet again.

'So, what is the story?'

'You were right about Hannah,' Mullan said, looking towards, but not at me. 'I did like her. And I think she liked me too. But we all fancied her back then. She was so pretty and such a good person, like a genuinely good person. She wasn't bitchy like some of the other girls, she didn't laugh at you when you said something stupid. She was nice.'

It was as if he'd never quite grown up past his teens, beyond that point when the boy's greatest fear is being laughed at by a girl he likes. I knew, from sad experience, that he was not unusual in that regard: I'd lost track of the number of domestic violence scenes I'd attended where the words, 'She started laughing at me,' echoed past blood-stained walls.

'We all liked her,' Mullan said. 'Charlie came up with this stupid bet that whoever had sex with her first won.'

'Won what?' McCay asked.

Mullan looked at her blankly. 'I . . . I don't know.'

'Bragging rights,' I said, the whole thing saddening me with its seediness.

Mullan shrugged. 'I guess,' he agreed.

'So who did win?' McCay asked, keen to get to the crux of the story and sensing that the ending might prove to be a waste of her efforts.

'Charlie came up with the bet,' I said, taking Mullan back to his original point. Whatever he needed to tell us, he'd worked out at some level already. Our job was to listen and to follow wherever his mind took us.

'I hated the idea of it,' Mullan said. 'But he said it was just a joke. He didn't mean anything serious by it. But he only said that after we became friends, me and Hannah.'

He paused, moving across and sitting on the same wall as me, though at the far end, away from me.

'How did you become friends?'

'We both did Art,' he said. 'I used to doodle, cartoons and stuff. Then when *Pokémon* really hit, I got into anime and started doing anime drawings. She liked it too. One day, in Art, I drew her as an anime character in my sketch pad and she flipped out. It was the coolest thing she'd seen, she said. I tore out the corner I'd drawn it on and gave it to her.'

'She had it on her bedroom wall,' I said. 'It's still there.'

Mullan looked wounded by the revelation, tears brightening his eyes.

'We hit it off then. I didn't tell the others then because . . . I don't know . . . it was our secret, just between us. Telling them would have spoiled it in some way. Or jinxed it.'

McCay nodded and, moving across, sat between us, though the curvature of the wall meant I could still see Mullan unobstructed.

'Did you start dating?' she asked, shifting her position and laying the phone on the wall next to her, unobtrusively.

'Not like that,' Mullan said. 'She was a friend. Once or twice we held hands when we were sitting in Art, under the

277

table, like, so no one else could see but us. She had the finest fingers and her skin was always cool to the touch. We went out for a walk one night and I tried to kiss her. It was really messy, like a disaster, and I got really annoyed because I thought I'd screwed up what we had, but she was so cool about it. Said she didn't know if she was ready, but when she was, it would be with me.'

'How did that make you feel?' McCay asked, again interrupting the flow of Mullan's recollections.

'I was okay with it, I swear,' Mullan said. 'She was friendly with everyone, but I didn't think there were any other boys or anything. She chatted with everyone the same, so I wasn't jealous, if that's what you mean. Anyway, a few nights later, she kissed me, kind of out of the blue. She said she wanted to see if she liked it. Looking back, it was probably nothing, a peck on the lips, but then it was amazing for me. But she just sat back when we'd finished and stared at her shoes and asked me not to tell anyone. Of course, I promised I wouldn't. And I didn't. But the problem was, Charlie and Brook were getting worse about her, some of the things they were saying. They started spreading that she was frigid because she hadn't dated anyone. Then Charlie started a rumour that she was a dyke, that that was the only reason she'd not gone out with anyone. I guess she heard because she asked me the week of the club whether I was going and when she said she was, I said I would. She asked me to bring some condoms. My dad owned the chemists where I work now so it was easy for me to lift a packet, you know?'

McCay nodded, but thankfully had the sense to say nothing now.

'That night, we'd a few drinks. I dropped my wallet on the bus and Charlie lifted it up. It was thick, what with the johnnies inside it, and he made a joke about me being loaded, there was so much money in it. He nearly went ballistic when he saw the condoms, took the piss about me fancying my luck, all that shite. He took one out and said if I was getting my hole, he was going to as well. Maybe some of the Letterkenny girls would be slappers.'

He looked to McCay, as if aware of his diction choices. 'That's what he said, not me,' he added.

'That's okay, Riley,' McCay said. 'I understand. Hannah must have been hurt by it all. Or embarrassed?'

'She was up the front of the bus, thankfully,' Mullan said, shaking his head. 'We'd sat down the back because Brooklyn was taking speed and we'd a bag of cans we didn't want the bus driver seeing us drink. I didn't drink much, but I figured that night I could use something to build up the courage to, you know, with Hannah. I'd never had sex before,' he added, simply.

'Anyway, we got to the club and Brooklyn was being an asshole right from the start. I was trying to stay with Hannah as much as I could, but the two lads kept hanging around, trying to flirt with her. Her mate, Leah, had met some lad from Omagh, so Hannah was stuck with all three of us when she tried to talk to me. Brook was off his head, bouncing around the place. Charlie started getting angry drunk when he realised he was getting nowhere with her. I think he noticed me and her getting on okay because at one stage he called her a dyke and headed off, looking for a girl. Hannah got upset and her and Leah went to the toilets. Apparently

Charlie met her there again and started on her, calling her all kinds of things, a Fenian bitch, all that kind of crap. She wasn't; her dad was, but her mum wasn't, so she was at school with us.'

I nodded, absently, the social importance of the minutiae of people's religious background still grimly fresh in our collective memory.

'His da was in the Lodge and he started on her about Drumcree and about the parade's commission, like it was her fault. Called her a plastic prod, all that shite.'

Everything about his story depressed me, everything it said about human nature and about the tribalism we'd fallen into back then; tribalism that had not really gone too far away even now.

'He didn't mean half of it,' Mullan said. 'It was the drink talking mostly, but still. On the bus on the way home, I sat with Hannah, 'cause Leah was snogging that lad she met. She asked me if Charlie meant what he said, if other people at school thought the same of her. I told her he was talking shite, that no one thought that. Then she asked if I'd heard she was a dyke. I couldn't tell her it was Charlie who'd spread it, so I said nothing, said that I knew she wasn't sure. She held my hand, put her head on my shoulder and I sat there, afraid to move in case I disturbed her. I could see us reflected in the bus window. We looked happy, you know? Like a normal couple. Then I saw Charlie's reflection, and he knew. He was sneering at me, like a really dirty smile.'

He stopped talking and sat for a moment in silence. I looked across and could see that he was wiping tears from his eyes, the memory of that evening overwhelming him.

'Anyway, we got to Strabane and she asked me if I wanted to get some food. I didn't, but I got off the bus with her and instead of going across to the chippy, she led me down that road, behind us.' He nodded towards his rear, where an access road ran down alongside the new library and the rear of the Alley theatre.

'We stopped at the doorway over there,' he said, turning his head and gesturing further along the same road. There I could see, set in from the thick wall of the building, an old double wood-panelled delivery entrance for the shop that had once been housed there. The doorway was deep-set enough that someone standing in there would not be visible from further along the road and would, even from here, be bathed in shadow.

'She told me she wanted to do it. That she was fed up with what everyone was saying about her and if she was going to do it, she wanted it to be with me,' he said, then began to sob. McCay got up and moved to the other side of him, putting her arm around his shoulder in comfort, but he shrugged her off and I saw then the resolve that had brought him to us this evening, the need to confess, to tell his story. Hannah's story.

'I'm okay. I need to get this out,' he said, and shifted away a space from McCay. 'I need to tell you. I was shitting myself; I don't even know if I was excited or what I was. I put on the johnny and that and only just started when she began to panic and asked me to stop. That it was hurting her. I stopped and stood there, with my pants around my ankles and she started to cry. She said she didn't want to. I told her that was okay; I was dying to at that stage, but then she looked at me funny and said, "I don't want to at all. Not with boys." Then I knew. The dyke thing had hurt her because it was true.'

I felt sick at the thought of what was to come next, already knowing how the story would end.

'Then we heard laughing,' Mullan spat. 'I looked over and Charlie and Brooklyn were standing just the other side of this.' He indicated the area where we sat with a nod of his head. 'They'd followed us down and were watching us. They'd seen it all. Charlie was pissing himself laughing. Hannah panicked and started to run, but I don't know if she knew where she was going. They went after her to shush her and I was standing with my pants down. By the time I got the johnny off and my trousers up, they were already down here. I . . .' He paused again. 'I . . .' He stopped and looked across at me, his face slick with tears. 'I didn't go down to her, right away. I should have and I didn't. I was angry and embarrassed and . . .' He swallowed dryly, staring at me, willing me to complete the sentence for him.

'Afraid?'

He nodded.

'By the time I got down there, Brooklyn was already on top of her. She was lying in here, right here.' He patted the earth behind him with his hand. 'I pulled him off her, but it was too late. Charlie was panicking a bit at that stage too. Him and Brooklyn started to run. I told them we should stay, to make sure she was okay. Charlie said, if I stayed, it would look like I was to blame. I'd been with her too. Brook had lost it at that stage; he was tripping, shouting at the lights, shouting about shadows and all kinds of shit. Charlie said that she'd be okay, that Brook couldn't have hurt her that much. That it was all his fault anyway. If anyone asked, it was all him. That he would cover for me, not tell anyone what had happened. That he'd keep me out of it.'

'And did he?'

Mullan considered the question, then nodded.

'Did he . . . was he involved in raping Hannah?'

Mullan shrugged. 'I don't know. The only one I saw was Brooklyn. We reported him as soon as we knew Hannah wasn't well.'

'But not before.'

Mullan shook his head. 'I was . . .' His eyes brightened again. 'I was too much of a coward. I was just a kid.'

'So was she,' I said.

'Did you tell anyone else the truth?' McCay asked, keen to get as many details as possible.

'I told Jack.'

'Jack Grimes?'

He nodded.

'You're nodding,' McCay said, and I realised it was for the benefit of her recording. 'But that's not in your statement.'

'Jack spoke to me,' he said. 'He told me what to say. He went through it with me.'

'Why? Why leave out everything about Charlie picking a fight with her?'

Another shrug. 'He wanted to protect us, I guess. You'd need to ask him.'

'Why did you remain friends with them?' I asked. 'Afterwards.'

He shrugged. 'I felt bad about Brooklyn. Everything got pinned on him. But I brought her down there; I started it. And I owed Charlie for keeping me out of it. My parents would have freaked if they'd known.'

'But you didn't do anything wrong,' McCay said.

'I left her here,' Mullan said, simply. 'I could have helped her and I didn't. Charlie and me came up with a story that Brooklyn vanished off somewhere. He was so off his head; he didn't remember anything anyway and it had been his fault. Charlie convinced me.'

'And you agreed?'

'He said he was looking out for me. He'd found something on the ground that put *me* with Hannah, not Brooklyn, but that he'd kept it to keep me out of things. The way Charlie put it, the bad people got punished and the good people didn't.'

'Except Hannah,' I said.

'Except Hannah,' he agreed.

'What had he found?'

'I think it was the condom wrapper or something, but I don't know. He just told me not to worry. That he would keep me right.'

'And what did you have to do in return?'

'Nothing,' Mullan said. 'Nothing. He's my mate. He's a good friend.'

'Not like Brooklyn?'

'Brook wasn't all bad,' Mullan said. 'His old man treated him like shit, beat him senseless at times. We used to see him with cuts still bleeding on his back from where he hit him with his belt buckle.'

'And now?'

284

'He contacted Charlie and me when he got out. He wasn't meant to, but he did. We were the only people who knew *Brooklyn*, you know, rather than Gerard or whatever his name was. I think it mattered to him to have people who still called him Brook when they talked to him, people who knew that person. But he'd changed: he wasn't him any more. He got nasty with us, threatening. Saying there was stuff from that night he knew but hadn't said.'

'He began to remember?'

'He began to suspect, at least,' Mullan said. 'He talked about voices urging him to do it. He said he remembered me there. Remembered seeing me stripped, with a condom on. He wanted us to do him favours.'

'Drugs?'

Mullan nodded.

'And anime sketches?'

Another nod. 'Charlie must have told him that that was how me and Hannah had become friends. The first time he asked me, it wasn't too bad; the picture was of a girl he said was eighteen. She was dressed and everything, so I thought it was harmless. And he paid me a few quid for doing it. I wanted to keep him on side, you know. After all this time, if something came out?'

'But?'

'Then it started getting too much. The girls were getting that bit younger, the pictures a bit more explicit. I refused to do one and he said he'd tell everyone the truth. That me and Charlie had been there. That we'd been part of it. So I kept doing them. The pictures. And kept getting him whatever drugs he needed.'

'Until he died.'

Mullan nodded.

'That must have been a relief.'

He realised, after a second, the implication of my comments and he shook his head. 'I had nothing to do with that. I swear,' he said. 'It didn't do me any favours anyway because you started asking all these questions and things were going to come out.'

'So, you're getting your story in first.'

'I'm getting my story told,' Mullan said. 'I owe it to Hannah for the truth to be known. But, like I said, it was Brooklyn who killed her. He banged her head off the wall to stop her shouting and he killed her.'

He was done. He slumped slightly where he sat, started picking the moss from between the stonework of the wall. 'The worst that I did was that I did nothing.'

'You were a kid,' McCay said, echoing his previous defence.

'You were a coward,' I said, echoing his own admonition.

'I know,' he said.

Chapter Forty-One

'What happens now?' he asked.

'I don't know,' I said. Cathy McCay was trying hard not to show her glee at the end of the tale, her project now firmly back on track. 'I'll have to speak to the PSNI about it, give them a copy of that,' I added, motioning at her phone.

She instinctively moved the phone to her other hand, further away from me. 'It won't affect your story,' I said. 'But it is a record of what happened. A more accurate witness statement than the one given twenty years ago.'

'What do you think they'll do?'

'I don't know,' I said. 'The Historical Enquiries Team seems to be in some sort of limbo and this case is technically closed already. They may do nothing. Or they may charge you with obstruction for giving a false statement. Though if Jack Grimes did coach you on that, I can't see it happening.'

He nodded, seeming to derive no pleasure from my suggestion that likely nothing would happen to him as a result of what he had told us.

'Why now?' I asked. 'Why not when Harris got out?'

'Because of this,' he said, gesturing at McCay and me. 'Because all of this won't end until the full story is told. And I guess it needs to end.'

I nodded. 'That makes sense.'

'I owed it to Hannah, just like you said.'

I called Jim Hendry as I drove back across the border and explained what had happened. 'You should have called me,' he said.

'He agreed to speak to me and the journalist,' I said. 'It was like he was setting the record straight before anyone else got a chance to tell their side of things. She's recorded the whole thing and sent it to me; I'll send it on to you now.'

'Did you believe him?'

'I think I did,' I said. 'He'd no reason to lie. He doesn't come out of it covered in glory, you know? But it puts the focus on McDaid.'

'And on Jack Grimes, if he did coach the kid on what to say in his statement.'

'I'm sorry, Jim. I know that puts you in an awkward position.'

'Like we didn't see that coming. I've more news on your friend, Porter. We've pulled various child-porn images off his phone.'

'Have you charged him?'

'Not yet,' Hendry said. 'We told him we'd contact him when we're done with his phone. We'll see what we have altogether before we decide what to do. He'll probably explain it away as part of the decoy scheme, but, whatever excuse he comes up with, he's crossed the threshold. I don't see that internal review Patterson was touting today doing anything but exonerating you. We'd not have found that stuff if not for your right hook anyway, so enjoy your leave.'

'It's not quite what Patterson said,' I told him, explaining what had happened to my father.

'Shit. Sorry to hear that, Ben,' he said. 'Leave Mullan and the rest to me. I'll keep you updated.'

Tom was already at the house when I got back over the border. We embraced quickly in the hallway and he asked me what the hospital had told me. He'd called and been given fairly much the same story. They hoped to have more to tell us in the morning. On a whim, I packed an overnight bag of bed clothes and toiletries, and Tom and I drove up to the hospital to drop them off. A different ward sister was on duty and agreed to allow one of us to take the bag in and briefly say hello. It seemed only fair that Tom should go in, I having seen my father earlier.

When he came back down the corridor, only a few moments later, his eyes were wet with tears.

'Has something happened?' I asked, panic rising.

'He's not good,' Tom managed. 'He doesn't look good, Ben.'

I stared through the double doors, in at the corridor, busy with the evening shift moving briskly from room to room, in one of which my father lay, as if willing someone to change their mind and come down and allow me in. But no one did and, impotent and lost, we headed home to wait.

*   *   *

When the phone rang at 7.30 the next morning, I jumped up to answer it, my innards leaden with dread. It was Jim Hendry.

'Sorry for the early shout,' he said. 'I thought you'd want to know. We've just pulled Riley Mullan out of the river. He's dead.'

Day Six

14 March 2020

Chapter Forty-Two

Debbie had been woken by the call and she stood now as I got dressed.

'You don't have to go, you know,' she said. 'You're on leave.'

'I need to, Debs,' I said.

'No, you don't,' she said. 'Your father is sick. You need to be here, with Tom and with him if you're called.'

'I . . .' I stopped lacing my boots and stared at her. 'I called him a coward,' I said, after briefly summarising the story he had told us.

'You were right,' Debbie said. 'He was a coward. That's not on you.'

'But what if that pushed him over the edge? What if that's what caused him to go in the river?'

'The comment of someone he's barely met before will have pushed him more than his own memories of how he failed someone he loved? You think that's the final straw?'

'I shouldn't have said it. I should have held my tongue and—'

'You're not responsible for everything that happens, Ben,' Debs snapped. 'We've had this conversation before. You're not to blame for everything and you're not in control of everything.'

'But I need to be,' I said. 'I need to . . . I need to—'

'Need to what?'

'I need to put things in order,' I said. 'I need to control the small stuff I can control because otherwise I'm just getting drowned by the big stuff I can't.'

'You know, finding out who killed Brooklyn Hayes, or whatever his name is, won't change what's happening with your dad. Or with Penny and Shane.'

'I know that,' I said. 'I'm not stupid.'

'It's all going to be okay,' Debs said, sitting beside me and putting her hand on my arm. 'Things change and we'll change with them.'

'But I don't want them to change,' I said. 'And I know that's stupid, but I don't want them to. And the only thing that's certain at the moment, unchangeable, is that someone killed Brooklyn Harris. I can work out who it was.'

'And when you do? What then?'

I'd not considered the question before. What then? Face what lay ahead for my father?

'I . . . I don't know.'

'We're your constant, Ben,' Debs said. 'Me and the kids.'

'I know,' I said. 'I know that. But they're drifting away from me—'

'From us,' Debs said. 'As we did from our folks. And their kids will from them.'

'I know that,' I repeated. 'That doesn't make it any less shit to have to go through.'

'I know,' Debs agreed. 'But it's all we have.'

'My dad's going to die,' I said, articulating the unspoken truth that had gnawed at me for months now, making concrete with those words something that I'd tried hard to avoid facing. Even as I did, I could feel the room shifting a little round me and I had to put my hands down onto the bed to steady myself.

Debs nodded tearfully. 'And I'm sorry.'

'I didn't expect you here,' Hendry said when I pulled up at the site where Mullan's body was already being zipped into a body bag. The spot was just across the river from Lifford, not far down from the main bridge connecting Lifford and Strabane. I could see, from where we stood, across to the spot where, almost eighteen years ago, I'd met Jim Hendry as we stood over the body of Angela Cashell.

'How's your dad?' Hendry asked, bringing me back to the present.

'The same,' I said, Tom having already checked before I left the house. 'I'm going to phone in a bit once the doctors do their morning rounds. What have you got here?'

'Cut and dried,' Hendry said. 'Mullan phoned his parents last night, after he'd spoken with you and McCay, and told them he loved them. They panicked and called the PSNI in Omagh. They started a search for him there and we started here, knowing that he'd been in Strabane. We got a call after one a.m. saying someone on their way home from the pub, coming across the bridge, had looked down and seen someone going into the river, just above the new footbridge at Melvin. We went up and checked. His phone and wallet were lying on the grass by the embankment. There was no sign of him. The rescue teams were out through the evening and, just after dawn, he was spotted here.'

'No signs of foul play?'

'Nothing,' Hendry said. 'He just walked into the water by all accounts. Didn't pause, didn't try to turn back. He walked in and went under and, according to our witness, disappeared from sight. We'll get tox screens and that done, but this one is simple: he confessed himself to you and that journalist last night and, that done, said his goodbyes and killed himself.'

'I told him I thought he was a coward,' I said.

Hendry nodded. 'I heard, on the recording you sent,' he said.

I'd not realised that McCay had recorded even that part of the conversation.

'I can't help thinking—'

'That's your problem right there, Ben,' Hendry said. 'Thinking. I'm going to speak to Jack Grimes if you want to tag along. I don't see anything much happening now.'

I tried to accept what Hendry had said, but I couldn't. Mullan had articulated his worst view of himself and I'd confirmed it for him. I knew well enough that if you tell someone what you think of them harshly enough or often enough, confirm their own self-doubt, their own worst impression of themselves, they'll start to believe it; just like Brooklyn Harris, his identity assembled by his father in all the wrong ways.

Grimes initially refused to speak to us when he opened the door and saw both Hendry and me. Only when Hendry informed him of Mullan's apparent suicide did he renege and allow us in, retreating down the hallway himself in a sign of our invitation to follow him into the kitchen where he had been eating breakfast.

Hendry explained the purpose of our visit and played the recording of my conversation with Mullan from the previous evening. Grimes listened attentively, his toast sitting untouched on the plate next to his elbow. His expression softened at the sound of Mullan's voice, particularly at the sections where he seemed to break down, and I realised that the man still had some residual fondness for the boy.

To his mind, I suspected, Mullan would always be the underdeveloped ten-year-old who needed help toughening up. In reality, he hadn't toughened up at all, the weight of his choices having seemingly eaten at him until he could finally take no more and, his soul unburdened, he had stepped into the river to free himself from his own guilt. It had been narcissism to imagine that I was responsible for his actions.

Grimes groaned softly when Mullan mentioned that he had helped him write his statement on the events the night Hannah Row died and shook his head. He listened till the end and, when the recording was finished, said softly, 'He wasn't a coward.'

'I shouldn't have said it,' I agreed. 'I was wrong.'

'Not for saying it,' Grimes corrected me. 'You were wrong in your assessment. He told me the truth, as he saw it.'

'As he saw it?'

'How many crimes have you worked where you've got fifty different statements about the same event? How many different perspectives? Each person convinced they're telling you the truth. There's only *their* truth. Everything else we do is piecing those together to come up with something that seems the most accurate representation of all of those stories.'

'Is what he says here what he told you back then?' Hendry asked.

'More or less,' Grimes said. 'He was younger then, angrier, at Harris especially. But the details are pretty much as I remember them.'

'And did you coach him in his statement?' Hendry asked. I could tell he was getting angry now that he'd been party to something back then that he had known nothing about.

'I did,' Grimes said.

'Why? To protect Mullan?'

Grimes laughed coldly. 'Riley? No. I was protecting Sean Row. And you. And me. And him,' he added, pointing across at me.

'Really?' Hendry scoffed.

'What do you remember about that summer? 2001?'

'What should I remember?'

'This place was a powder keg, waiting to blow again,' Grimes said and, with that oft-used description of modern Northern Ireland, I recalled Ollie Costello's confused use of the phrase and understood now what he'd been trying to say when I spoke to him in Finnside. I wondered if he and Grimes had had this same conversation almost twenty years ago.

'We'd had years of suspicion and in-fighting. In 2000 devolution was suspended and then restarted. It was all stop-start politics, point scoring and legal challenges. But by 2001, there was a hint that things were changing, improving. After years of protests over Drumcree, there was a hope that things might not be quite as bad, that the fire had been contained. Then this,' he said, gesturing towards Hendry's phone, from which he had heard the statement.

'What?'

'The daughter of one of the Parades Commission is attacked and killed. Hours earlier, someone challenges her about her father's role in the Drumcree decision and then that same person is involved, at a remove, in her rape and killing.'

'Her death had nothing to do with Drumcree,' I said.

'Exactly,' Grimes agreed, snapping his fingers and pointing at me as if I'd proved his point for him.

'Then why not mention it?' I asked. 'It wasn't relevant in the end.'

'Because if it had been included . . .'

'People would have inferred relevance,' Hendry said.

Grimes nodded. 'People love to look for meaning where there is none. See things where there's nothing to see. Impose their own beliefs. This would have become a sectarian killing, a political killing. Not what it was but what people imagined it to be and could twist to their own purposes. Hannah deserved better than to become a political football. That's not who she was.'

'So you encouraged Mullan to lie, for that?' I asked.

'He didn't lie,' Grimes said. 'Brooklyn Harris hit Hannah Row. He raped Hannah Row. He went to jail for doing both those things. Anything further would have confused the issue. Riley had an abortive attempt at sex with her. Why is that relevant? Who needs to know?'

299

'And McDaid?'

'He's an unpleasant little shit,' Grimes said. 'But Harris was the one who killed Hannah Row and your dislike of Charlie McDaid doesn't change that fact. You talked about truth earlier. The only truths that matter are that Hannah died and Brooklyn did it.'

'He told the journalist who recorded Riley's statement last night a slightly different truth,' I said. 'He claimed the shadows urged him to rape her. That he heard voices.'

'He was off his head.'

'He was with McDaid,' I said. 'Riley told us that Brooklyn started hinting he remembered more than he'd told you, about them being there.'

'Brooklyn was a user, in every possible way,' Grimes said. 'Whatever he wanted, whatever he needed, he found out a way to get it. Usually from Riley because he was too soft to say no.'

'And McDaid?'

'He survives,' Grimes said. 'It's no surprise to me that of the three boys, he's the one left standing.'

'Do you think he was more actively involved in Hannah's death?' I asked. 'Honestly?'

'Honestly?' he repeated. 'I don't know. Perhaps. But we were limited. I was directed by powers above me to remove any of the possible political aspects of the case from statements. To do that reduced McDaid's role to almost nothing. That was the story we were telling; the story that best fitted the facts as they needed to be known for the time that it was.'

'You don't think Row's family needed the truth?'

'I asked you before about being a father. How do you think Sean Row would have felt if we'd suggested *his* job, *his* decisions, had cost him *his* daughter's life?'

I didn't answer the question, no answer being necessary.

'I knew the man. He was a good person, a good father. He'd nothing to do with her death either, so why even imply that he might have had? What good would that have done? The harm had been done, but with the case concluded the way it was, we'd minimised that harm to only that which was unavoidable. There was no cover-up of anything that mattered.'

'Everything matters,' I said. 'What did Charlie McDaid take from the scene?'

'I don't know,' Grimes said. 'That's the first I heard of it today. If he was looking out for Riley, he may have lifted the condom wrapper, like Riley said. Or the used condom.'

'What about Hannah's pants?' I asked.

Grimes nodded, accepting the possibility. 'We never found them.'

'What did you think happened to them, back then?'

Grimes shrugged. 'We wondered whether someone had come along the roadway and found them, perhaps over where Riley and she had been standing. But no one ever came forward.'

'Mind you, we didn't release the details of their absence to the press,' Hendry added. 'No one would have known to come forward.'

'The other option was that Harris had taken them and then dumped them somewhere. We searched the bus and his house, but with no success. I asked Riley if he'd taken them, and he swore he hadn't. He had no reason to lie.'

Hendry nodded. 'So, Mullan didn't mention them. Harris was so high that night, if he'd had them, he'd probably still have been in possession of them.'

'You think McDaid took them?' I asked. 'To "protect" Riley?'

'Or to protect them all?' Hendry said.

'Or for some imagined, personal bragging rights,' I said, thinking again of McDaid's bet with his two friends. 'Something so personal of Hannah's? Something intimate? That strikes me as more than just "protecting" people. It's another violation of the girl. A trophy. Or a memento.'

'Certainly, I'd imagine if they *weren't* found by a passer-by, but were deliberately taken, they'd have to have been taken by someone with a deep personal animus towards Hannah.'

I nodded.

'Whether he took them or not is irrelevant,' Grimes said. 'It was twenty years ago.'

'That night defined each of those kids,' I said. 'If McDaid took them, I'd bet he still has them somewhere. Especially if they were his insurance policy to keep Riley Mullan in line.'

'Getting a warrant to look for them is a different matter,' Grimes said. 'No one would allow you a search based on that, on supposition and inference. Especially not for a case that's already closed.'

Hendry nodded. 'He's right,' he said.

'Besides, you making Charlie McDaid a villain in your head doesn't mean he is one in real life,' Grimes added. 'Speaking of deep personal animus.'

'I don't have—' I began, only to be interrupted by the

buzzing of my phone. I didn't recognise the number. I excused myself and moved outside to take the call. It was the consultant from the hospital.

'Mr Devlin, I've been in with your father.'

'How is he?'

'He's comfortable. But, we should talk. Can you come in at noon to see me? I've rounds to complete before that but it's best we speak today.'

I felt my stomach constrict. I knew that the news would not be positive.

'Is it bad?'

'It's best we talk in person.'

'Can we see him?' I asked. 'He's alone up there.'

'You and your brother can see your father for a short while when you're in with me, subject to appropriate social-distancing measures.'

'Thank you, doctor,' I said.

I called Tom to tell him that I'd pick him up on my way past, then moved back inside to where Hendry and Grimes had seemingly concluded their conversation. I could guess by the tenor of their discussion that Hendry was explaining to Grimes why he'd gotten involved in examining the Row killing once more.

'I liked the Rows,' Grimes said. 'A decision was taken to try to protect them from greater harm. To protect the country from greater harm over a misreading of the Drumcree nonsense. But if McDaid was involved, if he did do more than we were told, than we found, I'll be the first to applaud seeing him in court. My only regret would be that Sean didn't live to see it, if that's how this ends.'

'Did you know him before Hannah's death?' I asked.

Grimes nodded.

'What was he like?'

'He was a real go-getter. Nothing stopped him. He'd a good head on his shoulders, sensible.'

'How did he respond to what happened to Hannah?'

'It broke him,' Grimes said. 'It almost killed him. He emigrated eventually. I heard he died.'

I nodded. 'In a road traffic accident in New Zealand.'

'That's a pity,' Grimes said. 'He'd a tough time of it, particularly with the kids. First Aidan's illness, then Hannah's death.'

'Aidan's illness?' I repeated. 'Was Aidan the one who was sick?'

'He'd some sort of cancer,' Grimes said. 'In his blood. He needed a bone-marrow transplant.'

'Who gave him the donation?' I asked, though of course, I already knew.

'Hannah,' Grimes said. 'She was the apple of her parents' eyes because of it. She saved her brother's life.'

Chapter Forty-Three

Hendry had someone call at both Mrs Row and Aidan Row's homes, but there was no answer at either place, no sign of life, by all accounts.

For myself, I headed back to Lifford, collected my brother, and we both went to the hospital. We were met at the door of the ward and directed down to a family room which was, in essence, an office into which had been placed a scattering of easy chairs and a straight-backed sofa that could fold out into a bed for those who needed to spend the night in close proximity to their loved ones.

Tom and I sat side by side on the sofa waiting. After a few moments, a doctor, who introduced himself as Nathan, though did not clarify if this was his first or last name, and the ward sister, Jenni, whom I had met the previous day, breezed into the room, wholly at ease in the familiarity of their surroundings. They took a chair each, at the other side of the room, and neither had approached us to shake hands, despite both Tom and me rising on their entry.

'Thank you for coming,' Nathan said. 'Ben?'

He nodded at Tom who, in turn, gestured towards me. 'That's him. I'm Tom, the other son.'

Nathan nodded. 'Thank you for coming,' he repeated. 'You know, I'm sure, that your father is very ill.'

I nodded, swallowing dryly and absurdly wishing I'd picked up a drink of water somewhere.

'He's dipped overnight,' Nathan said. 'Our tests have shown that he's in late phase four or early phase five of his illness.'

'His illness?'

'His heart is failing,' Nathan said simply. 'It's escalated quite quickly over the past twenty-four hours or so, since the event that brought him in here.'

I nodded as if this was something I'd hear every day, not knowing how else to respond.

'We can offer support at this stage, but any care we offer will be palliative in nature.'

'Is there nothing else that can be done?' Tom asked. 'No treatments?'

'None that will affect the outcome. Your father's heart is very badly damaged,' Nathan said, shaking his head in a show of benign sympathy.

'What about a transplant?'

Another shake of the head. 'Your father's age means he'd not be a priority.'

'He would be for us,' Tom said.

'I understand that,' Nathan said. 'Really, I do. But he'd be at the end of a long waiting list that he'd not survive, to be frank. And the surgery itself would be too much for him anyway. I'm afraid that's simply not an option.'

'We understand,' I said.

'We also need to discuss a DNR for your father.'

Tom looked at me.

'Do Not Resuscitate,' Nathan explained, misinterpreting his look.

'We know,' I said.

'Your father's illness will follow its own trajectory and pace now,' Nathan explained. 'The nursing staff will keep him as comfortable as possible, but I have instructed them, that, if he should suffer another cardiac event, we will not be intervening. It wouldn't be fair on your father.'

'Your daddy's on his own journey now,' Jenni, the staff nurse, offered. 'We'll make it as easy a journey as we can for him.'

'Thank you,' I managed.

'Thanks for everything you've done,' Tom added.

'Do you want to see him for a few minutes?' Jenni asked.
Tom nodded.

'How long . . . how long has he left?' I asked.

'No one can say with any accuracy,' Nathan said.

'I know. But in your experience, based on people with similar illnesses at this same point in the journey, how long would you guess?' I asked.

Nathan shrugged and looked to Jenni who, I realised from the gesture, was clearly more experienced than him.

'We could tell you that your daddy will pass at noon tomorrow to let you get ready but, you know, you'll still not be ready come noon tomorrow. I understand you want to know but, when it's his time, he'll go.'

'Should we stay here now, with him?'

'We could say there's no immediate risk within the next few hours, but certainly, over the next few days, I wouldn't be too far away from the hospital in case we have to call you urgently. This is just a guess, though. We've seen patients linger for weeks and patients who seemed strong go in

307

minutes. It's not an exact science. There are no easy answers, I'm afraid. One of you at a time can stay with him.'

I was reminded of what Jim Hendry had said to me about his own experience. Had I really imagined that finding out who had killed Brooklyn Harris would change anything? The world still turned, time still passed, people still died and were born and married and lived and fought and made up and danced and drank and sang and cried. And my father would die and these things would still go on everywhere else because what was happening here and now mattered only to us, to Tom and me and my family.

But then I also understood why it was so important to get to the truth, the essence of who had killed Brooklyn and Hannah and why Riley Mullan had stepped into a river. Each of their families deserved to know, as we now knew, why their loved one had died. It was the only way to help try to make sense of the one thing that could not be rationalised or intellectualised: that gulf in nature torn by the loss of one of us, that diminishment that each of us feels when part of us is taken from us, beyond our sight and comprehension. I had been selfish in my pursuit of the truth, for the truth was not mine to own. But it was still a worthy aim. And a necessary one.

Afterwards, I sat with my father in his room, a space like every hospital room, sterile and impersonal. He slept the whole time I was there, though when I took his thick hand in mine, I felt him give an almost imperceptible squeeze, as light as a kiss. I held his hand in both of mine and told him that I loved him and the briefest smile ghosted his lips.

Tom came in after me and I waited in the corridor. My phone rang, earning me a disapproving glance from one of the staff, so I moved out into the communal waiting area beyond the double doors to take the call. It was Dr Forbes from the Forensics Team.

'Inspector Devlin,' she said. 'How are you?'

'I'm . . . I'm okay,' I said, then added, because she had asked, 'I've just been told that my father is dying.'

'I'm so sorry,' she said. 'Oh, God, I'm so sorry.'

I didn't know why I had told her, other than because she was the first person to whom I was speaking since being told and I needed to tell someone.

'Thanks. It's . . . ah, I . . . I'm sorry. I shouldn't have told you that. How are you?'

'No. It's fine. Something like that, you need to talk about. I'm so sorry to hear it though. It's not an easy thing to deal with.'

'No,' I agreed.

'Look, I'll call you back later. Or is there someone else on your team I should call?'

'It's okay,' I said. 'I can pass on whatever you need.'

'Are you sure?' she asked. 'It's just . . . I've got back the tox screen on the blood you sent me from the Lifford murder scene. There's a cocktail of stuff showing up, but one thing really stands out. The person whose blood this was has high levels of arsenic trioxide in their system.'

'They're being poisoned?' I said, recognising only the word arsenic.

'Kind of. It's a chemo treatment for someone with acute myeloid leukaemia. Arsenic tends to be used when other treatments have failed.'

309

'Other treatments? Could that include a bone-marrow transplant?' I asked, suspecting I knew now whose blood it was we had found.

'Yeah,' she said. 'If the AML returned, arsenic would be the treatment.'

'I think the girl whose blood you matched had given a bone-marrow donation to her brother when they were younger. He gave us a cheek swab when we asked for a sample for comparison.'

'It wasn't a match, I'm guessing, but then it wouldn't be,' she said. 'Only the blood. Occasionally other cells change a little, but mainly it's just the blood. That would explain the blood match, then. But, based on the tox readings I have here, I think the person you're looking for is really quite ill. Is her brother ill?'

I thought back to seeing Aidan Row, the thinness, the beanie hat, the pallor of his skin. And I began to suspect I knew why we weren't able to find him or his mother.

'Thank you, Doctor Forbes,' I said.

'I hope your daddy's . . . I hope things go okay for you all. I'll be thinking of you,' she said.

I thanked her again and, following a hunch, dialled through to Altnagelvin hospital in Derry. Within two minutes, I knew where to find Aidan Row.

Chapter Forty-Four

The North West Cancer Centre had opened a few years previously, though it still had a state-of-the-art quality and a lightness and airiness imbued by the floor-to-ceiling windows and roofing that meant it retained a warmth in spite of the personal tragedies that drove each person to cross its threshold.

It hadn't taken long to work out that Aidan Row would be in Ward 50, where patients experiencing problems while on chemo were treated. Row had looked ill when I'd first spoken with him, though only in retrospect did it make sense to me.

I'd sat with Tom and my father until the staff told us only one of us could stay. Tom said that, as I'd had several days with my dad staying with us, he'd like the chance to spend some time with him, which I knew was only reasonable.

After leaving my dad, but promising I'd be back later, I'd headed on down the back road through St Johnstone, snaking alongside the River Foyle which ran down through Derry and beyond. I didn't tell Hendry I was going down, nor did I call the PPU officers we'd met earlier, Fleming and Black.

Aidan Row's mother was sitting in the waiting area outside Ward 50 when I arrived, alongside Michael, Aidan's partner. They were eating sandwiches and drinking tea, which one of them had brought in from a local café. Mrs Row blanched when she saw me.

'I'd like to speak to Aidan, please,' I said.

'You can't come in here,' Michael said. 'You've no rights over here. Leave, please!'

A nurse, fiddling with her swipe card as she approached the doors into the ward glanced in our direction so I sat opposite the pair, hoping that in so doing I might lower the tenor of our conversation.

'I know what happened,' I explained. 'I know it was Aidan. His blood ties him to the house where Harris died. Hannah's blood.'

'Can't you just leave him alone?' Mrs Row said, her jaw quivering. 'Leave us in peace. You can see where he is. He's not . . . he's not coming back out of here again.'

'I understand that,' I said. 'And I'm sorry, Mrs Row. My own father is dying in hospital at the moment, so I understand exactly how you feel.'

'To lose both children? No, you don't,' she said.

'You're right,' I admitted. 'I don't. I *am* sorry. And to you, Michael. I'm not looking to arrest him, or charge him. I just need to know what happened that night.'

'Why?'

'Because, in the end, whether you thought Brooklyn Harris was a victim or not, everyone deserves having someone care, someone to understand why.'

'Can you not guess why?' Michael asked.

'Yes,' I said. 'But I have one or two questions about how as well.'

'I don't agree,' Mrs Row said. 'I don't agree to you speaking to my son.'

'I'm sorry, ma'am,' I said. 'The sister in the ward has already asked him would he see me. He said he would.'

'Why would he?' she asked, appealing more to Michael than to me.

'I don't know,' I said, anyway. In reality, I suspected that I did know. Aidan must have realised his own time was almost over; perhaps he felt the need to confess, to tell his story, too.

I sat on the window bench opposite his bed after the sister with whom I'd spoken came up and brought me down to the cubicle in which he lay. The door, a glass pane that could be wheeled open and closed, sat ajar and, beyond, I could hear a cleaner whistling as he mopped down the corridor floor and could catch snatches of conversation between two of the staff, discussing a night out they had planned. But here, inside the cubicle, the air was a held breath.

'How did you know?' Aidan Row rasped after I told him my suspicion.

'The blood, in the end,' I said. 'I thought it had to do with what had happened to Hannah, twenty years back, but it always came back to the blood.'

'It has always come back to my blood,' he managed, laughing wheezily for a moment at his own joke.

'What happened?'

'Are you recording this?' he asked, looking at me askance.

'No,' I said, raising my hands a little as if to indicate he could check me if he wished, though I knew he would not, could not, in his present condition.

'I'll deny it anyway,' he said.

'This is between me and you,' I said.

'A different type of confession from what you're used to?'

'You'd be surprised,' I said. 'In the end, most people want to tell someone, want their actions to be remembered, for good or ill.'

'And which is this? Good or ill?'

'I'm not sure,' I said. 'How did you know where to find Harris?'

Row lay back on his pillow, his breathing ragged. 'I knew he was in Lifford,' he said. 'So, I went and sat down at the bank machines and waited in the car. I knew he'd be out. At the bar. Sure enough I spotted him later. Followed him and saw where he went. He'd been drinking. I waited until it was late. Went in. Killed him.'

It was that simple, seemingly. As if describing a normal day at work.

'Did he wake?'

Row rocked his head back and forth lightly against the pillow.

'What caused you to bleed?'

'I take nose bleeds,' he said. 'The treatment means I bleed . . . bleed easily.'

'Did you know your blood would be the same as Hannah's?'

He shook his head. 'They told me. Back then. But I . . .' He chapped his lips dryly but refused my offer to bring him water with a light raising of his hand. 'I forgot. Until you said.'

'Why?'

Row looked me but did not speak.

'Why now?'

'Because he's dying,' a voice said and I turned to see Michael standing in the doorway.

Aidan squeezed his eyes shut in response to his partner's voice.

'For Hannah?' I asked.

'And for me,' Row said softly.

Michael must have guessed from my expression that I did not follow. 'Brooklyn Harris killed the only person who was a match for Aidan. Hannah's transplant saved him the last time but she's not here now; there's no donor now. When Harris killed Hannah, he killed Aidan too. It just took until now.'

Row coughed a rasping laugh. 'The longest life sentence ever.'

'You avenged your own death,' I said.

'And Hannah's,' Aidan said.

'How did you know he was there? In Lifford?' I asked, but Aidan Row had completed what he needed to say and I wondered why he had felt the need to tell me. I thought back to the first time I'd met him, when Joe had taken the cheek swab that Aidan already knew wouldn't place him in Harris' room. He could barely lift his hand.

'Good luck, Aidan,' I said, moving forward and offering my hand to him to shake.

'You're not meant to—' Michael began to say, but Aidan had already placed his hand in mine, his touch waxy and chilled, his grip non-existent, his hand resting as of one already dead.

315

'I sanitised before I came in,' I said, moving towards the door. 'Will you walk me out?'

'I'll be back in a second, Ade,' Michael said, then stepped back to let me past.

We walked the length of the corridor from Aidan's room, passing a small kitchen available for the use of families. I knocked and, after checking it was empty, stepped in. Michael followed me warily.

'Is Aidan's mum around?'

'I suggested she go over to the shop for a drink for him,' Michael said. 'I thought it best she didn't hear what Aidan had to say.'

I thought back to her response when I first told her the news of Brooklyn's death; her tears. They made more sense now. 'I think she already knows,' I said.

'There are some secrets he'd rather keep.'

'I thought you should know,' I said. 'Riley Mullan died last night.'

Michael searched for the name but clearly without success for he shook his head to indicate he had no idea whom I meant.

'He was one of the three boys who were there the night Hannah was killed,' I explained. 'He told us a little more of what happened that night.'

Michael paled. 'Was Brooklyn Harris not the person who killed Hannah?'

'He was,' I said. 'But there were others there. Riley himself and another youth called Charlie McDaid. They may have been more involved than the RUC admitted at the time.'

316

Michael shook his head. 'I know Charlie McDaid; he helped Ade draw up his will. He's a good guy.'

'I'm not convinced he is,' I said. 'I think he may have been involved in some way in the attack on Hannah.'

'But Harris confessed to killing her.'

'And Aidan has confessed to killing him.'

'I don't follow,' Michael said, folding his arms and leaning against the counter on which sat a toaster and an opened loaf of bread.

'I mention them,' I said, 'because I wondered if Charlie McDaid was the one who told Aidan where to find Brooklyn Harris?'

'I'm not sure,' Michael said.

'Could you check?' I asked. 'For me?'

'Why would I?' Michael asked.

'I shook Aidan's hand there,' I said. 'He has no grip. No strength. I'd wondered why he'd agreed to confess to me, until I saw him. Then I knew. He didn't avenge his death: you did.'

'That's ridiculous,' Michael blustered, moving from where he leaned against the counter, shifting across the small space, away from me.

'The person who stabbed Brooklyn Harris used enough force to crack through his sternum. Pulled a horsetail of blood across the ceiling in the movement. I'm not convinced Aidan could even have held a knife, never mind wield it with that force. But he's dying anyway and no matter what he tells me now, the courts and the PSNI can do nothing worse to him than Harris already has. But the dead don't avenge their own passing. It's the ones left behind who feel

317

that pain, who need to balance that debt. So, while I know Aidan was there and I'm sure that you only acted on his behalf, his surrogate, I've no doubt it was your hand on the knife.'

'But Aidan has confessed,' Michael said.

'So did Brooklyn Harris,' I said. 'I thought the police then were wrong to accept that, even if it was for the greater good, as they saw it. But I feel differently now. Harris killed Hannah and Aidan both, the night he smashed her head off a wall. But you're the one who's been given the life sentence now, of grief. Nothing I do will change that.'

Tears sprang to the man's eyes, his expression crumpling.

'Someone told me that no matter how this ended, it could not end happily. There couldn't be a just end. Whether Brooklyn got what he deserved or not, the one person who's been pulling strings and directing everyone else to his tune is Charlie McDaid. And he's the one person who has avoided any responsibility. So, I need to know, taking Aidan's confession at face value, who told him that Brooklyn Harris was in Lifford?'

Michael pulled a phone from his pocket. 'I've Ade's phone now so I can respond to people texting him. He can't even type any more,' he explained. I watched as he navigated through various apps before he held the phone out to me showing me a message. At the top of the screen was the account name, Charlie McD. The message simply read '*Brooklyn Harris is staying in Lifford tonight. He's looking for another girl, just like Hannah. He'll never stop. I thought you should know.*'

As we walked back up the ward towards the exit, we met Mrs Row, who had bought juice for both Aidan and Michael.

She handed it to Michael then squeezed his hand as he took it. 'You're so tired-looking,' she said. 'You should get some rest. I'll sit with Ade.' The gesture, so simple, so maternal, caught me off guard.

Death may have stolen from her one child already and a second one soon, may have shaken her sense of who she was, but in that moment, with someone else's child, she was still, instinctively, a mother.

Chapter Forty-Five

I called Joe McCready as I left the hospital and explained what I'd been told by Aidan Row and Michael. Or a part of it at least. I then repeated the call with Jim Hendry.

'You were half right,' Hendry said. 'It was a murder victim avenging their own death; just not the victim you thought.'

'They were all victims,' I said. 'Harris, too.' And Michael, robbed of the person he loved. It was almost like Debs had explained Shakespeare to me: an initial act of corruption had rippled out and everyone touched by the waves had to die. Harris, Mullan, Hannah, Aidan. Only Charlie McDaid remained.

'Can we charge McDaid with inciting violence at least?' I asked. 'Give us enough to search his house and offices?'

'He didn't incite violence, though,' Hendry said. 'He passed on information. You know the prosecution service won't go for that.'

'We must have something we can use,' I said.

'I'm sorry, Ben,' Hendry said. 'You've gone as far as you can. If McDaid was involved at all, it was a lifetime ago and he's gotten away with it. It happens.'

I was driving up towards the roundabout where the Tinneys art installation stood, already indicating to take right across to Lifford when, on a spur, I changed my mind and went straight on, up the bypass and onwards to Omagh.

McDaid was seeing clients when I went into his office, so I told his secretary I would wait to see him. The others gathered in the room were attempting to socially distance, and one or two wore face masks while they waited to be called, so I stood in the doorway. Finally, as his waiting room began thinning out, I was told that he could spare a few minutes to speak to me.

'Inspector Devlin,' he said when I went in. 'I'd offer you a seat but I'm afraid I've only a moment. What can I do for you now?'

'I thought you should know that Riley Mullan died last night,' I said.

'Oh,' he said, seemingly stunned by the news. 'I'd not heard. Thank you for letting me . . . How did he die?'

'He was recovered from the river this morning,' I said. 'The PSNI are not looking for anyone else in connection with it.'

McDaid lowered his head, reverentially. 'I'm truly sorry to hear that. Riley was a good mate. Had been for years.'

'You went through a lot together, the pair of you.'

He smiled briefly, sadly. 'We did.'

'You're the only one left now,' I said. 'From the night of Hannah's death.'

His expression darkened, his brows pulling together. 'I'm not sure what you mean by that.'

'You see, Riley spoke to me last night. Myself and a journalist. He wanted to offer his confession. Give us his version of what really happened that evening.'

321

'His version?' McDaid said, his expression implacable now.

I nodded, taking the seat McDaid had not offered. He sat, likewise.

'He told us that he and Hannah got together that night. That she and he liked each other. That they began to have intercourse and she asked him to stop.'

'I don't know anything about that,' he said, shaking his head slowly.

'He said that you and Brooklyn Harris spied on them while this was happening and that you and Harris chased after Hannah when she realised and ran away in embarrassment.'

He scoffed now. 'That's rubbish,' he said. 'Riley was a nice guy but he was a fantasist. It's nonsense, I'm afraid.'

'He said you had spread stories about Hannah in school, because she wasn't interested in you.'

'Names in school?' McDaid asked, incredulously, rising as he did so. 'I think we've reached peak waste of my time now. I have clients to see.'

'He told us about the underwear,' I said.

'What?' McDaid asked, not moving now. I got the sense he was working hard to keep his gaze fixed on mine.

'He said you kept Hannah's pants that evening. You told him you'd done it to protect him, but that's not true, is it?'

'I've no idea what you're talking about,' McDaid said, but he still made no motion for the door.

'It was you who sicced Porter on Brooklyn the first time, wasn't it?'

'Why would I do that?' McDaid asked.

'Brooklyn claimed he could remember more about that night. About someone urging him on, telling him to rape Hannah. He began to suspect you were both there, you and Riley.'

'He was off his face on speed,' McDaid said.

'He was calling in favours when he got out, though,' I said. 'Riley was doing his drawings for him, for all those girls he was meeting online. And keeping him in whatever prescription drugs he needed. Which made me wonder what he was looking for from you? Then I worked it out. You set him up for Porter, then convinced him that you'd talked Porter down from using what he had. Porter told the PSNI he was advised not to use the footage he had of Harris, that he would incriminate himself.'

'This is all fascinating. But entirely circumstantial and, in the case of everything Riley has said, hearsay from someone so unhinged he committed suicide hours after saying it.'

'I know Porter contacted you the evening that he discovered Brooklyn was in Lifford.'

'It's not against the law for someone to contact their solicitor,' McDaid said.

'No,' I agreed. 'You see, initially, I thought he'd asked you whether he should doorstep Brooklyn again and you'd talked him down. But now I'm thinking that maybe you tried to encourage him to do it and he refused. So you had to take a different approach.'

'What approach might that be?'

'You contacted Aidan Row and told him instead.'

McDaid swallowed now, the act spoiling his attempt at a scoff. 'Really?'

'I saw your message to him,' I said. 'And he followed through for you.'

'That proves nothing,' McDaid said. 'As a friend, I thought he should be aware that Brooklyn was in the local area. That was all.'

'Well, as a friend, I'm telling you now something *I* shouldn't,' I said. 'Porter is going to be charged with child sex-image offences. He'll be looking at serious time away. You don't think he'll offer up someone as a way to reduce his sentence? Especially someone who encouraged him to press assault charges against me and hand over his phone with the footage of the incident. The very same phone the images were found on that will incriminate him? How do you think that'll play out when he starts to connect the dots and sees you've been using him from start to finish?'

'You need to leave, Inspector,' McDaid said. 'I have people waiting.'

I nodded and stood. 'Once that happens, the PSNI will get the warrant they need and sooner or later Hannah Row's underwear will be found once they tear your house apart. And the thing is, you don't look out for anyone but yourself. So I'm betting that when they are found, *your* DNA will be on them, too. Even after all these years.'

I knew it was a gamble, a desperate move. But it was the only move I had left.

Chapter Forty-Six

I called Hendry immediately.

'Do you still have Porter's phone?' I asked.

'It's sitting on my desk,' Jim said. 'He's to collect it.'

'Keep an eye on it,' I said. 'I spoke to McDaid there.'

'You what?'

'I stuck in a hook to see what would happen. I told him that Mullan told us McDaid had taken Hannah's underwear and that Porter was facing charges. That he'll turn and squeal on him to reduce his sentence.'

I'd barely finished speaking when I heard the dull drone of a phone buzzing on the other end of the line.

Hendry laughed. 'That's him now. I'll let it go to voicemail.'

'If I'm right,' I said. 'If he still has the underwear, he'll need to dispose of it. Soon.'

'Are you planning on watching him to see if he does?'

I grunted.

'Do you want company?'

'Always,' I said.

Minutes later, I watched as McDaid walked out the front door of his building and crossed to his car. I dialled through to his office and asked to speak to him.

'Mr McDaid has gone home sick,' his secretary said. 'Would you like to leave a message?'

'I'll catch him later,' I said, hanging up.

I stayed at a distance behind him as I followed him back to his house, phoning Hendry to tell him where I was. I guessed McDaid wouldn't destroy the underwear, if indeed that was what he was going for, in his own home, lest it should be searched and the evidence uncovered.

Still, as I sat outside, I began to worry that perhaps he would burn them in his back garden. Or even just wash them, thereby destroying whatever trace evidence might remain on the garment.

I moved around to the rear of the house, keeping close to the wall, peering in through the window. There was no sign of him in the kitchen, which was visible from where I stood. Nor could I see him in any of the downstairs rooms.

Then I caught a glimpse of him, rushing down the stairs and appearing briefly in the hallway, before he headed back out the front door. He had a blue bag in his hand.

I rounded the corner of the house again and appeared behind him as he moved towards his car. Only then did he see that my car was parked across the driveway, blocking his exit, my having remembered Porter's mistake the evening he'd door-stepped Harris.

'There's nowhere to go,' I said.

He turned to look at me, his expression feral.

'You fucking—'

'Give them to me,' I said, pointing at the parcel he held. 'I'm guessing they're Hannah's.'

'You've no jurisdiction here. Nothing!' he spat. 'Get off my property.'

'He doesn't. But I do,' Jim Hendry said, appearing at the foot of the driveway, his warrant card in his hand. 'I'd like to speak to you, Mr McDaid.'

McDaid looked from one of us to the other, clearly considering his options. If he could just run, dispose of the blue bag somewhere, he'd be free. I could see him weighing up his choices of which direction to go, either past Hendry or past me. He chose me.

Though I was ready for him coming at me, still he knocked me to the ground with ease, his youth and rugby experience giving him a distinct advantage over me. I held on to his leg as he tried to move away past me, scrambling back up from the ground where he had fallen as he'd taken me down. He kicked back, connecting with my cheek and I felt the pain balloon in it with the contact. Still, I clung to him, desperate not to let go, not to let him slip away from me.

He kicked again, this time stunning me, my field of vision flaring momentarily white. I felt his leg moving as my grip loosened so I hung on all the harder, wrapping myself around his ankle and foot, willing myself to hold on, just a bit longer.

He kicked wildly to get away from me, using his free foot to dislodge me, but I held on there, clinging like death, knowing that, no matter what, I could not let go now.

And, after a moment, I felt his kicking lessen. Looking up, I saw that Hendry stood over him now, the blue bag in his grip, McDaid lying on his back on the grass, beaten.

Hendry opened the bag and glanced in, his expression darkening.

'What the hell is this?' he asked, pulling out what looked like a circuit board.

That brief moment of confusion was punctuated by the ringing of my phone. It was my brother, Tom.

Chapter Forty-Seven

Tom stared at me when I arrived, though knew better than to ask about the bruises that had swollen on my cheek and forehead.

'Was it worth it?' he managed.

'I hope so,' I said.

My father was stirring. I knew, since both of us were now being allowed in to see him together, that this evening would only end one way and, as I walked into his room, I felt so body tired, I didn't know if I had the stamina to face what lay ahead of us.

He smiled mildly when he saw us. 'My two boys,' he said.

I could not trust myself to speak, so instead I took his hand and sat next to him, feeling again the rough texture of his skin, the warmth of him, the thickness of his fingers that had somehow retained a dexterity that had allowed him to tease seedlings apart in the garden as he'd worked, burying them knuckle deep in the rich soil, handling them with almost paternal pride.

Like the pride he had in both of us, I knew.

'We're both here, Dad,' Tom said. 'We're with you.'

'I'm glad,' he said. 'I didn't want to have to go alone.'

I felt the heat of the tears running down my face and realised that I'd been crying for some moments. He looked at me and, with a soft click of his tongue, raised his hand and wiped my cheek.

'It's okay, Ben,' he said. 'I'm ready to see your mother.'

'I love you, Daddy,' I said and, in that moment, felt again as though I were eight years old, saying goodnight to my parents, the simplicity of the love I felt for them never clearer. I was, I knew then, still that child and, no matter what happened, he would always be my father and, even in his absence, I would always be his son, just as Mrs Row would always be a mother, despite the loss of her children.

'Son,' he said softly, his hand warm against my skin. 'My son.'

With his touch, his word, my father had assembled me.

'I love you too,' he said. 'I love you both so much.'

We sat like that for a few minutes. At one stage, I could see that he was dry, his lips smacking lightly as he tried to speak and, dipping the small water kit sponge into the glass of water next to his bed, I offered some to him, as if on a hyssop stick. He sucked at it lightly, then laid his head back.

I could tell you more, but the rest of that evening is personal to my father and Tom and to me. Suffice to say, we spoke about all that we needed to say until he went to sleep. Then we sat together, my brother and I, whispering through the darkness, comforting each other with the security of our shared memories, reaffirming with every word, who we were and whence we'd come.

We sat with him all night, each of us holding one of his hands. And we remained with him, watching vigil with him until the morning, when he was gone.

Epilogue

26 June 2020
We all lost things that late spring.

The lockdown started in earnest soon after my father's funeral and most people found themselves confined to their homes and local areas. The kids initially enjoyed the novelty of it, almost like an extended school break, but that soon waned as the death toll increased and the weeks rolled by. Still, we were together and I took comfort from knowing each night, as I locked the front door, that my children were safely inside with me.

Yet, socially, we lost our freedom to move about, our joy in meeting friends with an embrace, our chance to sit with our extended families and share food or a drink, our chance to walk unimpeded through a shopping centre, to sit in a cinema or theatre, to play our sports, to listen to live music, to gather in pubs and celebrate our national saint's Feast Day together. And, beyond all that, many lost their jobs, their livelihoods, their businesses, their mental resilience challenged like never before.

And beyond that still, most importantly, many lost their lives, their loved ones.

As Covid spread through the country, care homes bore a particular brunt and, in the middle of April, I took a call from Louise McGowan in Finnside to inform me that Ollie Costello had succumbed to the illness. Due to the restrictions, and his cause of death, I was unable to attend his funeral, though Patterson assured me that, when things had returned to normal, we would hold a memorial in his honour.

In the space of two months, I had lost two paternal figures from my life.

I was wrong, in part, about Charlie McDaid. He did not have Hannah Row's underwear and, indeed, still claimed never to have them or to have been involved in the assault. The lack of DNA evidence meant that, in that regard at least, there was nothing to tie McDaid to Hannah's assault and killing.

However, the hard drive that Hendry had taken from him, and held on to while McDaid was investigated over failing to stop for a police officer and an assault on me, offered up other riches. Not least was a digital trail leading back to the profile of Sara Burke. Bob Porter, facing his own child-pornography charges, admitted that Charlie McDaid had designed Sara Burke and had been the one to make contact with Harris, before contacting Porter and telling him what he had done. His hope had been that there would be enough to incriminate Brooklyn Harris and have him returned to prison if Northern Justice flagged up Harris' behaviour to the police. When Tom Fleming of the PPU informed Porter that the sting information was inadmissible, McDaid had to look for an alternative arrangement to deal with Harris. He eventually found it in Aidan Row.

Though we could never connect him to Hannah Row's attack, his eagerness to target Harris suggested that there must have been some truth in our belief that Harris had accused McDaid of being involved in the original assault in some way. In this instance, though, we were unable to prove it and I had to accept that I may have been wrong. Perhaps.

The PSNI continue to investigate his involvement with Bob Porter. The assault review involving myself and the latter man found in my favour and Patterson reinstated me, once I'd taken my sympathetic leave following my father's death.

'We'll need you back firing on all cylinders,' Patterson said. 'You know the rule; if you fall off a horse, best get back in the saddle as quickly as you can.'

I stopped short of pointing out that losing a parent was not the same as falling from a horse for, in a strange way, I understood that he meant it as a show of sympathy and support.

'We're going to be a man down when young McCready gets his new promotion,' he'd added.

Joe was up for inspector and was awaiting the next available vacancy. He was ready to move on. While he didn't say it, I suspected he was annoyed that I'd not involved him in the final hours of the investigation and that, with Aidan Row's passing a few days after my father's, he'd lost any chance of successfully closing the case.

Jim Hendry called me in late April to see how we were managing in the lockdown.

'We're okay,' I said. 'How's life north of the border?'

'Between this and Brexit looming large, we're going to be hitting a perfect storm of shit later in the year,' he said. 'I'm not sure I have the energy to face it.'

There was a pause while he allowed that comment to sit.

'So, you asked for an early exit?'

'I've applied for it,' he said. 'I'll find out in a few months if I got it. There's so much uncertainty at the moment, with everything going on, I don't know whether the package I'm looking for will be available. I don't know if I can afford to retire with anything less.'

'I'll be sad to see you go,' I said. 'You've been a good friend.'

'I'm not away yet,' he said.

'Thanks for having my back that day, with McDaid,' I said. 'And even before that. I know you were in a tight spot over it.'

'Sure what else would I be doing if I wasn't getting your arse out of trouble?' he asked, his accompanying laugh cut a little short.

'Keep in touch,' I said.

'I will. I'll let you know if I hear anything, but our place is so bloody slow it could be next year before I get word. If Brexit's happened by then, we can meet at that new wall I told you they'd be building on the border and pass gifts across the frontier!'

Though I was able to pretend an interest in all the things that were happening around me through those months, the truth was that, following my father's death, I felt set apart from the rest of the world, as if I was an observer rather than a participant in my own existence. Debs seemed to sense this and, though she continued with normal routines and conversation within the house, I could tell by the way she'd smile at me when I remained vacant in the midst of a discussion, or missed a question directed at me, that she knew my mind was elsewhere.

The grief came in waves, overwhelming initially and then, gradually, easing in frequency, if not in intensity. I gathered up the items belonging to my father which he had left in our house and put them in a travel bag. It remains still in my wardrobe.

In those weeks, I felt as if I had joined a club, the rules for membership of which only other bereaved could understand. And on some days, I wished the club had its own membership badge I could wear, something to mark me as among the freshly wounded in the hope that strangers might know and friends remember and so handle me with a gentleness commensurate with the rawness of my grief. But people, with the best will, forget, and time passes, and life continues.

One night in June, I sat up late, flicking through the channels for something to watch. I put on Netflix and noticed my father's subaccount, set up by Shane. Opening it, I saw that he had been watching a movie, *Saving Mr Banks*, and had clearly stopped halfway through. Something about it, the incompleteness of it, upset me, knowing there was a story he would never finish, a tale whose ending he would never again have a chance to know. I thought of watching the end of it myself, on his behalf, but knew that, viewing it from my perspective now, rather than his then, there was no point: it would have ended differently for him.

One evening, later that month, Debs suggested we go for a walk together. The travel restrictions were still in place and we had to remain within our own area, so we headed down the road a little and along a laneway that had once run into the pine forest near our home and which opened out, eventually, at an old graveyard. The forest had been cut down at some point without my realising it, and, like Persephone gone, the world seemed less verdant as a result, as if in mourning at its passing.

We reached the graveyard after a short climb. Years back it had flooded, the ancient stonework breaking and releasing, with the floodwaters, the remains of some of the dead. The council had reinterred them and cemented over the ground where they lay to avoid a repeat of the incident. But the spot was always quiet, the graves for the most part long since forgotten. From this elevation, we could see across to Strabane, and a stretch down the Foyle valley towards Derry and, behind us, our own home where, even from this distance, we could see the kids sitting out on the front step where the strongest mobile signal could be sourced.

'How are you doing?' Debs asked, taking my hand where we stood.

'Okay,' I said. 'I'm getting there.'

'It'll take some time, Ben,' she said. 'To figure out your place in the world again.'

'I know,' I said. 'It's just a bit strange that my dad, the person who gave me my sense of myself after Mum passed, is the one I need to talk with to find it again and yet is the very person I can't talk to any more.'

'You can talk to me,' she said.

'It's not the same,' I said. 'Fathers and sons, you know?'

She nodded.

I looked down to our house. 'The lockdown has helped, strangely,' I said. 'It's like this one huge thing has changed, but the rest of the world stopped for a few months. The kids and that being at home. It's like life has hit a pause in some places, even as it's barrelled completely out of control in others.'

'Take comfort wherever you find it,' Debs said. 'There's no right or wrong way to deal with it.'

'I know.'

'But however things change, I'm still here. I'm always here.'

I looked at her and saw her again properly for the first time in months. I'd been so focused on my dad, my work, myself, I'd lost sight of that one constant.

'I know, Debs,' I said, taking her hand in mine and, lifting it to my lips, kissing it. 'Thank you.'

And that's how we stood, that evening, as the sun crested the hills to the west, gilding the edges of the clouds and setting the sky alight and, for that moment at least, I felt more like *me*.

I was my father's son, my mother's son, my children's father, Debbie's husband and the man who had loved her fiercely since first he met her, all tied together by family, by blood. As my father had known and had told me, and as I now understood even more deeply, that was all that mattered in the end. Family conferred on me all that I needed to know about myself, about who I was.

And as long as I had that foundation, all that was broken would reassemble, everything lost would find its place, in time.

Acknowledgements

Thanks to all those involved in helping this story on its journey from my desk to the bookstore shelf, especially the team at Constable. Special thanks to Krystyna Green, Amanda Keats and Joanne Gledhill.

I've been incredibly lucky to meet so many people through writing who've become good friends. My thanks to my fellow crime authors who've been so supportive of me and my books, particularly over the past few years. Thanks too to Angela McMahon for her help and guidance and to Dave Torrans and the team in No Alibis, the spiritual home for so many of us writing here in Northern Ireland.

Thanks to Dave Headley, who has been such a good friend to Devlin and to me for the past decade or more, and to Emily Hickman for all her work on my behalf.

My thanks to my colleagues and students in Holy Cross College. Most people are lucky to have one career they love – I've been blessed in finding two.

For a book about family, sincere thanks to mine: to the McGilloways, Dohertys, O'Neills and Kerlins. Thanks in particular to Carmel, Joe and Dermot for all their support through the years. I owe a debt of love and gratitude that can never be fully repaid to my mum, Katrina. And as I write, my dad, Laurence, Devlin's fiercest supporter, is never far from me, now more than ever. His memory and spirit imbue every part of this book. He was the best man I have ever known and I miss him every day.

Finally, my love and thanks to my wife, Tanya, and our kids, Ben, Tom, David and Lucy, whose love gives life its meaning for me. I'm a very lucky man indeed.

Delve into a new gripping standalone tale
from Brian McGilloway.
The Last Crossing is available to order now.

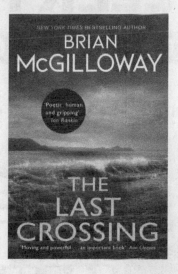

Tony, Hugh and Karen thought they'd seen the last of
each other thirty years ago. Half a lifetime has passed
and memories have been buried. But when they are
asked to reunite – to lay ghosts to rest for the good
of the future – they all have their own reasons to agree.
As they take the ferry from Northern Ireland to Scotland
the past is brought into terrible focus – some things are
impossible to leave behind.

In *The Last Crossing*, memory is unreliable, truth shifts
and slips and the lingering legacy of the Troubles
threatens the present once again.

Kazuo Ishiguro is the author of five previous novels: *A Pale View of Hills* (1982, Winifred Holtby Prize), *An Artist of the Floating World* (1986, Whitbread Book of the Year Award, Premio Scanno, shortlisted for the Booker Prize), *The Remains of the Day* (1989, winner of the Booker Prize), *The Unconsoled* (1995, winner of the Cheltenham Prize) and *When We Were Orphans* (2000, shortlisted for the Booker Prize). He received an OBE for services to literature in 1995, and the French decoration of Chevalier de l'Ordre des Arts et des Lettres in 1998.

by the same author

A PALE VIEW OF HILLS
AN ARTIST OF THE FLOATING WORLD
THE REMAINS OF THE DAY
THE UNCONSOLED
WHEN WE WERE ORPHANS